Praise for Z. A. Maxfield's *Crossing Borders*

A Literary Nymphs *Golden Blush Recommended Read!*

"*Crossing Borders* was truly a pleasure to read from beginning to end... It's a rare author who is able to put so many different emotions into their writing and I'm pleased to say, Z.A. Maxfield has done it well. There are really too many good things to say about this wonderful gay romance to adequately cover in a review, so my suggestion would be to buy this gem and read it yourself."

—*Literary Nymphs Review*

Awarded Five Angels by *Fallen Angel Reviews*!

"What a wonderful love story. I found myself being quickly drawn in to this story, first by the humor and then by the romance. Z. A. Maxfield tells a story that pulled me into so many different emotions. I found myself laughing out loud through some parts and crying through others."

—April, *Fallen Angel Reviews*

"*Crossing Borders* is a little jewel and it was such a joy to read that when I finished the book, all 218 pages of it, I thought 'that was a brilliant piece of writing'. ...Z.A. Maxfield is a delightfully fresh voice among all the 'noise' of the M/M romance genre. I can't say enough good things about *Crossing Borders* but I can highly recommend that you buy this book. It's a keeper."

LooseId®

ISBN 10: 1-59632-783-9
ISBN 13: 978-1-59632-783-2
CROSSING BORDERS

Originally released in e-book format in July 2008

Cover Art by Anne Cain and April Martinez
Cover Design by April Martinez

Printed in the U.S.A. by
Lightning Source, Inc.
1246 Heil Quaker Blvd
La Vergne TN 37086
www.lightningsource.com

CROSSING BORDERS

Z. A. Maxfield

Dedication

For Marri, who slid over one seat during The Rocky Horror Picture Show *(so we could talk) twenty-five years ago, and has been right beside me ever since.*

Chapter One

It seemed unimaginably sudden when Tristan decided this was the last day he'd look at some guy out of the corner of his eye and think, maybe, *yeah*, that would be so...damn. He'd been feeling it all along, the nagging and awkward insistence of his brain over the ease of his body getting lucky. There wasn't a girl in his circle of friends who didn't come on to him, but lately his body had been vibing more insistently in a different key, and with every month that passed and every insipid date with his girlfriend Tiffany-call-me-Viper, he'd realized it wasn't something he could run from anymore. Because when Viper stood him up, Tristan looked at her brother, whatever *his* name was, when he answered the door all embarrassed and thoughtful and guilty somehow, and he thought, *Damn, I should have asked you out instead.*

"She's gone out with another dude... Sorry," Viper's brother said. Like that was a bad thing. "I think she's kind of over you, you know?" He hung on the door a little, and Tristan noticed right away that he was aroused and trying to hide it. "Sorry, man," he said again.

Tristan held his hand out and smacked the door, stopping it as it was closing. Mesmerized, fascinated, and trying not to look at the spot of moisture growing against the faded blue of the man's jeans, he said, "Hey, wait --"

But then what's-his-name looked behind him at a girl with blonde hair and seriously kissed lips. She slid her arms around his waist under his shirt. Tristan turned to leave. "Never mind," he added as he carefully stepped down the brick stairs to the sidewalk. "Tell Viper I said 'bye."

"Sure thing," said Viper's brother as he closed the door.

Jeez... *Viper.* Tristan felt bad about feeling nothing at all.

So even though the decision seemed sudden, as he boarded up and down the large rolling hills on State College Boulevard, Tristan was aware that the choice he was making today came from a long and sometimes Byzantine series of personal dialogues. If Viper didn't do it for him, it wasn't going to get done. He felt relieved somehow, unencumbered. He felt the wind blow through his hair and through his life as it wafted out all the garbage he'd been doing for years that meant nothing to him.

Viper was cool and funny and sexy and willing, and he couldn't care less. Because he wanted Viper's brother, or more precisely, the leaking, sweet-as-candy cock that tented his faded Levis, even though it was probably making its way into the blonde chick even as Tristan thought about it. And he thought about it a lot. So, okay, once he admitted he wanted it, the next logical step was figuring out where *the hell* to get it.

Tristan pushed off the ground hard, sorry again that he'd loaned his car to his sister, Lily. It was hard climbing the hill that crested at the State College intersection with Bastanchury Boulevard, where on clear days you could see the LA downtown skyline. Worth it though, because once he topped that hill, he would freefall all the way down to Imperial Highway, then turn right, and after a block or two, cross the street to go to Borders, because that was *the plan.*

Being nothing if not thorough, Tristan had worked on *the plan* in his spare time, day and night it seemed, since Viper had called to officially dump him. Still, there didn't seem to be an actual *viable* plan until he heard two girls talking about Borders in Art History class. He'd deliberately listened in as they chatted together amiably about using books as bait to lure and trap unwary men in the bookstore café. If he hadn't already decided he'd be better off with dick than pussy, their predatory attitude would have put him off for life anyway. How crafty. How Machiavellian. *How marvelous.*

The plan.

Tristan kicked the back of his skateboard so the front leapt into his hand. The move was as natural to him as breathing, something he was doing now in an unnatural, anticipatory way. Coming down that hill, his muscles bunching, the board rocking, the force of gravity and the wind pushing him was exhilarating, but not the cause of his rapid heart rate. Not the only cause.

Tristan entered Borders, getting a feel for the place, trying to figure out the best way to case the layout. It wasn't the largest Borders he'd been to, but he nevertheless found one shelf of gay lit sandwiched between a corner of African American literature and two shelves of what looked like lesbian romance novels. Right there, right in the damn front of the store, albeit back in the corner, but still…damn. *Right in the front of the store.*

Tristan had printed off a number of titles, a laundry list of must-reads he'd gotten off an Amazon reviewer's Web site. He picked up three books, two contemporary novels, and Armistead Maupin's *Tales of the City.* He searched around in the poetry and literature sections and found Allen Ginsberg's *Howl* and a book by Keith Hale called *Clicking Beat on the Brink of Nada.* Whatever. He hoped he didn't have time to read them. He just wanted to use the books to start a conversation that would end with him getting laid. He hedged his bets by grabbing a guide to gay Las Vegas nightlife on his way through the travel section and adding it to the pile he set on a table, staking out his territory. He ordered a cup of coffee and a rice crispy treat. He was going to sit glued in that seat, all day -- all night if he had to -- until somebody talked to him or kicked his ass out. That was *the plan*, and Tristan was all about *the plan.* He was sure his intentions couldn't have been any more obvious if he'd brought a box of Twinkies and unwrapped them, shoving them into his mouth and licking the cream out one by one. But *obvious* was a large part of *the plan*.

On the way over, it did occur to Tristan that this might not be the sanest moment of his life, but he couldn't allow lack of information or common sense to get in the way of true desperation. He knew it was crazy and ruefully acknowledged the fact that no normal person would try something like this. He'd grown up not ten minutes from here, and someone he knew was bound to show up. In life there were lookers and leapers. Tristan had to admit he was a leaper.

Tristan had toyed briefly with warning his mother beforehand, but thought he'd like to at least have a homosexual experience before bringing up the whole "I'm gay" thing. Like his tongue piercing, his mom always found the bright side quicker when things were a fait accompli. He played with the bead on his tongue now, a nervous habit of long standing. He willed himself to relax his shoulders, picked up the contemporary novel *Chemistry* by DeSimone, and started to read.

After a few minutes, Tristan chanced a look around, checking all the men out in the near vicinity…*and froze*. Standing in line for coffee was the last person he wanted to see today. Really, the last person he wanted to see ever. Up until now, things had gone smoothly enough. Maybe too smoothly, because he'd had absolutely no warning he was about to see the ubiquitous Officer Helmet. And damn, he was wearing civilian clothing, as though he didn't just sleep in his stinking cruiser, lying in wait to give out those without-a-helmet tickets to kids on skateboards. Tristan eyed him warily. He wore khaki cargo shorts and a Hawaiian shirt, with Vans and those little short socks you could hardly see. He had brown, tanned legs with a tribal tattoo around one ankle. In normal clothes he looked younger; his bedhead hair was golden blond, and he needed a shave. He had really shocking blue eyes. Jeez. Officer Helmet was…

"Sparky!" Tristan heard him hide his ruthlessness behind laughter. "You read?" He raised his eyebrows, and Tristan slammed his head down on the table with a thud. He brought his coffee and about fifteen packets of sugar and some creamers the short distance to plop himself down in the very last, the quintessentially worst place he could possibly be. Tristan could tell he was having fun today. He had a look that screamed "gotcha" as he relaxed his long legs and prepared to lay siege.

"Officer Helmet," said Tristan through clenched teeth. "Imagine seeing you in a bookstore." Tristan looked at him and sighed. He looked *good.* This could not be Officer Helmet. Maybe he had a twin?

"So. Sparky." Tristan saw him scan the book collection on the tiny table. His eyes returned to Tristan's face, and he was silent for an interminable moment. "Taking a gay lit class?"

"Yep," said Tristan. "On the money. When are they going to make you Detective Helmet?"

"It's not going to happen anytime soon, so you've still got to watch yourself at the skate park. I see you have your skateboard." He grinned. "Did you leave your helmet in the gay literature section?"

"No," lied Tristan agilely. "I gave it to my girlfriend Viper to hold. She's getting her hair done. Officer Helmet."

"I know Viper… Listen, Sparky, I'm off duty, so why don't you call me Michael?"

"Why don't you quit calling me Sparky? The whole red hair freckles thing has been done to death, man. Sparky, Rusty, Red, Rory -- I'm over it." For Tristan, it was a rare outburst of honesty with "the Man."

"That's not why I call you Sparky," said Michael, starting to pour sugar after sugar into his coffee and adding what seemed like an avalanche of cream.

"What?" asked Tristan. "Then why?"

"Not telling you," said Michael. "Do you go to Cal State Fullerton?" He indicated the stack of books on the table.

Tristan snorted. "I went to Troy Tech, so no. I go to UCI."

"Well, excuse me. *I* went to CSUF, so it didn't seem like an insult." Michael still looked fairly complacent, so Tristan didn't think he'd been stung.

"Sorry," he muttered. "What was your major, and why'd you become a cop?" Was he curious? Really? He'd have to reflect on that.

"Communications, and I wanted to be a cop, so I became one. It's not like it's the last resort of the educationally impaired. Besides, it appeals to my rabid, power-starved nature to exercise authority over the weak and helpless."

There was that grin again. *Damn.* Pretty teeth. Lopsided grin. Tristan didn't want to laugh, didn't want Officer Helmet to be funny. But before he could stop himself he laughed through his nose and almost snorted out his coffee. "That, I believe," he said. He wondered if he could just go back to *the plan* now. Or ever. The Man -- Michael looked like he was comfortable, which was the exact opposite of how Tristan felt.

"Do you know that yours was the first ticket I ever wrote?" Michael said suddenly, and Tristan stared at him. "Of course, I'm still looking to give you the second, but you're fast and have an uncanny sense of when I'm around. Tell me the truth. You guys post lookouts, don't you? Every time I cruise by the skate park, the only people there are dads and little kids with all kinds of pads and helmets. The magic is gone."

Tristan gave a light laugh. "Surely you don't expect me to reveal trade secrets." He leaned over as if inviting Michael into his confidence. "Dude, the helmet? It gives me hat hair."

An indefinable look passed over Michael's face as he said, "Sparky, sometime I'm going to take you to the morgue and let you see what an un-helmeted head looks like. Did you know the human head cracks open just like a watermelon with very little pressure, and then gray stuff starts coming out?" He played with the empty sugar packets. "I hate that shit."

Tristan said nothing; what could he say? He hadn't thought Officer Helmet had a reason for ticketing him besides the obvious one: that he could. Not for anything did he want to see this person as a man with his best interests at heart. That would be just…not good. He pressed his lips together and remained silent for a while.

"Sorry," murmured Michael. "Okay, so what's your major? What happens in Sparky's head at school?"

"Physics," said Tristan.

"Yeah," said Michael. "Figures. That's you, all about energy, always in motion. I only ever see you running away. Makes perfect sense."

"Hm," said Tristan, thinking that Officer Helmet ought to know that firsthand; he'd chased him enough. "If you didn't have to wear that bulky cop suit and those oxfords, you could probably catch me." He figured the man was faster dressed as he was now, and freer to move.

"Could I?" asked Michael, considering. "Think so?"

"Look," said Tristan, taking his phone out and checking his messages pointedly. "I'd love to stay and chat with a guy who gave me a really expensive ticket for not wearing a damn helmet, but I'm waiting for someone, and if they come and see me chatting amiably with the Man, well…there goes my credibility, you know?"

"Blowing me off, Sparky?" asked Michael, reaching out and taking Tristan's phone. "Oh, hey, cool -- a new one."

"Yeah," said Tristan, trying and failing to retrieve it. "Well, about the blowing off thing? In a word, yes."

"No, let me play with your phone for a second," said Michael, holding it out of his reach. "It's cool." The little electronic gizmo bleeped happily in his large, square hands.

"Yeah, okay," said Tristan looking around. He hadn't forgotten *the plan*; Officer Helmet had just postponed it. "Um, not to be rude or anything."

"Oh, all right," said Michael, picking up his coffee and his trash and muttering about how some people just don't seem to understand the word civility anymore. "Hey, Sparky?" he asked before he walked away.

"Yeah," said Tristan, finding something pretty compelling in the eyes he'd never noticed were Ty-D-Bowl blue. "What?"

"What are you doing here?" asked Officer Helmet. "Really?"

Well, shit. "I'm here, Michael, to get laid, not that it's any of your damn business, because I checked. Unless I'm selling it, which I'm not. I'm of age, and I'm free, white, and single, so *butt out*," Tristan said in a rush.

Michael looked at Tristan and then at the stack of books he had on the table, his blue eyes burning a big, gaping hole in his confidence. "You sure that's what you want?" he said, concern on his face. "The way you want it?"

"Yeah," said Tristan, now sure he was as red as his hair. "I want that. It's what I wanted all along."

Michael sighed. "In that case, Officer Michael Truax says, 'safety first,' Sparky. Try to remember that, okay?"

Chapter Two

Tristan thought he could breathe again when Michael walked away, but as if to say "no such luck," the man plopped his hairy policeman's ass right down at an adjacent table and grinned. Tristan's head smacked his stack of books again, hard. He did his best to ignore Michael, who for his part, got up and retrieved *Gay Las Vegas Nightlife* from Tristan's table and returned to his with an unrepentant, shitty smile on his face. He placed the book flat, Tristan noticed, so the cover wasn't visible. Obviously he wasn't there to pursue his own version of the plan.

A few minutes passed, and Tristan noticed a dark-haired man in old-guy trousers and a button-down shirt looking at his stack of books. Really looking, kind of staring and straining his neck to see the titles that were scattered by now on the table. Tristan pushed his long red hair behind his ear in a nervous gesture. He worried his tongue piercing. The man eventually stopped right next to his table.

"Say, those are some interesting titles," he said mildly, smiling. Tristan looked up, it seemed, a long way. The man was tall and not bad looking, but older than Tristan would have hoped for.

"Um, yeah." He smiled back. Not above a little trolling. Not above trying to leave with someone before it was like last call and true desperation set in.

"Can I sit down?" asked the guy.

"Sure," said Tristan. He wondered if there was some kind of code, or slang, or secret message he wouldn't know if someone used it on him. Tristan thought he might need a Captain Queer decoder ring or a spirit guide. His cell phone beeped with a text message, and he jumped. Picking it up, he held it to read the screen.

Married, probably with kids, wedding band tan line. Just thought you should know. Officer Helmet. Oh, shit!

He took the time to text back, *LOL* and prepared to talk to the man, regardless of Officer damn Helmet's sour observation. But he checked, and damned if the man didn't have a tan line, right there where his ring would have gone had he been wearing it. Maybe the man was a literature buff and just wanted to talk about prose.

"So, uh," said the man. "My name's Terry. What do you like about that stuff?" He nodded toward the stack of books on the table.

"You planning on lecturing me about the evils of my lifestyle?" asked Tristan a little defensively because, face it, *Michael* made him feel defensive.

"No, I'm planning on asking you if you have your own place." Terry smiled. "For various reasons, I don't use mine for tricking." He gave Tristan a look. *Okay, no decoder rings necessary.*

"Sorry," said Tristan. "No can do, I've used up all my infidelity tolerance minutes this month."

"Oh," said Terry, taking it better than he ought to have. "Guess I picked the wrong month." He laughed as he moved on, as though he hadn't just propositioned a boy and gotten shot down.

"What are you now -- my wing man?" said Tristan, barely loud enough for Michael to hear him.

"Serve and protect, little man," said Michael with a laugh. "It's my job."

"Don't you have a relationship of your own you can go screw up?" Tristan said, rubbing his freckly forehead with the palm of one hand.

"Nope," said Michael. "I'm off duty on relationships too, for the moment. Don't look now, but here comes another one."

Tristan gave him an exasperated stare, but the man was right -- someone was definitely checking him out. Tristan got up to retrieve another coffee, and when he came back, he spun his chair and straddled it, his head resting on his hands, now folded on the back of the chair.

Michael nearly gagged on his coffee, he was laughing so hard.

"Um...hi," said a guy about his age, sort of an earnest, nervous-looking kid. "Oh, my gosh! I love that book," he said, pointing to *Clicking Beat on the Brink of Nada*. "Have you read it yet?" The boy had preternaturally dark hair and faded green eyes. He was pretty and thin, and he seemed nice.

"No," said Tristan. "I just --"

"Oh, you won't believe it. He is such a fabulous writer! It's my book for when I'm feeling all emo, you know?" He put his hands in front of his mouth and squealed, "Oh, you have *Chemistry*! I've been dying to read that, another emo read, but what can I say?"

"Well, I just --" said Tristan. The boy had a way of using his earnest eyes to advantage that made Tristan want to lean in.

"Love doesn't always have to be tragic, does it? Do you think so? I mean, they always make it seem like love has to end in a suicide pact or something, but I think just having a healthy, normal relationship is possible, don't you?" He sighed.

"Well, healthy is good, of course," began Tristan when his phone beeped, signaling another text message. He glared at Michael, but looked at it anyway.

OMG! U never get 2 talk again, it read.

He texted, *ROFL F U* in all caps and returned his attention to the boy in question. “So, do you like to do anything besides reading?” he asked.

“Oh, sure! I’m in a club at school that cosplays Harry Potter. I’m Snape.” He tried to look suitably evil and failed.

Tristan pasted a smile on his face. Someone from the Harry Potter wannabe costume club. This was not good. This was so very, very not good. “What school?” he asked, dreading the answer.

The boy leaned forward. “As soon as I tell you, you’ll think I’m some spoiled rich kid.” He pouted. He shrugged and looked as though Tristan was pressuring him for an answer, even though he hadn’t said a word. “Oh, all right, I go to Villa Park High.” He grinned. Tristan knew Villa Park High -- very rich kids, very permissive parents.

Oh, heaven and all the saints preserve us. “So that would make you, uh, how old?” asked Tristan.

“How old do you think? People always tell me I look twenty-two.”

“Somebody’s completely deluded,” muttered Tristan. “I’m nineteen, and I thought you were about my age.”

“Ha-ha, I’m sixteen,” said the boy, and something inside Tristan went *twitch.*

“Um,” he said, trying to think fast on his feet. “Look, I don’t want to be rude, but I’m waiting for someone, and they won’t like it if I’m not alone. You know?”

“Oh,” said the boy, now clearly disappointed. “I see, maybe next time, then?”

“Sure,” said Tristan, watching him walk away.

His cell phone beeped that he had a text, and he read it. *Try ‘impedimenta!’ next time.*

?! he typed.

R U doing catch and release? came the next text.

R U going to STOP? he texted back.

Michael shook his head and mouthed, "Probably not." Tristan was getting hungry, his stomach not quite used to eating only a rice crispy treat for lunch. He gathered all his hair and held it off his neck for a minute, hoping the cool air would feel good. He was burning up, probably with shame if he thought about it too long, so he wasn't going to.

Tristan chanced a look a Michael at that moment and found those blue eyes watching him. They held a hint of something troubled, and he read concern there and something else. Something obscure that made him feel even warmer than he had before he'd picked his hair up. Tristan dropped it and smoothed it behind his ears, a gesture he knew was dorky, and found he didn't know what to do with his hands. He smoothed them over the pages of his book and worried his tongue bead a little more.

He glanced up to find Michael's mesmerizing eyes on him again and had a very strange thought. It was such a strange thought that it took some time to percolate through all the layers of horror and disbelief that underlay it until it reached Tristan's brain. He looked up again to find the blue eyes still watching, something eerie, something hot and vaguely predatory radiating from them. Seeing his hungry gaze, Tristan did something crazy. Something he had seen Viper do a hundred times when she was bored and she wanted to distract him from whatever he was doing. He raked the front part of his long hair up off his face with one hand, following the curve of his head down until it rested on the nape of his neck. He looked at Officer Helmet from under his lashes, and then he licked his lips.

Pow. Michael's coffee went right over the side of the table and broke open on the ground with a splat. Tristan stared, dumbfounded, as the man blushed deeply and mopped up the floor with about a hundred of those recycled, brown paper napkins. Michael murmured some self-deprecating comments and sheepishly went back to the counter to refuel. Tristan went back to his books, steadfastly refusing to look up even when he was certain Michael was looking at him. He had no idea what to do with his newfound knowledge, or even if he'd read Michael's awkward behavior right. *Had he read it right*? Well…hell. No way, *no way* was Officer Helmet hitting on him.

Tristan's cell phone beeped. *Why aren't u laughing?* it read.

Why do you call me Sparky? he sent back. It seemed a long, long time before he got an answer. He even put his phone down, thinking Michael wasn't going to reply.

Tristan's phone beeped at last, and he flipped it open to read, *Not telling you.*

Well, shit.

Michael got up and walked to Tristan's table, taking his former seat. "Well? What's new?" he asked.

"C over Lambda," sighed Tristan. "Are you a stalker, or what?"

"What," Michael replied, shaking his head. "I'm just here to drop off my mom's car keys."

"You have a *mother*?" Tristan asked incredulously.

Michael just looked at him. "Very funny."

"I, um," Tristan said. "I have to go." He picked up his pile of books, including the one Michael was still looking at, and walked away.

"Hey, you forgot your skateboard," said Michael, holding it up.

Tristan flamed up and returned for it, finding he had a much harder time carrying his load back than he did bringing it to the café in the first place. He wondered if that was because of the heady anticipation he'd felt on engineering the plan, and the sick, twisted way he felt now, watching it go so catastrophically awry. He felt Michael following him, but Tristan refused to turn and acknowledge him.

Officer Helmet was not part of the plan. The plan was about strangers, about someone with whom he could have hot, rabid man-sex. Not someone he knew. Not someone he saw every weekend stalking him at the skate park, trying to give him a ticket. Not someone who made a crusade of trying to protect his head. *If that's even what's going on here*, he thought.

Tristan went to the gay lit section and replaced the novels he'd taken down, a little OCD kicking in as he nervously placed them in alphabetical order by author and then straightened the spines for good measure. He returned the other books, all the while aware of Michael following him at a discreet distance. At last he was ready to bag his plan -- *the plan* -- for the day, hoping to escape, if not with his dignity, at least with his life.

He reached the enclosed foyer entrance where Borders kept the bargain books, and he thought he was home free until he heard a voice behind him say, "Not so fast, Sparky, I don't see a helmet."

"I'm just going to walk it home, Officer, I promise," he prevaricated, turning to find the man standing so close, Tristan's nose bumped his chest. "Ow."

"I tell you what, I'm sorry I blew your little fishing expedition. Are you hungry? I'm going to eat at Lucille's across the parking lot, and if you want, you can join me. Then I can run you home." He raised his eyebrows in a question. "It beats getting a ticket, which you surely would. Because I can *make* that happen."

Tristan's mouth flew open, then closed, then opened again. "That's extortion…that's a total misuse of your authority. You ought to be ashamed."

"It's just barbecue at Lucille's. Not the movie *Deliverance*, which if you ask me, it could have been. You're lucky I stepped in; you could have ended up getting really hurt, or worse." He looked grim. "I'm hungry; are you coming?"

"Uh," said Tristan, whose own stomach had been rumbling for more than an hour. As soon as he hit the parking lot, he could smell the smokers going, the rich mesquite barbecue smell something that teased and taunted him every time he came to this Borders anyway, so he just said, "Well, okay. I'm hungry, and I love that place."

It didn't take them long to walk across the parking lot and into the loud, smoky restaurant. They were seated immediately because it was between the lunch and dinner rush. Tristan ordered a berry lemonade, and Michael, a Corona.

"You're drinking?" asked Tristan, incredulous.

"It *is* my day off," replied Michael, amused. "The sandwiches are huge. You want to split a tri-tip sandwich and get some onion straws?"

"Uh, yeah," said Tristan. Tri-tip was his favorite. "Sure." He didn't know where to put his feet or his hands or his eyes. A sense of the unreal began to wash over him in waves. "If anyone I know sees me here eating lunch with you, my life is over."

"Because I'm a cop," said Michael.

"Well…yeah," said Tristan stupidly.

"Yet you were looking to pick up some gay guy for an afternoon of what?"

"What? What do you think, *what*? Not that it's any of your business, but yes, that was *the plan*," said Tristan.

"What about Viper, the goth chick? She's a doll." Michael grimaced. "Well, more like a voodoo doll, but she'll be cute when she's over the whole blood sport thing." Michael shot him a searching glance. "You don't really want to change your whole life on a whim, Sparky, and tricking with strangers like that? Can get you dead. It's fun chasing the next rush, but…"

"Is that what you think? That I'm into the weird stuff, and I want to walk on the wild side?" The waitress brought their drinks, and they took the time out to thank her politely. Tristan unwrapped his straw and placed it in his lemonade. "Like, next you'll see me all tatted up on some old guy's leash with a ball gag in my mouth." He held his napkin in front of his mouth so he wouldn't laugh so hard he spit his lemonade out.

"Well, isn't that like you? Big motion, big air, big rush?" asked Michael, and to Tristan it seemed he really was trying to understand. To be…a friend. How totally weird.

"Well, yeah," said Tristan carefully. "I'm kind of an adrenaline junkie. I like to do stuff that's not particularly safe sometimes."

"But putting yourself in the hands of strangers? That's not so good, yeah?" said Michael with concern in his eyes.

"This is too bizarre. I can picture you having the same talk with Viper about me. With Viper, I'm the guy, right? I'm the predator. Now I'm the one that needs to be protected? I'm a guy," said Tristan. "I can take care of myself. Anyway, how do you know I'm not some serious Dom, and you shouldn't be warning those guys about me?"

Michael smiled, but said nothing. He squeezed the lime through the neck of his bottle and took a sip, savoring the way the bitter bubbles tingled in his mouth. When the waitress came back, he ordered for both of them.

Michael relaxed back in his seat, but Tristan found himself fidgeting. He arranged and rearranged his silver and picked his right leg up, sitting on it, getting comfortable. In constant motion, he was rapping on the table when the onion straws came.

"Oh, I love these," said Tristan, taking the first one and eating it with his eyes closed like a sacrament.

Michael picked up a few and ate them, dipping them first into the sauce. “Me too. I come here a lot because I’m always doing stuff for my mom. She works at Borders.”

“She does?” *Just my damn luck.* “Just that one, right? Not the one in Savi Ranch?”

“You little shit! You’re already thinking of taking your show on the road.” Michael laughed. “I’m not here to kill your fun, Sparky. I just want you to be careful. I’m sure I’ve said enough on the subject; just eat your lunch and I’ll take you back to your house. You still live with your folks? Didn’t you want to go the dorm route?”

“No, not really. My dad passed away a couple of years ago, and I like to hang around with my mom and help her with my brothers and sister.” He blushed, thinking that sounded stupid. “Free room and board doesn’t suck, either.”

“Well, it’s UCI, so it’s close, right?” said Michael. “That’s lucky, anyway.”

Tristan pushed the straw around in his lemonade and didn’t look up.

“What?” asked Michael.

“I could have gone someplace else. I got into Stanford and Georgetown. My mom doesn’t know.” He pushed a lemon around, finally digging it out and sucking on it, ripping the flesh away with his teeth, his tongue lapping at the bitter white pith. He shuddered. “Lemons, man, it’s a total love-hate relationship.” He looked up to find Michael’s eyes on him in a way that made him burn. Michael broke eye contact first and picked up his cell phone, playing with it.

“You’re a good guy, Sparky,” said Michael finally, as their sandwich came. They traded sides, fought over the pickle, and generally managed a good-natured lunch together.

"Have you got brothers or sisters?" Tristan asked, amazed to find that he wasn't just making small talk; he was actually interested.

"Nope, it's just me and Mom. My dad didn't hang around after I was on the way." He swirled the last sip of beer around in the bottle and downed it. "I bought a duplex in Fullerton, and she lives in the other place. She's what you might call a free spirit."

Tristan grimaced. "I don't know if I like getting to know stuff about you. It's like playing cards with the enemy on Christmas Eve."

"I'm not the enemy, Sparky," said Michael, picking up his phone again. He held it for a few minutes, fidgeting with it, then Tristan's beeped to indicate he had a text.

Hey, Sparky, it read. Michael smiled over at Tristan, who fumbled with his own phone, making Michael's phone beep.

Hey, Officer Helmet.

Tristan grinned and said, "I hope you have unlimited text messages on your plan. You're kind of like my friends, texting each other in church."

"I'm shocked," said Michael.

Tristan's phone read, *U text in church?*

Yep, he sent back. Out loud he said, "The phones are all set on vibrate, and every so often someone will jump, and it's like, 'Can I get an *amen*.'"

Ask me again, Tristan read on his cell phone.

Ask what? he sent back.

Why I call you Sparky. Michael fumbled with the keys, not looking up.

Well, sure, why? Tristan sent back.

You light me up, came the answer, and Tristan's nimble fingers stopped on the keys. He stared hard at the small screen on his phone, the text message right there, waiting to see if he would send a reply. He just sat and stared till his phone turned off, unable to look up into the oh-so-blue eyes of the man who had sent it.

Chapter Three

"'Scuse me," Tristan said, getting up and walking quickly to the men's room. He opened the door and made a straight path to the one stall with a door and sat on the edge of the toilet, hardly daring to breathe until it became an absolute biological imperative. *I light him up*, he thought, all the breath whooshing from his lungs at once. The phone beeped again.

I M R U? it said. Well, shit. He didn't need his Captain Queer decoder ring for that, either.

What the hell? he typed, stupidly. No way, *no way* was that man gay. Michael was just messing with him, trying to scare him off the deal. Scared *straight* like the documentary, except with cops instead of felons and more consensual man-sex.

Need a hand? Michael sent with a smiley icon, and Tristan nearly dropped the phone in the toilet.

Who R U? Tristan sent back. He heard the door to the bathroom open and moved his feet from the floor to the toilet like a third grader, to hide.

"I'm the guy you caught today, Sparky," said Michael's amused, musical voice. "I paid the tab, time to go. I know you're in there."

"Oh, all right," said Tristan, stepping down and unlocking the stall door. "If you're through messing with me, I guess I could use that ride home now." He marched out, keeping his eyes down, prepared to follow Michael out of the bathroom.

"Okay, come on." Michael walked casually through the restaurant and out the door and across the parking lot, still holding Tristan's skateboard. He used a remote to unlock a monstrous black truck with four doors and light bars everywhere. He tossed the skateboard into the back seat and got in, watching as Tristan climbed up. He waited until Tristan buckled his seatbelt.

"I live down State College," Tristan said. "Past the university." He still didn't look up. His fishing expedition had gone so spectacularly wrong he was already coming up with a new plan, one which involved never leaving the house again and maybe enjoying gay porn for a while.

"Sparky, look at me." Michael didn't start the car, he continued patiently in a war of wills with Tristan, who didn't really want to see those mocking eyes ever again.

"No. I get your point. I'm scared *straight* already."

"Jeez, I hope not." Michael put his hand on Tristan's face and turned it toward him. "I really, really hope not." He pressed a kiss to Tristan's lips, running his tongue gently along the fuller lower lip, which stuck out as if Tristan was pouting.

"What are you doing?" asked Tristan shrilly.

"What do you mean? You were trying to get picked up, so I picked you up." Michael ran his hands through his hair. "Are you kidding? What normally happens when you do that whole gay book thing?"

"I don't get picked up by cops." Tristan neglected to mention that so far, he hadn't gotten picked up at all. Except he had, hadn't he? And he hadn't even felt it.

"Nothing wrong with cops unless you're doing something illegal," said Michael. He laid his head back on his headrest and looked anything but comfortable.

"Well, I wasn't, so I don't know what you want with me," said Tristan.

"Are you an idiot?" Michael asked, and Tristan felt the blood heat his face. He knew he was turning an ugly shade of red.

"Wait, don't tell me, I go with you, and it's a one-way ticket to county lockup for soliciting a cop, right?" asked Tristan, disgusted. "Gonna let the inmates scare me straight, huh?"

"Sparky, you are out of your mind," said Michael. "This is like teaching queer remedial at the continuation high school. You were fishing, and you caught *me*. Don't you get that?"

"Oh, *hell no*." Tristan just stared.

Michael rolled his eyes and started the car. "I'll drop you, don't worry about it," he said, his face impassive.

"Look, it's not that --"

"Save it," snapped Michael. "Just save it."

"Okay." Tristan was unable to think. Michael's big truck slid through the now worsening late afternoon traffic on Associated, and the sun was beginning to set. Michael's mouth was compressed into a thin white line, but the rest of his body was still relaxed and easy, and Tristan thought it might be costing him an effort to keep it that way.

Eventually, on Yorba Linda Boulevard, Michael casually asked, "Okay, where to from here?"

"Um, left on State College," Tristan said, directing him the rest of the short drive. When they pulled into the driveway of Tristan's house, he sat there for a minute, completely unsure of what to do. "Look, I can pay for my lunch."

"Nah, it was a pleasure," said Michael. "See you around, kid. Wear a helmet, man, really."

"Oh, yeah, maybe...okay," said Tristan, starting the climb down from the tall truck. "Hey, thanks for everything."

"Sure thing," Michael said, and Tristan closed the car door.

From that moment forward, Tristan's brain seemed to work in slow motion. Michael threw the truck in reverse and backed slowly out of the driveway, safe and sane as always, driving away at the perfect speed for Tristan's suburban street. Tristan watched Michael's truck crawl away with its lights already on in the gloomy dusk exacerbated by the trees overarching his street as if it had nothing to do with him.

It wasn't until Michael's truck was about fifty meters away that a series of emotional aftershocks slammed through Tristan, and before he knew it, he was running down the street, chasing that truck, slamming his skateboard beneath his feet and building up speed until he caught the fender on the passenger side.

Once there, he couldn't help but just enjoy the ride for a minute, knowing that when Michael glanced in the passenger-side mirror, his life was probably over. What seemed a too-short time later, the truck slowed to a stop, and the driver's side door opened and then slammed shut with a loud *ka-blam* that reverberated through the quiet neighborhood.

"Tell me," said Michael, pinching his nose like he was trying to stop a nosebleed, "that I didn't see what I just saw." Tristan noticed the vein throbbing on his temple and had second thoughts.

"Well, I…um." He couldn't explain that he'd had a blast of something he'd never felt, like all his cells jumping, like a magnetic wave that pushed him and pulled him toward that truck at the same time. Something like *wanting*, but that word was so shallow, and what he felt was so deep. "I wanted to catch you, you know, before you left." How could he not have noticed how soft Officer -- Michael's hair looked and how the stubble on his chin looked golden in the dying light? How blue his eyes were in his tanned face?

Michael crossed his arms. "Say it," he said implacably.

"It," said Tristan, snarky, and Michael turned to leave. "No, wait. Yeah, *yes.* I wanted to catch you. You…fish. Me…reeling you in."

"Fair enough," said Michael, with a half smile. "But we're going to work on your communication skills." He walked around to the passenger side of the truck and politely held the door open for Tristan, who numbly got in, skateboard in hand. "Do you need to do anything at home? Get anything?" he asked.

"Uh, no," said Tristan, just staring, hardly daring to believe all the new things he was doing this day.

"Quick stop first," said Michael, who said nothing more until they pulled up in front of Play It Again Sports. Michael got out and came around to him.

"What are we doing here?" asked Tristan.

"You are getting a helmet that you will wear every damn time you board from now on because my heart just can't take the strain." Michael held his hand out to help Tristan down from the truck, but Tristan ignored it and leaped lightly down by himself.

"Dude --" he began, but Michael cut him off.

"No. Don't 'dude' me -- it's not negotiable." He pushed Tristan against the door of his truck. "I don't do this; I don't just pick up guys. I've chased you and watched you and wanted you for two years now, even though I felt like some kind of loathsome pervert because you're younger than me. If you want anonymous, this isn't it. Make up your mind. I like your head, and I want you to protect it."

"Jeez," said Tristan. "Stop barking at me. I can't think when you bark."

"Sorry." Michael's lips quirked a little.

"I was kind of looking for anonymous, but maybe you could just blindfold me or something?" he asked.

“Oh, Sparky,” sighed Michael, taking his arm and marching him into the store. “The things you say.”

Chapter Four

They settled on a black, nondescript helmet of the variety that every self-respecting professional skater wears and every smart-ass skater loathes. "There," said Michael with a satisfied grin. "That's done. I didn't think it would take offering my body, but I am a dedicated peace officer, and whatever works, since public safety is job one, right?" He led Tristan back to the truck, but turned when Tristan stopped. "What's up?" he asked.

"This just feels weird," Tristan admitted.

"I know." Michael's smile reassured him. "Come on, let's go." He handed Tristan up into the passenger seat before walking around and getting in himself. He put the key in the ignition. He started up the truck and turned on the radio, and Tristan was shocked and relieved to find they had the same taste in music. He allowed the quiet between them to continue, even though it was in his nature to fill up gaps in a conversation, choosing instead the safety of silence. He noticed they were driving through the older part of Fullerton, by the city college, where there were picturesque Craftsman-style houses on streets with big trees and bigger roots tearing up the sidewalk. Here and there, places with weird rooflines that made them look just like Snow White's dwarves' cottage dotted the suburban landscape. The houses looked like they were built in the twenties or thirties, and he wondered what kind of place Michael had.

They pulled into the long driveway between two small identical houses, both Craftsman-style, with steps leading up to wide, welcoming porches. In the back there were two stand-alone garages. Michael pulled in front of the one on the left.

"This place is so great!" said Tristan enthusiastically as they walked around the house and up the front porch steps. "You said it's yours? Did you win the lotto?"

"No," said Michael. "I started buying and fixing up these old places in high school, when the market sucked and people were selling them for nothing. At first I got my mom involved because -- would you believe? -- realtors didn't want to show property to a sixteen-year-old. I've been buying and selling ever since. Of course, now the market is so inflated, I'm kind of standing pat, but I have income property, so that's fine with me. It means less construction work on my off hours."

"Wow," said Tristan, as Michael unlocked the door. The place, to his eyes, was perfect. The focal point was the wood, the highly polished floors, painted white crown molding, and built-in cabinets bearing workmanship so fine, it was some of the best Tristan had ever seen. "Oh, this is…it's so detailed." He ran his hand over the molding around the door leading to the hallway from the living room. "My dad was an architect; he would have loved this. Not because the design is genius or anything; this was probably built back in the thirties, wasn't it?" Michael nodded. "But the workmanship is so fine."

He went with Michael for the tour, down the long hallway, living and dining room on the left, two bedrooms with a bath between them on the right, kitchen and service porch, as Michael called it, in back. "Awesome," he said, "You did it perfectly. So many people get these places and trick them out with clutter everywhere, 'home sweet home' and all that charming crap, but here" -- he spun in the middle of the living room -- "the house is the star."

"Thank you," said Michael quietly. "That's nice…thank you."

"It's beautiful." Tristan went to the fireplace and traced the woodwork on the mantle. "Especially this," he said, noting the delicate carving, the way the moldings were layered and built up together to create an intricate pattern.

Michael rolled his eyes. "My mom's would make you cry. It's so cutesy it looks like Smurfs live there. Moms. What can you do?" He smiled and walked back toward the kitchen, Tristan following.

"Speaking of moms, I'm going to leave a message with mine," said Tristan, going out to the small back porch, noticing the Dutch door with delight as he exited. "Great touch," he said. "The door."

He turned and left a message, saying he was at a friend's and didn't know when he'd be back, or if… He nervously looked behind him to see Michael reaching into an old-fashioned fridge for a beer. He snapped his phone shut and returned to the kitchen.

"What did you tell her?" asked Michael. "Listen, do you have a curfew…or…"

"No, I don't," said Tristan quickly. "Not really, I'm, uh -- I told her I'd be back, or maybe not. She knows she can reach me on the phone. She trusts me."

"Does she have any idea that you do this? Does Viper? I hope you always use protection. What does Viper say when you go cruising for cock? Doesn't she mind that you walk both sides of the street?"

Tristan's head spun, and his face burned. "Well, sure, I use protection," he answered that question first. "Jeez. As for Viper, she actually…um…she dumped me. But it's not exactly like I'm busted up over it." He nodded at Michael's beer. "Aren't you going to offer me one?"

"No," said Michael flatly, giving him a look that said, "duh." "But I have soda, juice, and lemonade. Which do you want?"

"Lemonade," said Tristan. "Do you have a fresh lemon?"

"Yeah, hang on." Michael went out the back door, returning minutes later with some lemons. He got a knife and an old-fashioned bar juicer down from one of the cabinets and turned to Tristan. "Make yourself useful and juice these while I make the sugar syrup."

"Okay." Tristan cut the lemons and placed them into the metal container before pressing the large lever to squeeze the juice into a bowl.

Michael took out a saucepan and added water and sugar to it.

"I didn't mean for you to have to go to all this trouble," he murmured under his breath as Michael lit the old-fashioned stove.

"This isn't trouble, Sparky, this is domestic foreplay. The syrup has to cool, and while it does, I'm going to suck you dry," Michael said in his rich, melodious voice. "Going to make you scream, baby, and when you land, the lemonade will be --"

The knife clattered out of Tristan's hand, and he cried out, "Shit!" He grabbed a paper towel and wrapped it around his cut finger, murmuring "Ow, ow, ow. Lemon juice. Ow."

"Oh, here." Michael came over and placed his hand under the faucet, running cool water over it and studying the cut on Tristan's finger carefully. "Not deep. I'll get a first-aid kit. Don't move," he said, and Tristan stayed right there, feeling like an asshole, until Michael came back.

"Here," said Michael, moving Tristan under the light while he put antibacterial ointment and a good, tight fabric Band-Aid over the cut. "Careful not to get lemon juice in that," he teased.

"Ya think?" said Tristan.

Michael moved then, suddenly, and took Tristan's head between his hands, stroking his hair and bringing him in for a long, slow kiss. Tristan relaxed into it little by little, first opening his lips to Michael, allowing the other man to invade him with his tongue, and then tentatively sending his own tongue out to play, exploring. He stepped into Michael's body, into his embrace. Tristan felt the strength there, the hard muscles, the anxious cock pressing against his own, and also the gentleness with which Michael wielded all that strength, and fell in love. Well, seriously *in lust*, for the first time, and he thought, *oh, crap*.

Michael turned off the stove, pushed Tristan up to the counter, and sank to his knees on the hard tile floor. He fumbled with Tristan's belt and then unbuttoned his pants, stroking him all the while through the fabric. Tristan's brain melted, and he just stared at the man on his knees before him, silently watching. When Michael freed Tristan's cock from his boxers and caressed him, Tristan sucked in a lungful of air and timidly stroked his hair, moving his uninjured hand unconsciously in the same rhythm Michael's hand used on his dick.

"Oh," he moaned, and dropped his head back at the first touch of Michael's mouth on his balls. "Hey, oh…"

Michael laved the sensitive flesh, stroking and sucking until Tristan felt boneless and slid a little, opening up for him, muttering a curse and getting a better grip on the counter with his injured hand.

"*Oh*!" he said when Michael licked up the underside of his cock, along the vein there.

"Latex okay?" Michael dug into his front pocket and produced a condom. "I can't without it," he added, looking right into Tristan's eyes, making sure he understood that they would have to play it safe.

"*Go*," said Tristan, his hands shaking. "Whatever, just…just don't stop."

Michael smiled, then hummed around Tristan's balls a little while he put the condom on with more stroking than was strictly necessary. He took his time and then wrapped his lips around the head of Tristan's cock, flicking his tongue a little at the slit in the top. Even through the latex, a bolt of electricity shot up Tristan's spine and crackled through his hair.

Tristan's knees buckled, and Michael grabbed his ass both to hold him up and bring him closer, swallowing Tristan's cock in one mind-boggling move that had Tristan's heart hammering in his throat as he came right then and there. Michael continued to squeeze, stroke, and suck him until he came down, eventually collapsing in a heap over Michael's shoulder. Michael slipped off the condom and knotted it, throwing it into the trash.

"That was…" Tristan tried to form words. "That was…oh, shit." He wrapped his arms around Michael's neck and buried his face there, sort of kissing and sort of biting, but mostly just hanging on in a possessive, primal instinct kind of way.

Michael sighed against his skin. "Let me guess, Sparky," he said, and his voice sounded like it came from somewhere very far away. "First fishing expedition?"

"Mmmhmm, yeah, well…" Tristan tried to find a way to deny it, wondering if cops could tell if you were lying better than girlfriends could and deciding that, yes, they probably could. "Yes. Okay. But it's not what you think. I have experience, so I didn't think it would be, you know, that different. Just, like, we'd use different holes and stuff."

"You're kidding me," said Michael, brushing the hair out of Tristan's eyes. Tristan thought Michael held his hair a little longer than necessary and wondered if he liked it, maybe, and just didn't want to let it go.

"Look, perhaps I was a little hasty," said Tristan, starting to panic. "But it's not like I haven't been hitting it with girls since I was fourteen, so…"

"It is *not* the same!" said Michael. "And you almost placed yourself in the hands of a total stranger. What do you do for brains outside of school, Sparky?"

"Hey, I do *not* need your insults. How does anyone get started having..."

"I'll tell you how," said Michael, gritting his teeth. "Most of us start like it's a joke between friends, you know, pretending it's just until we can get it with girls so let's jerk off together or whatever. Some of us get laid by older or more experienced men who may or may not care about our feelings, but are probably not into hurting our bodies, because it's hard to get it up if you're in pain. And then some of us get ourselves into really bad situations with strangers who don't care about us at all and end up getting used."

"Which were you?" asked Tristan gently, unable to stop touching Michael's face, conveying without words the tenderness he was feeling in that moment.

"All three."

Tristan tightened his grip on Michael. "I'm sorry. I thought it would be like picking up girls for sex, you know, at the mall or something." He smoothed the hair on the back of Michael's head, down to his neck. "Which I've done, so I'm not a total novice at this sort of thing."

"Oh, Sparky, a guy looks at you? You *are* the girl." He smiled and then shook his head. "Still want that lemonade?"

"Yes...no...I want" -- he tightened his grip on Michael -- "I want..."

"I know." Michael helped him to his feet. "Come on." He took Tristan's hand and walked him into the living room. "We probably ought to talk."

Chapter Five

Michael dimmed the lights until Tristan could just barely see. His living room was small, furnished with not much more than a large sofa on an oriental rug facing the fireplace.

"I really love this room," said Tristan, echoing his earlier sentiment. "It's like a room in an historic home, and it feels like the best place on earth for a good book. It must be great when you have the fire lit." He was babbling, and he knew it, but Michael didn't seem to mind too much.

"Yeah," said Michael. "Too hot for one today, but sometime soon it'll get cold enough. I don't use the heater; I just light the fireplaces."

"Fireplaces? Plural? There's more than one?"

"Yes, I have a Franklin stove in the bedroom with a gas log for warmth. I only need it once in a blue moon, but it's got character. I put one in my mom's place first because she asked me to, and then I liked it." He ran a hand through his hair. "I like old things. I wanted a house that felt like it wasn't all wired for cable and satellite and broadband. I wanted it to feel like a home, not an office."

"You nailed it," said Tristan, settling onto the couch and sinking into the soft cushions. The leather felt like a baby's skin against his hands, and he sighed. "How do you live without all that stuff, though? I don't watch an awful lot of television, but I have to admit to being a little bit of a *CSI* and *NUMB3RS* junkie."

"I have a television; it's just not obvious." He smiled. "I do have two bedrooms -- one I use as a media/office room, but you'd never know it unless you searched. The bathroom's big enough; the kitchen I kept old-fashioned by buying refurbished appliances. This house is all about the wood, so most of the effort has gone into the carvings and moldings." He seemed to look around again, as if he needed to check that it was still right, and then said nothing more.

The topic of Michael's house was, if not exhausted, momentarily worn out. Tristan had little idea what to say. He looked at his hands, which were folded carefully in his lap, and wondered if it would be okay to just reach over and grab Michael by the hair. That would be bad, he decided, probably.

Michael saved him by slipping an arm around his shoulders. "So let's start again, Sparky. Why are you here?"

"You're really going to keep bugging me till I tell you?"

Michael nodded.

"Here goes, okay? Even when I was a kid and I was reading those Dick and Jane books, I thought I'd probably be better off with Dick, you know? So Viper dumps me; she stands me up, see? Then her brother answers the door, and long story short, he was hard and leaking on his jeans because his girlfriend was there, and I thought, *Aha*! That's what I'm talking about. I mean I just *own* it. Sign me up for one of those! It was all I could do to keep from licking him, or just taking a big bite right through the denim, and I was only saved from the embarrassment of a lifetime because his girlfriend came up from behind him, with her mussed-up hair and kissed-up lips, and I thought, *Well, shit. Got to come up with a plan.*"

"And that was your whole plan? Borders, Gay Lit 101, and a cup of coffee with a rice crispy treat?"

"Well, yeah. I had condoms; I'm not stupid."

"My lucky day." Michael rolled his eyes.

"Look, I'm sorry you got involved, and thank you for lunch, man. Although, it's not like you didn't work really hard to *get* yourself involved. At least admit that," said Tristan.

"Sparky, when you're right, you're right." Still, Michael didn't move. He just sat there with his arm around Tristan, his own shoulders shaking with laughter.

"Anyway, I loaned my car to my sister, which is why I was boarding today, so I need a ride home," said Tristan. "Please?" He thought being polite couldn't hurt.

"Not taking you home."

"What?"

"Not returning you. I like you. I'm keeping you." He got up and asked again, as if he hadn't just said the strangest thing, "Still want that lemonade?"

"Um, yeah," said Tristan.

Michael held out his hand. "Then come help me make it," he said, pulling Tristan along like a toy. He lit the stove again, starting the sugar syrup, and mixed the lemon juice with water. "I think there are some frozen raspberries, if you want to add them, there in the freezer." When he'd finished boiling the syrup, he turned back to Tristan, who gripped the counter tightly with both hands. Michael faced him and put his arms around him, sliding his hands into the back pockets of Tristan's jeans. He nudged Tristan's feet apart and stepped between them.

"You were shorter when I ticketed you two years ago, but you've grown since then," said Michael. "I'm…"

"Ripped." Tristan slid his hands over Michael's strong arms, daring a caress of Michael's chest. "I'll bet you have great abs."

"Not really. I'm not strong, but I'm fast, even though I can never catch a certain hooligan when I chase him through the neighborhood behind the skate park."

"Well, if you'd just said you wanted to kiss me…"

"I wanted to kiss you then; I want to now. How about it?"

"Caught me," sang Tristan, looking into Michael's eyes.

Michael leaned in then, pulling Tristan's hips closer and tasting his lips with his tongue. Tristan opened to him and moaned a little when he felt Michael squeezing his ass. It was a good kind of squeeze. Hard, but not pinchy, and it brought him more in contact with Michael's cock, which felt damned fine.

Tristan brought his hands up and ran them through Michael's short hair, digging his fingers into the scalp a little, massaging him, holding him still, and using his thumbs to trace the features on Michael's wonderful face.

"So good," Tristan whispered between kisses, not even aware that he'd spoken until the words were out. "You're…so hot."

Michael moved from Tristan's lips, finding and licking the junction between neck and shoulder. Tristan dropped his head back to give him more skin, but miscalculated, and his head smacked back on the cabinets.

"Jeez, baby, looks like you need to wear that helmet inside too," murmured Michael against his skin. Michael moved back, and Tristan made a noise when he lost contact. Michael smiled. "Back soon," he said and went to stir the sugar syrup into the bowl of lemon juice Tristan had made earlier. He added the raspberries to the lemonade, poured the mixture into a pitcher, then placed it in the fridge. "It'll be a while before this cools to a nice drinking temperature."

"Yeah?" Tristan was still dazed.

"Yeah, a little while." He took a ribbon of Tristan's long red hair in his hand. "This is like fire," he said. "Red hair is often curly, but yours is like silk."

"Mmmhmm," said Tristan, being stroked and loving it, like a cat.

"You are so beautiful. I thought that the first time I ever saw you." Michael kissed him, hard, still holding his hair, winding it in his fist.

"Yeah?" Tristan liked the small tug, liked Michael's possession of him.

"Wanted you," said Michael.

"Me?" Tristan kissed him back, loving the taste of him, loving how his beard was scratchy, and his skin was tough from shaving.

"Started calling you Sparky because when I ticketed you that first time, I looked into your eyes, and this shock went straight to my balls," Michael said into his hair.

"No kidding, really?" Tristan wanted more skin, so he started to unbutton Michael's Hawaiian shirt. Under his assault, Michael's shirt opened in seconds. He stopped what he was doing and just gazed at Michael, his hands over his mouth.

"Sparky?"

"You are so…" Tristan stood back to look. "Oh." He couldn't stop himself; he went straight for one brown nipple encircled by blond hair sort of just calling him and wrapped his lips around it. He licked it, working it with the bead on his tongue, feeling it harden under his probing. He rubbed his face in the fuzz on Michael's chest, the crinkliness of it going straight to his cock, before taking over the other nipple.

"Oh, hey." Michael cupped the back of his head. "You…hey."

"Yeah, oh, this is good," he said against Michael's chest, his brain melting from the sensual stimulation. He tried to sink into Michael then, his face rubbing the tan flesh, his hands tracing the muscles. "I wish I could tell you how this makes me feel."

"Yeah."

Tristan moved like a blind man reaching out, wanting everything. He was trying to crawl inside Michael and feel him from the outside at the same time. Tristan's hands shook as they explored.

"It's been a while for me," Michael murmured.

"What can I…what should I do?" Tristan was at a loss.

"Oh." Michael cupped Tristan's face in a tender gesture. "I'm trying to think if I was ever that young."

"Hey." Tristan pulled back, stung. He might not know how to *ask* for what he wanted, but he for damn sure knew what he wanted. He caught Michael around the neck and pulled him in for a full-body embrace and a searing kiss that he was sure left little doubt that, though he might be young, he was not to be dismissed casually.

Michael took Tristan's shoulders in his hands and forced him back.

"What?" asked Tristan, bewildered. "No good?"

"Are you kidding?" said Michael. "I feel like a junior high school kid; I'm about to come in my pants."

Tristan's face burned. "I…well, me too." He laid his hands on Michael's chest, sliding them up to his shoulders, reaching out to bring Michael back. Tristan pulled Michael hard against the whole length of his body again and surged against him. "Do you have a load of laundry you need to do? Because I'm like, so close if I touch my fly button I'll go off."

"Sparky," Michael panted, his hips snapping against Tristan's in a powerful thrust as he forced the younger man against the counter, lining up their cocks through the fabric of their pants, using the zipper to scratch him a little. "The things you say sometimes make me think…"

Tristan came so fast his hips jerked, and he shook and slammed against Michael, who held him close and followed him over the edge. Their mouths joined then, in passionate combat, their lips fused and their tongues searching until their hearts slowed down a little. Michael gently lifted Tristan up onto the counter and held him.

Tristan wrapped his arms and legs around Michael and put his head down, his teeth grazing the space where Michael's neck met his strong shoulder. "So good," said Tristan with a sigh, clinging to him like a monkey "I want more… I want everything."

For an answer, Michael just rubbed his face in Tristan's hair. "Chased you lots, Sparky," he murmured into the stuff, marking the skin of Tristan's neck.

"Caught me," repeated Tristan, moaning softly at the burn and sting of the blood Michael was bringing to the surface of his delicate skin.

"Would you like to take a bath?" Michael asked. "I have a big tub."

"Are you planning to take it with me?" Tristan jumped down from the counter. He started across the kitchen to the hall door and turned to find Michael staring at him with hot eyes. "What?"

"You are so beautiful, Sparky," Michael said, pushing away from the counter to follow him.

Tristan dipped his head so his long hair would hide his face. "You make me feel beautiful." He allowed Michael to pass him and watched the way his body moved as he led him to the only bathroom in the small house, situated between the two bedrooms.

Michael's footfalls were silent, catlike on the hardwood floors compared to Tristan's, and Tristan had an idea that he did everything in that same measured, deliberate, and conscious way. He wondered if Michael brought dates home often, and if he did, were they more like him? Were they older, more sedate, more grounded and less likely to do something as stupid as humping him like a puppy while he tried to make lemonade? By the time Tristan heard Michael turn on the water, his face was on fire.

"What's up?" asked Michael.

"Nothing really," said Tristan, looking around what seemed to him a relatively large bathroom. Like every other part of the house, this room was beautiful, spare, and presumably carefully remodeled. The focal point was an enormous claw-foot bathtub, slipper shaped, with a high back. It impacted the eye, thought Tristan, the graceful, essentially fluid shape of the tub against a geometric backdrop of gray and cream tiles. It was exactly the kind of bathroom that Tristan pictured for mystery novels and trendy bed and breakfasts. It was a monochromatic man's room with no place for extra paper, or his sister's endless zippy bags for cosmetics.

Michael slipped his shirt off and looked straight at Tristan while he removed his sticky jeans and shorts. "That's a feeling I wasn't nostalgic about."

"It's not an everyday occurrence for me, either." Tristan looked at Michael, whose body was fit and tanned and ripped. Michael had lied -- the man had abs to die for. "I think if I hang out with you much I'd better get used to it," he said thickly.

Michael turned a slightly pink shade at that revelation and came over to help Tristan out of his clothes. He kissed all the skin he found as he revealed it, peeling off Tristan's shirt and undoing the belt on his jeans. When they were both naked, they stood and stared at each other for a long time. Michael broke the connection first by turning away and picking a stick lighter off a shelf to light candles. He dimmed the overhead lights until the room was lit by only the candles' glow.

The tub was pure luxury, all white porcelain and surrounded by a silky white fabric shower curtain that Michael pushed out of the way as he sank in first, his back against the raised lip of the tub. He looked…so hot. Tristan was still, and Michael watched him quietly.

"I, uh, guess I should…" said Tristan, slipping into the water without a splash. He sat at the foot of the tub, facing Michael, and squeezed himself over to the side of the faucet. Tristan looked anywhere but at Michael's eyes, which he knew would be amused at his expense.

"Oh, no, you don't," said Michael softly. "I get to hold you; it's my tub, my rules."

"Oh, okay." Tristan practically swam through the water to sit with his back to Michael's chest. He felt the man inhale and exhale, his own chest rising and falling with Michael's. "This is nice."

Michael picked up a tiny bottle and poured a little of its contents into the water, swishing it around. The smell of something vaguely familiar teased at Tristan, and he closed his eyes, trying to place it.

"A little aromatherapy," said Michael. "Nice after a long day of arguing with unrepentant criminals."

"Christmas…" said Tristan. "It smells like Christmas."

"Yeah, I guess. It's probably the rosemary; it has an evergreen smell. It kind of reminds me of food," said Michael. "But then again, so does everything. I'm kind of a foodie."

"I got that when you made sugar syrup for the lemonade," said Tristan. "FYI, even mothers don't do that anymore."

"My mother does," said Michael.

"Figures." Tristan ran his hand through the water a little, moving it in ripples. Michael's arm came around him then, stroking the taut muscles on his stomach, slipping lower to brush his cock, which responded with shocking enthusiasm.

Tristan could feel Michael smile against his neck. "You respond so instantly."

Tristan tried to hide his face in his wet hands.

"No, Sparky, it's not a bad thing. I like that. Are you kidding? It's hot."

"I'm like that with you." Tristan put his hand over his shoulder to hold Michael's head where it was, next to the skin on his neck. Michael's touch was making him sigh and shake and want things he was afraid to ask for. "Not everyone."

"There's something I want to ask you." Michael kept his voice carefully neutral. "Am I even remotely someone you could see yourself with? Dating, I mean? Not just a trick from Borders because you were curious, but someone real to be with. I don't mind being, you know, just the guy you caught on your very first fishing expedition."

"Oh, no!" said Tristan. "That feels, like, a million dumb ideas ago." He stroked Michael's hair thoughtfully, glad his back was turned so he didn't have to have look him in the eyes. He didn't even stop to wonder why that seemed so much more intimate than bathing with the man. "I think you may have saved me from, at best, an embarrassing afternoon."

"I'm glad you think so," said Michael, who seemed to be waiting for an answer to his question.

"I didn't expect to find someone I liked," Tristan began. "I just wanted to know how it felt to be with a man. Maybe figure out, you know, how to do it. Anonymously, sort of, so I wouldn't have to look like a total asshole to that same guy twice. That's really dumb, isn't it?"

"No, but it wasn't really safe or well thought-out," said Michael. "Would you want to hear your sister say that?"

"I'm a man, Michael. Stop comparing me to a girl."

Michael splashed him a little. "You're young, Sparky, and slim and delicate in your coloring. Sure, you shave, but not much, not like I do. You still have baby hands," he said, holding one up, the pruny fingers white and soft and freckled. "Look, no veins." Michael held his own up by comparison. The veins were prominent, the multiple scars he'd gotten from woodworking and construction like a tracery of white lines against the tan background. "All I'm saying is that when a guy like me looks at you, as innocent as you are, as genuine, as naive, he feels protective. Someone else may choose to exploit you."

"I see."

"I can do anonymous, Sparky, I can show you what you want to know," he whispered.

Tristan froze. "You don't know what you're getting into. I think I may have a really long, slow learning curve." Tristan couldn't look at him.

"Mmmhmm, that's what I thought," said Michael.

"Um, you'd probably better, you know, plan on spending some time with me. It could be months before I get it right."

"Maybe more."

Tristan could feel the easing of tension in Michael's body and hoped it was because he'd gotten the answer right. "So, if you don't want to invest that kind of time with me, then maybe that's something you ought to say right up front," said Tristan. "Because I can do, like, anonymous, but it wouldn't be my first choice. Anymore."

"Sparky?" said Michael, turning him and kissing him so deeply that Tristan started seeing spots in his field of vision. "Anonymous isn't even on the menu anymore, okay?"

"Oh, okay." Tristan was relieved and frightened all at once. "So, then, what *is* on the menu?"

"You, my redhead, are going to" -- he whispered a word into Tristan's ear that made the blood drain from Tristan's face, then return with a rush of heat that singed his eyebrows -- "me through the mattress." As if to illustrate his point, he slid Tristan's naked body over his own, rubbing their cocks together briefly, aided by the silky bath oil he'd added to the water. "Feels good. You're gonna make me fly, right, Sparky?"

"Oh, I…yeah…I hope so." Tristan bit his lip. Michael looked happy, *so that was good…right?*

Chapter Six

Okay…okay, get a grip. I've done this before, Tristan thought as he dried himself off with one of Michael's awesome, luxurious bath towels. He wasn't exactly stalling for time, but he wasn't hurrying, either. He'd asked for this, schemed for it, planned for it, and gotten it, but in reality, it wouldn't be as easy as he thought to slide between the sheets and just screw the man. Michael had left him alone in the bathroom, presumably to put their clothes in the wash or something, and would wait for him in the bedroom. Tristan was grateful for the privacy. He carefully hung the dirty towel up on a hook, looking down at himself. Thoughts like, maybe he wasn't the most manly guy he'd ever seen, whirled around his confused head.

Tristan had gotten a good, long look at Michael as he left the bathroom, and now his heart thudded painfully from sheer nerves. Michael was beautiful. Smart and funny and sexy and everything Tristan had ever wanted. He was caring and powerful, and at the same time gentle and oh-so-hot. Tristan was afraid he'd do something stupid and uncool like launch himself at the man like the winged monkeys from *The Wizard of Oz*. He sat down hard on the lid of the toilet.

Okay, it's official, he thought. *I'm gay. I'm a done deal.* He put his head in his hands and just sat there. He was no way going to be able to do this without shaming himself, or Michael, or all of their collective ancestors.

"Sparky?" called Michael's voice from the hallway. "You aren't losing your nerve, are you?"

On the money, Detective Helmet. "Just a minute."

"Can I come in?" asked Michael, sounding concerned now.

"Sure." Tristan heard the door open.

"Usually people use that with the lid up," teased Michael, coming over to hunker down in front of him. He drew Tristan's hair back like a drape and held it in his hands. "You're under no obligations here, you know."

"I know that." Tristan leaned into Michael's hand.

"What are you thinking?"

"Seriously, dude, did you just *hear* yourself? I thought once I went over to the dark side I'd never hear those words again."

"Sparky," warned Michael. "No jokes, what's up?"

Tristan took Michael's face between both his outstretched hands and kissed him gently. "I never wanted anything in my life more than I want to be really, really good for you."

"What?" This obviously wasn't what Michael had expected to hear.

"You've already taken me places light-years more amazing than I've ever been before, Michael, and I want to do that for you too…I just…" Tristan bit his lip.

"Shh… Let's just go, okay? Let's just go together. We can do that, right?" He stood up, and with a friendly smile, took Tristan's hand and led him to his bed.

They slid between the sheets, which were soft and silky against Tristan's naked skin. Michael's touch began a slow burn in his body that was sensual and crazy. Tristan's pulse beat everywhere, his blood thrumming endlessly through his veins as Michael kissed him and stole his breath. He began to explore Michael hesitantly, feeling heat come off Michael's skin in waves.

He touched and teased, licked and bit his way all around Michael's willing body, turning him this way and that, finding new and exotic destinations with every movement of his head, his hands, even his feet. Every cell in his body tingled with awareness, as if they were whispering his lover's name in his blood. Dazed, he looked down at Michael from where he lay on top of him, his long red hair forming a curtain around their faces.

"How do you want it?" Tristan whispered, afraid to speak too loudly, afraid to shatter the magic of the moment.

"I want to see you," said Michael. "I want to watch your face." He reached under the pillow for lube and a condom, and held them out for Tristan, who took them from him.

"I don't want to hurt you," said Tristan, in an agony of indecision. He understood the concept, but…

"Here, look, okay?" Michael said taking Tristan's hand. He separated Tristan's index finger and put a generous amount of lube on it. "It's this first, yeah?" he said, raising his eyebrows at Tristan, who almost couldn't keep from looking away. "Then this," he said pulling up the second finger. "Then this," he pulled up the third, until Tristan was looking at the three fingers on his own hand, right in front of his eyes. "Then it's you, and you make me fly."

"Oh, my…" said Tristan, still looking stupidly at his fingers. "Make you fly."

"Yeah, baby. I want you -- you know that, right? Like today sometime, maybe?" He smiled such a sweet smile Tristan had the absurd idea he could lick it off like candy.

Tristan looked back at his fingers, slick with lube, shining in the candlelight. "Today sometime…"

"I'll tell you a secret -- there's a surprise inside." Michael laughed and watched him through lowered lashes.

Tristan looked down at him. "A surprise? What the hell…"

"We'll both know when you find it," said Michael. "We're going someplace only you can take me, right? I want that; *I want you.* Don't worry. You can't hurt me."

Tristan looked at his hand again and then at Michael's eyes. "When we make love, you will call me Tristan," he commanded. "Sparky makes me sound like a damned firehouse dog."

"We'll see how you do first," said Michael, issuing a teasing challenge. "I like you, baby, want to feel you inside me... Ready?"

"Yeah." Tristan took the lube and condom from him. "I am."

Tristan slid the covers off them and moved down over Michael's body, kissing and licking his way to the warm and secret places he had yet to explore. He fingered and played with Michael's dick, loving the smooth, hard feel of it in his hands, turning it and lifting it, letting it leak onto his hands, teasing the veins and the ridges and the slit at the top with his tongue. He tasted the salty skin and the slightly bitter, briny fluid, and moved beneath it to the crinkly blond hair on Michael's balls, so fascinating in their sac. He mouthed them as Michael had done to him, first one and then the other, drawing a surprised gasp and a slight moan from the man himself. He moved them and licked backward from them, down the long strip of sensitive skin to the puckered hole he found there. He flicked his tongue against it, hardly daring to breathe for fear Michael would stop him, but he heard a sharp intake of breath and nothing more, so he did it again, wanting to feel, to touch, to taste every part of this man.

"Sparky," said Michael, his voice a little hoarse, a little shocked. "You don't have to..."

Tristan nipped the skin lightly, shutting him up. He lifted his still-slick index finger and slowly, almost reverently, slid it into the tight pink hole until it reached the first knuckle. "Tell me if I hurt you," he said to Michael, needing to connect as he made each minute discovery on Michael's body. Tristan experienced every ripple and quake of Michael's skin with a focus of laser-like intensity that heightened his own pleasure until his skin glowed with sweat, and he was breathing as if he'd run a race.

"You can't hurt me," Michael repeated, taking Tristan momentarily away from his intense concentration, surprising him a little.

"Hm?" Tristan slipped his finger in further, moving it tentatively around, and getting a satisfied moan for his efforts. "Oh, good."

Tristan moved the finger again, in and out, until Michael was moving with him, meeting him. Tristan used the lube to slick the second finger, and he slid it in with the first. Michael shifted, sighing, and Tristan pushed a little harder, working him now with his hand, allowing Michael to push back to meet his thrusting fingers. When Michael moved against him, Tristan pushed his face into Michael's golden skin, wanting to inhale and devour him. Never in his life had he wanted anyone this badly.

"That's so good, Sparky," said Michael. He patted Tristan's head where it lay on his thigh, where Tristan watched his hand gliding in and out of his lover's body. Tristan couldn't take his eyes away, watching his fingers, watching Michael's cock jerk as he stroked him from the inside. It was the hottest thing Tristan had ever seen. He slicked up the third finger and slid it past the tight ring of muscle to join the first two.

Michael moaned and thrashed a little, his head going side to side as he rocked against Tristan's hand. "Yes," he sighed. "Sparky, *yes*." He caressed Tristan's hair with the same rhythm Tristan was using to stroke him. His hips lifted and jerked as he took Tristan's fingers inside and squeezed them so tightly Tristan thought he'd die with longing to feel that on his cock. He wiggled his hand experimentally, curving his fingers upward, and Michael's hips shot off the bed. Michael bit down hard on his lower lip.

"Found it," said Tristan, hitting it again and again, as Michael writhed and moaned beneath him.

"Sparky!" Michael cried out, his voice a warning and a plea. "Now, *please*."

Tristan opened the condom package and wasted no time getting it rolled over his cock. "I'm going to…you know…" said Tristan. "Coming in, okay?"

"Go," said Michael, between clenched teeth.

Tristan pushed into him, each second of resistance followed by each exquisite sensation of yielding adding to the fire already burning inside his body.

"*Michael*," hissed Tristan, kissing his lips and moving slowly inside him. He pulled out, almost his whole length, and then pushed back in, loving the feel of the tight channel embracing his hypersensitive cock. Michael rippled and trembled beneath him, the sensation, the squeezing heat like nothing he'd ever experienced.

"Hard, Sparky," said Michael. "Push me hard…I want to feel you tomorrow…next week."

Tristan responded by setting up a rhythm of hard, sharp, shallow thrusts, changing his angle till he felt that jolt of pleasure go through Michael as it had done when he'd used his fingers.

"My name is Tristan," he said over a particularly aggressive jab. "Call. Me. Tristan," he said, using his body for punctuation.

As Tristan nailed Michael's gland time and time again, Michael started to call out to him, closing his eyes and stroking his own cock, pushing back hard against Tristan, urging him on with a litany of words, some sexy, some vulgar, and some that were just nonsense.

Tristan pounded into him, his balls slapping against Michael's ass crack. Looking for a better angle, Michael moved his legs over Tristan's shoulders without losing contact, which allowed Tristan to watch as Michael stroked himself sensually as if his pleasure was building along with Tristan's.

"Good," grunted Tristan. "So good. Come for me, Michael. Come on my cock, let me see it." He wanted to see that beautiful dick come rockets of hot liquid on Michael's tan stomach. The thought made his eyes cross and his flesh burn. He wanted to see that…could already smell it and taste it on his tongue.

"*Tristan*," cried Michael, looking him right in the eye. "Harder… Harder, Tristan…"

Tristan slammed home, and Michael came in his own hand, the white cream ribboning onto his chest. Michael's head dropped back, and his eyes closed as he bit his lip so hard he drew blood.

Tristan was a goner as soon as he saw Michael come. Nothing could have prepared him for how beautiful Michael became when he slipped over the edge in pleasure. "Michael." Tristan's hips snapped harder in response, his rhythm broken, his hips jerking of their own volition.

Michael's hole fluttered around him, his muscles clenching as he rode his release.

"So beautiful…Michael… You are so beautiful…" Tristan filled the latex a short second later, feeling the heat swirl around him inside Michael's body, burning him alive.

His energy gone, Tristan collapsed, still inside Michael, letting the man's legs fall gently to the bed. Sticky warmth squeezed between them. Without thinking, he kissed and licked Michael's lips where they'd been bitten, feeling the warm blood on his tongue.

"Michael," said Tristan with wonder, tasting blood and salty, sweaty skin and something unknown that was just Michael. He hissed as his limp cock slid from Michael's body.

Rolling with him, Michael held him fast, not responding as words were inadequate to describe how he felt. Instead, he wrapped himself around Tristan, showing him with his body that it was good. He put a hand between them, slipping the latex off Tristan's cock, tying it off and throwing it in the trash. He felt Tristan sigh where he lay bonelessly in his arms.

The intensity of the experience rolled over Michael in waves. He stroked and rocked Tristan in a state of slight shock, still trembling in the aftermath of the best orgasm of his life. He had meant, as the older, wiser, and more experienced of the two, to show Tristan the ropes, as it were, to aid him and build his confidence. He clung to Tristan even as he closed his eyes and slowly shook his head. Life was full of irony. This boy, this cocky college sophomore with his freckled, white baby hands and soft-as-a-girl's skin owned him. *Owned him.*

It was a lot to take in.

Michael sighed, realizing that Tristan's breathing was even, and his facial features were lax and childlike. Michael kissed his sleeping lover, stroking the silky red hair off his face. He'd be damned if he'd stare at that beautiful sleeping face all night, he thought. Yet, Michael yawned, maybe just for a few more minutes, so he could commit this to memory, in case. *Just a few more minutes...*

Chapter Seven

By three in the morning Michael knew he wasn't going to sleep and that his study of the boy/man sleeping beside him was bordering on the obsessive. He decided to get up and grab a snack, maybe something they could both eat in bed, and move the laundry from the washer into the dryer. He fixed a quick plate of things to nibble, cheese and meats and some veggies with ranch dressing. He padded around the house, checking locks and windows. Picking up the food and a couple of water bottles, Michael finally returned to the bedroom.

When he entered it was to find Tristan sitting up in bed with the blanket around his shoulders. Michael placed the food on the nightstand and climbed in beside him.

"All right?" he asked.

When he didn't get an answer, he put his hand on Tristan's shoulder, only to find it icy and trembling. Tristan's whole body shook under his touch, and concerned now, Michael drew an unresisting Tristan to him. The boy melted into his warmth, sinking into him like a frightened animal.

"Hey," said Michael, stroking his hair. "Hey." When Tristan didn't answer him, he asked gently, "Regrets?"

"*Iacta alea est.*" Tristan buried his face in Michael's neck. "Go figure. I remember that on the night when I'm having the hottest sex of my life."

"Really? The hottest sex of your life?" Michael grinned, but when Tristan growled at him a little, he tightened his arms. "I...what does it mean? Beyond habeas corpus and ex post facto, I'm a little weak in Latin."

"It means 'the die has been cast.'" Tristan was shaking less, and Michael, taking this as a good sign, kept him talking. "That's what people say when they've done something...irrevocable."

"You know, people don't really say that, Sparky," he couldn't help mentioning. "It's kind of..."

"Obscure, I know. I'm babbling." He took a deep breath. Michael just stroked his back in circles, keeping contact. Tristan leaned into his touch, soaking it in like a sponge. "I've crossed the Rubicon," he sighed. "It was a World Civilization multiple choice question. A. Crossed the Rubicon, B. Played with dice. C. I'm babbling again, aren't I?"

Michael digested this, wondering what to say, wanting to say the perfect thing even though his heart was breaking. *This* was why he rarely dated men who weren't already openly gay, he thought briefly.

"You got off with a guy -- you didn't start a civil war. Nothing we did tonight is anything you haven't already done with a girl. You said it yourself, right? Different holes. You haven't been invaded, you haven't...well, you just haven't." He closed his mouth, thinking that was probably his best option at this point. Regrets...well, they happened, didn't they?

He got up to light the stove and take the chill off the air, and because it gave him something to do. It was a gas log, so all he had to do was turn a key and light it with a stick lighter. When he returned to Tristan, the boy had tears running down his face. *Shit.*

"Oh, hey, Tristan," he sighed. "I'm so sorry, I didn't...I shouldn't have..."

"Shut up, will you? I'm having a moment here." He burrowed back into Michael's arms, and Michael held him, his chin on Tristan's head.

"I can move to the couch," said Michael. "Or set you up in there."

"You aren't going anywhere." Tristan tightened his hold on Michael.

"Okay…well. Can we have your moment together, then? I'm in the dark here." Michael sighed.

"Sorry." Tristan looked over at the nightstand. "Is that food?" He crawled over to take the plate and a bottle of water. He rearranged the pillows and sat with his back to the headboard, still wrapped in the blankets. Holding out the second bottle of water, he motioned Michael over. Warily, Michael came to him, sitting next to Tristan, their shoulders touching. Tristan smiled at him around a piece of sharp cheddar cheese, and he was reminded why he'd taken a chance with him in the first place.

""What's going on in that head of yours, and how can I help?" he said finally, giving in to the urge to take a couple of carrots and some celery for himself.

"Didn't you have a moment?" Tristan asked him. "Didn't it all yawn out widely before you that the path you chose was leading you someplace completely foreign?" This time he staked claim to a bite of salami. "If I eat this, will you still kiss me?"

Michael snorted. "Yep."

"So, anyway, I'm thinking, okay, there goes the wedding, the kids, the grandkids, and most of the public displays of affection. There goes that shot at socially sanctioned relationships, married filing jointly, being a soccer dad, watching my babies get born." His eyes glistened with tears that began to fall just as he said the word babies. "I saw my little brothers get born."

Michael put an arm around him. "It doesn't have to mean anything, Sparky. It's just one night."

"But it does mean something. That's why it was so… This didn't happen to you?" he asked again, his beautiful blue eyes sparkling with unshed tears.

"You mean, like, did I all of a sudden realize there goes my seventy-fifth wedding anniversary shout-out from Willard Scott?"

Tristan made a disgusting noise and snagged another piece of salami. "Well, did it? Happen to you?"

"Not all at once, no," said Michael, thinking back. "I doubt I ever did anything as…suddenly as you seem to. I have to say, I think you may be smarter than me. You think more moves ahead. Plus, I grew up in an unconventional family."

"Ah," said Tristan. "I see." The silence between them lengthened, during which they heard only the hissing and crackling of the gas log.

Tristan turned to him suddenly. "I'll never be sorry, ever," he said simply.

Michael listened to what Tristan said and tried to understand its meaning. He took a long, slow swallow of water. "I guess when you want me to know what that means, you'll tell me."

Tristan's hand smoothed over the column of Michael's throat before resting lightly on his Adam's apple. It fluttered there briefly and then slid down to caress a shoulder. "Can we…do you think we can slam the door on Willard Scott?" He put the food back on the nightstand. "Will you… *I want you.* I want it to be you…"

Michael understood what he meant, but he needed the words. "Sparky?"

"I want you inside me, Michael, I want you." Tristan lowered his lashes. "I want… Tonight's been like magic. I want it to be you, tonight. Will you?"

Michael bit back the flip reply that came readily to his lips. He wanted time to think, to consider the consequences. He for sure didn't want to be the cause of anyone's tears or regrets. Hadn't been, as far as he knew, up till now. He rubbed his face with both hands, giving himself a minute. He didn't feel Tristan stiffen next to him, didn't see the deep flush burn his cheeks, so he was wholly unprepared for what came next.

"Shit," said Tristan, tossing off the covers. "Where are my clothes? Maybe I should have made it a multiple choice question."

"Hey," said Michael. "Hey!" He threw his legs over the side of the bed, his feet hitting the wood floor with a slap.

"I'm sorry I took a brief time out of your evening to ponder my life. Won't happen again. TMI, I know." Tristan stalked out of the room toward the sound of the dryer.

"Look, you're overreacting to a pause in the conversation. Can you just stop?" Michael took Tristan's shoulders and spun him around to face him. "You opened the dialogue -- at least be man enough to stay and see where it goes. Come back to bed where you're not cold." Michael pulled Tristan along the hall by the hand and pushed him gently back into the bed.

Tristan just looked at him, still flushed and stiff. "What?"

"Look, you've got to know, you're the first person who's ever cried after having sex with me. That's a little intimidating." He sighed. "I just needed time to think. I don't want to hurt you any more than I already have."

"You haven't hurt me; when did you hurt me?"

"I just thought, maybe, if we took it a little slower… That whole crying thing? Never again, man." He touched Tristan's face lightly. "I was just trying to think how I'd feel if you regretted it later. If you felt bad about it, whether I wanted to live with that. Surprise, Sparky -- it's not just about you."

"I'm sorry." Tristan hung his head.

"Are you gay?" asked Michael with a sigh. "Is that your truth?"

"Mmmhmm," Tristan said into the night. "Yep. Totally gay. And I'm apparently a chick too, because here we are, talking instead of screwing."

Michael rolled his eyes. "Come here." He slid his arms around Tristan, laughing a little. "You wouldn't believe how much I like you right now."

"Yep, nothing like a --" He was kissed out of that thought, and didn't have many more before Michael slid his hands along his back and stimulated his skin to goose bumps. "Oh," he breathed.

"You taste sweet," said Michael. "Don't ever be afraid to talk to me, and don't run away when you don't get the answer you want... I want you to be happy."

"Okay," said Tristan in a small voice as Michael found a sensitive spot on his hipbone with his lips. "In that case..."

Michael stopped what he was doing and gave him his full attention. "What?"

"When it's dark, when it's just us, would you please call me by my given name?" he asked, his eyes serious. "It's important to me. It makes me feel like we're..." He was going to say "lovers," but lost his nerve.

"That's fine, Tristan," said Michael seriously. "You won't hold it against me if I slip every now and then till it becomes a habit?"

"No."

"Thank you for telling me," he murmured going back to Tristan's skin with his lips. "It's nice when I know what you want."

"I want you," Tristan said breathlessly.

Michael smiled against his most sensitive skin, rubbing his face in the crisp red curls he found there. He hummed a little next to Tristan's balls, earning a moan. "Could you hand me the lube?" he asked, right next to Tristan's cock.

Shaking fingers passed a small bottle to him.

"You're sure, Sp -- Tristan?" he asked one final time.

"Yes," whispered Tristan. Michael nodded. He touched, tasted, and explored every inch of Tristan's most private real estate, until Tristan writhed beneath him. When he slid a lube-slicked finger tentatively into Tristan's tightly puckered hole, Tristan stiffened against the invasion, then willed himself to relax. Michael gently moved the finger, stroking Tristan's thigh with his free hand, and little by little, slid it in.

"Lift your knees a little," he said, and Tristan felt another finger moving tentatively at his entrance. At the invasion, Tristan shifted restlessly and sucked in a lungful of air. "Don't forget to breathe out as well." Michael smiled.

"It feels...I..." Michael found Tristan's gland and ran a finger over it gently. "Oh, shit!" cried Tristan, jerking up, eyes wide. Michael did it again. Tristan was melting mentally, incapable of speech when Michael added a third finger. He pushed back against Michael's hand, numbly reaching for pleasure.

"Turn over," said Michael, his fingers still scissoring inside Tristan's hole. Tristan began to protest, but Michael merely helped him turn, saying, "Trust me?"

Tristan nodded, unable to speak. He felt full and dizzy and so damn needy. He wanted to say something, to protest not being able to see Michael, but then he heard a condom package open and felt Michael moving up behind him. Michael gently lifted Tristan's hips and slid a couple of pillows under them, nudging Tristan's legs apart as far as they would go. He lifted him to his knees, and then...Tristan felt him at his back, his hard cock ready to slide into his most private place. He began holding his breath then, partly from fear and partly excitement.

Everything Michael had done so far, touching him and filling him, had made him burn with need. He wanted to feel it all again, wanted that jolt of erotic lightning when Michael touched him just the right way. He was mindless with it, brainless, boneless. When Michael gathered himself to slide his slickly lubricated and gloved-up cock into Tristan's tight channel, he went slowly and very deliberately, as if totally focused on any movement or sound from his partner. Tristan felt the burn, then a searing kind of pain that frightened him and made his dick go limp. He heard himself hiss and gasp at the same time, vaguely wondering how that was possible.

"Michael," he cried out. "It's…it hurts…I…" Even as he said it, Michael was kissing his back, caressing his skin, soothing him, and the burn began to fade so he could think again.

"So tight," Michael said hoarsely. "I'm sorry. Breathe for me, okay? Deep breaths."

Tristan gave little nervous laugh. "That's your cop voice, Officer Helmet." He still sounded shallow, shocked. "I feel like I should be having a baby."

"Shh," said Michael, feeling Tristan's small laugh in the flutter around his cock. "Just breathe, okay?" He reached around and began to stroke Tristan's cock, going lower to fondle his balls. Tristan's body was still full of him, still shocked, but slowly loosened up, trusting him. The thought filled him with awe, that his Sparky trusted him with this.

Tristan dropped his head down to the pillow, and Michael knew when Tristan tentatively rocked his hips that the pleasure had started to chase away the pain. "Oh, Michael," he cried out when Michael started pumping Tristan's cock lazily, still not moving inside him. "Oh!" he cried the first time Michael moved, a short withdrawal, a slow slide back. "That feels...oh, damn..."

Michael took that as permission to move, and move he did, starting with slow, gentle thrusts, pumping Tristan's cock at the same time, finding a rhythm, then changing it as he felt himself racing toward release too soon. Tristan had begun to moan into the pillow, his butt coming up, pushing back, looking for more. Michael changed his angle, sitting up on his knees and taking Tristan's hips in his hands, curling his toes for traction. Michael pushed hard into Tristan's perfect ass, nailing his gland and slapping the fronts of his thighs against the backs of Tristan's as his lover, on all fours before him, took all of him and more. Tristan was shaking, melting around Michael's cock, almost keening into the pillow.

"Touch yourself, Tristan," said Michael, between thrusts. He was still bringing himself to the brink, then backing off. Sweat ran into his eyes, and he doubted he could hold off much longer. He began to make long, sweeping strokes, each one brushing by Tristan's gland, and he felt Tristan's orgasm when it came, in his stiffening body and the clamping of his asshole around Michael's cock, the sweet ass jerking beneath him with each thrust as he rode the waves of his release. He heard Tristan scream his name into the pillow. Michael grinned. *Noisy.* Michael let himself go right then, the sight of Tristan's body filled with pleasure, the smell of him, the noises he was making, all setting off a chain reaction of mini explosions that started in his balls and the base of his spine, and traveled through his body to his brain until he saw spots. He thought he might have shouted and hoped he called out Tristan and not Sparky.

They stayed rocking like that, on their knees, with Michael draped over Tristan's back and Tristan still probably biting the pillow, until Michael softened and slid out of Tristan's body. He removed and tied off the condom, tossing it toward the trash, and pulled Tristan with him. Michael rolled onto his side, spooning up to Tristan in a more comfortable, sleepable parody of how they'd made love.

Tristan said nothing, and oddly, this didn't worry Michael much. Maybe it was the way that Tristan snuggled back into him, or maybe it was the way he pressed Michael's hands to his body, or the fact that he hooked his foot around Michael's ankle and rubbed Michael's calf with it that made Michael think Tristan would be okay till he drifted off to sleep again.

Michael lay there wondering what morning would bring. That morning, or rather, now it was yesterday morning, he realized, he sure the hell hadn't known he'd be here like this, loving the boy for whom he'd written his first citation. He grinned into the darkness, circling the thinner man's waist with both arms. Sometimes good things *did* come if you waited long enough.

Chapter Eight

Monday morning Tristan went with two of his friends from school to Diho Bakery, a Taiwanese place close to UCI that made hot, fresh meat buns and sweet bean-curd pastries. He laughed and joked and played like always, but every so often he'd remember the previous Friday night and get caught up in it. His face flushed, and he worried his friends could read the new knowledge there. He'd eaten breakfast with Michael the previous Saturday after spending the night, straddling his lap and feeding him cereal, and being fed fruit in return. They'd shared coffee and then skin, showering and sliding together until the water turned cold. Tristan couldn't take his eyes or his hands off his new lover, and apparently, he couldn't get his mind off him, either.

"Hey, Tris," said Jonathon for the third time. "Dude, you deaf or what?"

"No, sorry," said Tristan, mastering his thought processes. It was midterms, and if he didn't get a grip, his test scores would be low and his social life nonexistent for the rest of the quarter. "What?"

"I asked, are you seeing Viper again, or did you find someone new? You're marked, man; it's like you're dating a Hoover."

"Oh." He slapped a hand to the side of his neck where it met his shoulder. He knew he should have left his hair down. His mom had noticed too and given him a hard stare that morning before he took the boys to school. "No, not Viper, I met someone."

"As usual, you work fast. Have you forgotten geeks aren't supposed to get laid? It's like a natural law or something. We're supposed to languish undiscovered in our labs while our jock buddies get all the goodies."

Daniel spoke up. "Our boy Tristan here is a jock and a geek. Slap a skateboard under any one of us, gentleman, and you'd have --"

"Broken bones," interrupted Tristan, choosing a cream bun for breakfast and a pork bun for lunch. "I've got to study more, or I'm hosed. How are you doing? I'm working on a paper comparing and contrasting Heisenberg and Schrödinger, and I've got three midterms, including one in German, which I *will* fail unless I give it adequate time."

"That hardly leaves any time for us to live vicariously through your mad ninja love skills. When are you going to see her again?" asked Jonathon as they walked to Daniel's car. "We can get together for poker afterward and dish."

"Seriously, dude," said Tristan. "Did you just say dish?" He got into the back seat with his pastries.

"I've got too many sisters, but you know what I mean; it's the only way I'll even get close to getting laid this year." Jonathan looked disgusted. "Michelle's at NYU, and I won't see her until her winter break. Poker is good though, right? How about Friday?"

"I'm going out on Friday after I take my sister Lily to a party and make sure it's kosher," said Tristan. "She's gotten invited to some big Halloween thing by a girl from work, but the kids are college age, and the only way my mom will let her go is if I take her and check it out for a while to make sure it's not going to turn into one big orgy. Afterward, I'm meeting someone at another party." *Michael.* "Saturday's good, though."

"How does your mom let *you* out of the house if she has standards?" asked Daniel, nodding toward Tristan's neck.

"I guess she has substantially lowered expectations where I'm concerned. I think she's just relieved I survived the whole high school skateboard thing. She trusts my judgment," he said, privately thinking, *Not for long.* He would be seeing Michael after the party, meeting him at a dinner hosted by some of Michael's friends, and he worried, not for the first time, whether he'd fit in. *No way.* He sighed. "I don't know about that party after Lily's, though…" He imagined a room full of cops glaring at him.

"Aren't you looking forward to it?" asked Jonathon.

"Hm, what, poker?" Tristan asked. "Sure."

"Not that. Friday. Your date."

"Oh, yeah, but it's midterms," he lied. "I can't help but think if I don't get back to school and start studying, I'll go down in flames…"

"You'll do fine. You always do," said Daniel around a cream bun. "Let's go." He started up his Honda Element, and they drove the short distance back to school. He had philosophy at nine, and he couldn't be late. He walked alone to his class, a lecture hall filled with students, only a small percentage of whom were interested in the philosophy class for more than just the fact that it fulfilled a requirement.

Tristan liked philosophy as much as he liked physics and was considering pursuing either a double major or making philosophy his minor. His brain liked to run as much as his body did, the two entities pulling him in two different directions constantly, creating an agitation that was rarely subdued for any length of time. He recognized that it was in the nature of both to be in constant motion. Thinking of Michael, of their evening together, engaged both his mind and his body to such an extent it threatened to shut all other functions down at once. He had a minute or two before class and was standing outside, wondering if he should get a water bottle, when his phone beeped.

It was a text message from Michael. *Hey, Sparky*, it read. The man loved to text. *How R U?*

Good, he texted back. *Still melted.*

My favorite, Michael wrote. Then, *C U Friday?*

Yep, around 10:30? asked Tristan, making sure.

K TTYL, he received.

K, Tristan thumbed and sent. He looked around, aware that the blush that stained his face must look like a beacon on his fair skin. A couple of girls with their hands over their mouths watched him, whispering confidences and giggling at him. He smiled sheepishly, and they fled, giggling some more.

That morning on the drive in to school, Tristan's heart had practically stopped every time he saw a black-and-white, and not for the usual reasons. He was very much afraid that at any moment he'd begin rhapsodizing over the gray blue sky or the crisp autumn air. It was only a matter of time before he'd be dotting the *i's* in his lecture notes with little hearts. It wasn't that he felt particularly authentic doing any of these things; he just couldn't stop himself. He was so disgusted by lunchtime that he ate half of his barbecued pork meat bun before he realized that it was someone else's leek and mushroom.

The sunlight broke through a crack in the clouds, and his face warmed, the light and heat like an old friend after a few overcast days. Even that sent his heart skittering in his chest, reminding him of physical things, like Michael's mouth on his skin, the warmth of the Franklin stove in the bedroom, and the way Michael took him from behind. It was an act of possession that made his body feel like it was no longer his own. He burned to belong to Michael like that again and had to sit there forcing himself, over and over, to return his mind to school where it belonged.

By Wednesday, he'd fought to put enough distance on the physical sensations that he was doing pretty well in school. Michael's frequent and sometimes imaginative text messages threatened to ruin it, though, like when he received the one during his German midterm that read, *R U nekkid?* Or the one that read, *Officer Helmet says spread 'em*, he got while eating dinner at Denny's with his mom and two brothers.

At night Tristan jogged at nearby Craig Regional Park, sometimes joined by his younger brothers, sometimes alone. Only by exhausting himself was Tristan able to find sleep at the end of the day, instead of lying in his bed with his heart racing in his throat and his hand on his cock. When the physical need overwhelmed him, he took long, hot showers, bringing himself to release again and again with Michael's face in his imagination and Michael's name on his lips.

* * *

By Friday, Tristan had all his tests taken and all his homework turned in. He had no classes on Fridays, so his morning was free, although he always took his brothers to school while his mom took his sister, who had earlier classes. On his way, he caught sight of a black-and-white that might have been Michael's, but had no way to find out, short of getting a ticket. When he'd dropped the boys off and returned home, he pressed the costume he planned to wear to Lily's party.

Strictly speaking, one party was a Halloween party, and the other wasn't. Michael's friends were not having a costume party, even though it was that time of year. But it would be much worse to embarrass Lily by showing up dressed as a chaperone than to go to Michael's party dressed as a samurai. Lily was self-conscious about his presence anyway. She was young and out of sorts and was acting emotional a lot of the time, which is why his mother asked him to check the party out, deciding not to do it herself.

"I promised Mom I'd go, Lily," he told her on the way. "It's better that it's me than Mom walking in there and checking things out, right?"

"You don't understand anything," snapped Lily right away. "How can I show up with my *brother*, for heaven's sake? That's like tying a pork chop around my neck."

"Thank you, I love you too," he said, sighing.

"You know what I mean." She glared straight ahead.

"Just tell everyone I'm your feudal era bodyguard," he said, trying to lighten her up. "It could be worse; I could have gone as Barney or something."

"Shut up," she said. "And when we get there, I don't know you; you never saw me before in your life."

"Then how am I going to explain why I'm showing everyone your naked baby pictures?" He pulled into one of the few parking spots still left on the street where the party was located. "I think you should be nice to me. I'm giving up half a date to be here so you could come, and you know I won't be as hard on this thing as Mom would."

"Yeah" -- she had the grace to blush -- "I know. I just don't get --"

"When people care about you, they protect you. That's good, right?" he said, thinking of helmet hair and how much he still loathed it.

"Yes, I guess."

"Well, then, let's get your goth-fairy ass in there and knock them dead, and I promise you, one whiff of drugs and you are so outta there, your head will spin. Are we on the same page?"

"Yes," she repeated. "No drugs."

"What about booze? What's your prime directive?"

"No booze for me, none for anyone I drive with, no hanging alone with anyone who's been drinking, phone call immediately if I get in any one of those situations. Only drink what I can open fresh for the first time, never put it down until it's finished, never take anything to drink from anyone else ever, period."

"Good girl, let's go get 'em." He slipped out of his car and put a reverse-blade sword through his belt. Going as Ruroni Kenshin, the redheaded wandering samurai from the Japanese comic of the same name, was a no-brainer for Tristan, with his thin frame and long red hair.

The traditional hakama pants, which had seven folds -- five in the front, and two in the back -- were fascinating by themselves. There was a complex way to tie them on, and for that reason alone they appealed to Tristan. He also enjoyed the tunic, with the sleeves he would sometimes tie up with a long sash so he could wash up without getting them dirty. Ultra authentic.

Tristan carried himself a little differently when he wore the costume, and he was sure it was because he'd read the graphic novels at an impressionable age, devouring them on lazy Saturday afternoons with his dad. He still carried the character of the quiet samurai in his heart with what he now realized must have been a crush. The red X on his cheek was made with a Sharpie marker that evening, and all in all, he thought he made a dashing figure.

Apparently, more than one of Lily's girlfriends agreed, and he had to fight the urge to leave before it was strictly okay for him to do it. He moved randomly from room to room, checking out the party-goers inconspicuously, and ascertained that the host's parents were home, even if they were barricaded upstairs while the kids were down. It seemed to him as though the owner of the house had a couple of older kids who were doing the same thing he was, chaperoning, and one in particular appeared to be acting as a bouncer, which would be music to his mother's ears. After an hour or so, he figured Lily was safe enough in this crow may have been a little beer, but none visible, actually. didn't smell it on anyone's breath. He knew the kid w acting as bouncer was vigilant, because they'd discussed the of having younger sibs to watch over.

Lily was making ferocious, unsociable eye contact with hi so he smiled at her and nodded his head at the door, indicating that he was leaving, and then he told her that their mom would pick her up at one in the morning, and she'd better be watching for a text and ready to go by then. It was only a brief drive to his own party and Michael from there.

Michael. Just the thought was enough to drive all the breath from his chest.

The dinner party given by Michael's friends was located in a house on pricey Skyline Drive in the part of town his father used to refer to as "haute Fullerton." The homes up here were beautiful and expansive, with massive windows and lovely views. Some of the older ones had large lots too, with fine backyards for outdoor entertaining, and Tristan had some friends from school in this neighborhood with properties large enough to keep horses. Horse trails wound around the hilly area, making it a kind of urban rural oasis. There was plenty of wildlife in the area too, raccoons and coyotes and other things like snakes that Tristan preferred not to think about too much. He parked his car on the road across from the address Michael had given him.

It was a fine, clear night, and the air was crisp enough that it was smoky from chimney fires. Tristan smelled the damp earth and the spicy scent of some wonderful kind of food as he strode up the cobbled walkway toward a gorgeous home. The entryway soared and a massive pendant light cast unusual shadows on the walls. Tristan knocked and took a deep breath. Michael had invited him here, he reminded himself. Michael wanted him here; he was a guest, not a beggar.

The entry door opened, and he stood facing a man about six ˍches shorter than he with a surprised expression on his face. Aren't you a little old to be trick-or-treating?"

"I'm here for Michael Truax. He asked that I meet him here." Tristan held onto his temper as the man just raised one eyebrow.

"I see…" The man turned around and called out, "My word, Michael, I had no idea you were babysitting tonight."

Chapter Nine

Tristan said nothing as he followed the man into his home. Nevertheless, he saw his evening tank before his eyes. He probably should have stayed with the kids at Lily's party; at least they appeared to be having some fun.

"Limit that razor-sharp tongue to politicians, Jeff, and leave my friends alone," said Michael, his mild tone belied by the warning in his eyes.

"Hey, Sparky." His warm eyes lit up.

Tristan felt the flush creep up his face. "Hey."

"This is my friend Jeff," Michael introduced him to the man who opened the door. "He can be civil; he just has to be reminded sometimes. Come, meet everyone else." He left their host and took Tristan to the rest of the group, who congregated in the large open kitchen. He took Tristan's hand in his, leading the way to the den area where more people milled around a table set with several attractive desserts. "Hungry?" he asked.

"I ate before my sister's party," said Tristan looking around. He definitely did not fit in. The room was full of thirty-somethings, all wearing business casual. Michael took him around, introducing him to the other guests, and he believed he'd remember their names about as long as it took them to forget his. Michael, bless him, introduced him as Tristan and not Sparky, and he loved him for it.

"Looks like a working breakfast at the stock exchange," he remarked to Michael when they were out of earshot. "You fit in here?"

"Yeah, well..." He looked around. "This is actually a group of Orange County investors that I work with sometimes on larger projects. Jeff has been looking into financing a resort in Lake Tahoe, and he wanted to run it past us. It just means handing out a prospectus and a short PowerPoint presentation. Actually, I rather hoped we'd be over it when you got here. The important fact is, I'm not your finance-a-resort-in-Lake-Tahoe kind of guy; the rest is just details and beer snacks."

"But still" -- Tristan grinned -- "an investment party. You sure know how to show a guy a good time."

"You look good, Sparky." He turned Tristan so he could see the back of the costume. "Very authentic. How goes the revolution?"

"Kyoto is ablaze, and the streets run with blood. The usual," said Tristan. "Thirsty work."

"Ah," said Michael. "What would you like? In your age range they seem to have water and some sodas."

"Water's fine."

Michael took Tristan to the huge Sub Zero built-in refrigerator and opened it, surprising him by pulling him behind the door and kissing him hard. "You look edible," he murmured against Tristan's lips. "Want the tour?"

"Of the fridge?"

"No." He closed the refrigerator, rolling his eyes. "Jeff, can I show Tristan the house?"

Jeff's eyes were knowing when he said, "Sure, just don't take too long." He checked his watch. "My presentation's going to be at eleven on the dot. I'm sure we can find a video game or a toy or something for your little friend."

"Jeff?" said Michael, irritated.

"Oh, all right." Jeff laughed at his friend's discomfort. the one who brought the little ninja boy, though, am I?"

"Hello," hissed Tristan. "*Samurai.*"

"Here" -- Michael handed Tristan a water and shot Je murderous look -- "let me show you the view from the gam room."

Michael took his hand again, rubbing it briskly between his own. He led Tristan to an enormous room with a pool table in the middle. It had video games and a jukebox. Tristan couldn't help but feel that Lily's party would have been wonderful in a place like this.

"Sorry about that," said Michael, jerking his head to indicate their erstwhile host. "He's a prick sometimes. He thinks that it's funny to talk down to people. I used to get it a lot because of the whole cop thing."

"Please tell me you beat the crap out of him and he stopped."

"Afraid not. I actually had to earn his respect." He rubbed small circles on Tristan's back, grinning. "'Course, it wasn't too difficult."

"I'll bet not. If he's ever seen you naked…"

"He has not!" Michael laughed. "Not that he hasn't tried."

"Well, then, I should get his respect, because I have," said Tristan, sliding his arms around Michael's waist. "And as a matter of fact, I haven't been able to get the image out of my head all week."

"Oh, yeah? Is that the only place it's been?" Michael pulled Tristan closer. "You didn't feel it anywhere else?"

Tristan's cock stiffened in response, and every cell in his body hummed that his lover was near. "What do you think?" he asked, starting to breathe irregularly. "What about you?"

"I hardly ever imagine myself naked; whatever could you an?" Michael's blue eyes held Tristan's. "As soon as this is over, n going to reacquaint you with every horizontal surface in my ιouse."

"Why limit yourself?"

"Laws of physics," said Michael against his mouth.

"Oh, laws," Tristan breathed. "It's just no fun if you can't break them."

"I did not hear that." He went serious all of a sudden. "Needed you all week."

"Me? I forgot all about you," lied Tristan, pressing his body closer so Michael could feel his throbbing cock.

With a grimace, Michael moved his body out of Tristan's grasp and took Tristan to the garden. There they discovered a fire bowl and a gazebo covered with hundreds of flickering white Christmas lights. The city shimmered in the distance with the lights of a thousand houses as Tristan drank in the view from the outdoor entertaining area.

"Warm enough?" Michael asked him, wrapping both arms around him from behind as they stood looking at the cars snaking along the freeway far below in the distance.

"Mm," said Tristan, his skin tingling with longing. He licked his lips, turning for another kiss. "Is this normal? I want to crawl inside you…it's like a drug."

Michael rubbed his face against Tristan's. "What's normal, anyway?"

"I've never felt this way," said Tristan. "It feels like my heart is going to explode out of my chest."

"Sparky," Michael whispered. He fit them together and kissed Tristan till his knees buckled. Tristan thought he heard a whimper in his own throat when Michael pulled away. "Back soon, then we'll blow this gig, okay?"

"Soon," echoed Tristan, whose eyes followed him all the way to the house. He returned his gaze to the view, breathing deeply. Once he regained mastery over his body, he studied the beautiful backyard more closely, walking along the lighted flagstone pathways and enjoying the earthy smells he found there.

Tristan was headed out to the small gazebo when a shadow moved away from the wall, and he discovered he and Michael had probably been observed by what he now saw was a boy, about fifteen years old, wearing all black, including fingernail polish, and drinking a beer.

"Oh, hey! I didn't see you there, you scared me," he said, taking in the sullen expression on the boy's face. Lily would have loved him instantly and written epic poetry to his eyebrows. "What's up?"

"Kenshin," the boy said, acknowledging his costume. "I didn't know Kenshin got off with men," he added.

"Well, it's not strictly in the canon, no," said Tristan hiding his embarrassment with a smile. "Sorry, we thought we were alone." He wanted to add that people should make their presence known, but didn't.

"It's okay, my dad's gay. I see worse than that all the time," said the boy. "And he's got the worst taste in men. I'd pay good money to see you and Officer Friendly there in bed." He grinned, intending, Tristan thought, to shock.

"Save your money for college," said Tristan. "Jeff's your dad?"

"Yeah, he, you know, ensured the dynasty before he went over to the dark side. I live here half the year and the other half with mom in Denver," he said.

"That must be odd; did your mom remarry?" asked Tristan.

"Why do you want to know?" said the boy.

"I don't know. Your dad's got my date -- I'm just making conversation." He sighed.

"Business parties suck," said the boy, and Tristan had to concur. "My name's Edward, by the way. My dad calls me Ned. Please call me Edward." He rolled his eyes. "Ned, man, it's like some English mystery on A&E. Hello, Ned. Morning, Ned. What's up, Neddie," he practically spat. He started to take a sip of his beer, but Tristan intercepted it.

"Here," he said, taking it away and pouring it out into the planter next to him. "I'm listening, so vent, don't drink."

"You shit! I'll just go get another one," he said petulantly.

"Fine, but talk to me first. I'm bored. Amaze me, Edward. My name's Tristan."

Edward barked out a laugh. "Your name means, like, of the sorrows, or something, doesn't it?"

"Actually, according to one Web site I saw, it comes from the Celtic or Gaelic word *drest*, the word for riot or tumult. I'm sure my parents would have sheared off if they'd known that. It fits, though, according to those who know me." He grinned and watched the boy digest this.

"I heard my dad jerking you around," said Edward quietly. "I hate these parties; he's like some petty noble plotting to enlarge his holdings. He won't be satisfied with what he has, ever. It takes up a lot of time to be that acquisitive."

Tristan bit his lip. His dad had been so different, perhaps less financially successful, but nevertheless, now irrevocably gone as well. "Well," he said carefully, "it's not like you need him to watch your Little League games anymore, right?"

Edward let out a breath. "I guess." He chucked the pod of some kind of plant over the fence down to the hillside below. "The cop's your guy, right? You're together?" he asked.

"Yeah," said Tristan, liking the way it sounded. "The cop is *my guy*."

"My dad used to make fun of him," he said, then laughed. "But it turns out he's some kind of financial genius, and now my dad wants him in on everything. I think he barely puts up with my dad. Sometimes I can see it in his eyes that he's losing his patience, like tonight."

"Michael isn't likely to let someone put down his friends." He didn't know how he knew it was true, he just did. "He's very…protective." He thought about the helmet and sighed.

"How long have you been --" began Edward, but they turned when they heard footsteps behind them. Tristan's heart skipped a beat when he saw Michael meandering along the lit pathway with Jeff, Edward's father, at his shoulder.

"Oh, shit, here he comes," said Edward, standing quickly.

"Neddie!" snapped Jeff. "I thought I told you to finish your homework while the guests were here."

"I was just taking a break, Dad," Edward said, hanging his head. "Sorry."

Tristan looked up at Michael with a bright smile, only to have it falter at the look on his face. "What?" he asked, as Michael came over to pick up the beer bottle, saying nothing. He walked the distance back to the house alone, throwing the bottle into the trash. Jeff, Edward, and Tristan stood uncertainly till he returned, still saying nothing.

"Michael," said Jeff, breaking the silence. "I'd prefer it if you took your friend home now, and in the future, will you let your friends know that to be a guest in my home requires that they be role models for my son?" He turned on his heel. "I thought you, of all people, wouldn't condone underage drinking. Come, Ned, your break is over."

Tristan remained grimly silent in the face of the pleading look thrown at him by Edward. He clearly would be in far more trouble if his dad knew his little Neddie was drinking the beer. Tristan kept his mouth shut, walking in silence behind them, next to Edward, two penitent children being chastened by adults, and he burned with shame and injustice, wanting to take Michael's head off at the root. He reached over carefully when the two grown-ups, as he now was beginning to think of them, were distracted, to squeeze Edward's hand sympathetically. The boy looked so pitifully grateful; he wondered if it would be possible for him to introduce Edward to his little brothers, who were basically good kids and might have liked to befriend him. He kept all his thoughts from Michael. Rage flowed through him, and the evening, for him anyway, seemed to be completely ruined.

"Thank you so much for inviting us," Michael was saying, holding the investment proposal in his hand. "I'll read this over and give it a lot of thought, okay?" He reached the door and only then did he look behind to see if Tristan had followed him. "Well, 'bye," he said to Jeff as he stepped out onto the porch.

"Thank you for everything," Tristan told their host stupidly, hating himself for observing the niceties with this so-not-nice man. "Good night."

Michael was still silent as he walked to his car, the sound of his footsteps reverberating on the quiet street. Tristan found himself thinking that in this, Michael was all cop and didn't really hold it against him. He'd seen the beer sitting there empty by Tristan and had no earthly reason to think it wasn't his. It wasn't his job to listen to excuses, he just had to act, every day, on what he saw and let the lawyers argue later. Tristan understood this in the abstract, but still would have liked the benefit of the doubt. Plus, it was just one lousy beer, wasn't it? He'd had more than that with his dad when he'd been alive, and Tristan had been much younger then.

"Say what you have to say, Michael," said Tristan, "My car is across the street. It's been a long night."

"So you thought you'd liven it up with a little beer?" he asked.

"It may interest you to know that not everyone is ready to throw the death penalty at someone who drinks a beer before their twenty-first birthday," said Tristan.

"I know that. They don't need to. Who do you think I help dig out of cars and take to the morgue every Friday and Saturday night? Have you forgotten you're driving, Sparky?"

"No, I haven't forgotten; I'm just adjusting my destination," he said tiredly. "I'm going home. I'll see you around, Officer."

"Is that your answer for everything? Just leave if someone doesn't like what you've done? Don't you feel anything is worth changing your behavior or your ideas for? Is having a beer so important that you'd just move on?"

Tristan was enraged. "You didn't even talk to me in there; you just treated me like I pissed on the rug and then marched out, towing me in your wake like a bad dog. Jeff sneered at me the minute I arrived, kept talking smack, but *nothing* shamed me the way you treated me in front of them in the end did." He got out his keys, glad his dad's old BMW had heated seats. The evening had grown cold, and his blood colder, as he walked away from Michael.

"Look, I was embarrassed, I admit it," said Michael. "Jeff's boy has some problems and has had some trouble with the law, and I saw you drinking with him and thought, *Oh, shit.* He doesn't get that this kid will look up to him and see someone to admire and emulate. Jeff had to practically surgically remove him from a bad crowd when he put him in private school. I know you're a good guy, but it's so important to show kids like him that alcohol isn't a panacea, you know?"

"I know. Thank you for everything, okay? I really just want to..."

Michael suddenly shifted, and without warning, caught Tristan in his arms, their lips meeting, their tongues sliding together like a dance.

"I just..." said Tristan between invasions, his body reacting instantly to his lover's nearness.

"Sparky, I don't want you to go, please," he said, his hands on either side of Tristan's face. "Come home with me." He looked at Tristan then, nudging Tristan's mouth with his lips, teasing, licking, his body starting a slow grind and burn that Tristan felt to his toes. He tasted Tristan's lips, and then, his eyes questioning, he sighed deeply. "I'm so stupid." He rested his forehead on Tristan's, his hands sliding down his arms and catching Tristan's hands in his own.

"What?" asked Tristan quietly. He didn't understand what was happening, his head still spinning from the assault on his lips.

"It wasn't your beer, was it?" Michael's voice was so low it came out more like a moan.

"Nope," said Tristan. His throat closed. He was silent, not trusting himself to speak.

"Why didn't you say something?" said Michael.

"Edward's dad is so charming, I couldn't help but be in awe," he said dryly.

"Follow me home?" asked Michael. "Please?"

"I told Edward that you were *my guy*, and then you treated me like warmed-over vomit. Is that going to happen every time you think I've made a mistake?" he asked, needing to know. "'Cause I'm going to tell you right now, I will *not* stay with someone who thinks they have the right to treat me like that. I had a dad. He was a great man, and you're not him. He never made me feel the way you did tonight, even when the house caught fire...just so you know."

"That's probably what made you such a good person, huh?" Something in Michael's tone of voice caught and held Tristan on the edge of the moment. "Sometimes I get so busy protecting the world from its own stupidity that I forget that it's okay to be kind. My mom tells me that a lot."

Biting his lip, Tristan tried to decide how much he wanted to say. "I poured that kid's beer out into the planter and told him he could vent instead of drink, because I'd listen." Tristan held his breath, wondering if Michael could see as clearly as he did that they were on the same page.

"Oh, Sparky." Michael stroked Tristan's face with the back of his hand. "I briefly forgot how very, very *shiny* you can be." He pulled a thick strand of hair free from the blue silk tie and held it to his lips, seeming to inhale it and caress it and rub his face on it at the same time. "I have a bed of sorts set up in front of the fireplace in the living room and a fire all ready to go. Please come home with me. Help me light it up, Sparky, will you?"

Tristan swallowed hard, looking at the amazing, upscale houses behind him. "After this dump? A classy establishment like yours is just what I need," he said, finding Michael's lips, which moved in as soon as he felt the tension leave Tristan's body. For a long moment they stood like that, lips joined and tongues entwined. Tristan broke the kiss to get into his car. "By the way, Edward said he'd pay good money to see us in bed together; maybe you should write up a proposal on that for your next little investment soiree."

"Sparky!" Michael barked with laughter on the way back to his car. He turned around with his hands over his face. "The things you say!"

Chapter Ten

It wasn't hard to follow Michael's truck down the hill and through town to his little house. Michael waved him into the driveway first, coming in behind him to sandwich his car between the house and the garage. Before Tristan even got out of the car, Michael was there, opening his door and taking him in his arms again.

"Is that your sword or are you just glad to see me?" he teased as he pulled Tristan to standing. "I can never remember that you're taller than me until we're standing like this. It's different from what I'm used to."

"Why is that?" asked Tristan as he walked around to the trunk, opening it and removing a small duffle. "Don't like looking up?"

"No, it's not that," said Michael. "I find I like it rather well, actually…" He took Tristan's hand and led him to the back door, using his key to open it and walking immediately to the panel to turn off the alarm. "I like it a lot." They stood in the dark kitchen together, holding hands.

Tristan had so many plans for this moment. He'd thought in obsessive detail about what he'd do with Michael when they were alone again. Just how he'd touch him and what he'd say. But standing there with only the porch light illuminating his face in the shadows of the kitchen, each and every one of those ideas fled, and he was content to stand and watch and wait, and see if the elemental nature of their first night gave him clues about what to do on their second. Minutes seemed to be ticking by.

"Fire," said Michael after a while, as though he'd had a long conversation in his head, but the only word that came out was that one. "Come with me." He motioned, and Tristan followed. There in front of the fireplace was, indeed, a futon covered in soft, fluffy-looking blankets and pillows. It was far enough away from the fire to be safe from stray sparks that might fly through the chain curtain, but close enough to be warm and smoky, and Tristan longed to lose himself there with Michael.

"Here," said Michael putting a match to the kindling he'd laid out earlier. "Sit here and let me look at you."

Tristan sat, perversely as though he really were the character Kenshin from his comic books, his knees folded, his feet under him, his hands on his thighs, waiting.

"I've been wanting" -- Michael took the blue fabric holding Tristan's hair up and pulled on it -- "to do that since I saw you come through the door at Jeff's house tonight." Tristan's hair fell to his shoulders like liquid fire. "Oh, Sparky."

"I think…I think I'll sit here till you figure out what to do with the rest of my clothes," said Tristan looking straight ahead.

"I was watching you at Jeff's," said Michael. "Imagining this." He moved behind Tristan and slid his arms around his waist, slipping the tunic wrap out of Tristan's hakama and sliding his hands under the fabric, up and up, to graze Tristan's nipples. He untied the simple garment and slid it off Tristan's shoulders, kissing skin as he uncovered it.

"Were you?" said Tristan, putting his hand over his shoulder to touch Michael's hair as Michael kissed the nape of his neck. "I think I like that."

"Mmmhmm." He fumbled with the fastenings on Tristan's pants. "These are different," he said, running his hands over the ties. Tristan took his hands and walked him through it, first untying the knot in the front, then untucking the toggle, the front ties, and the obi. "There's, like, a board in there?" he asked, feeling the stiff part of the pants in the small of Tristan's back.

"Yep," said Tristan, feeling like there was a board in front too, with Michael touching and undressing him. Baring his skin. Breathing hot breath on his neck and bare shoulders. "What about your costume? Let's get that off too."

"What?" asked Michael.

Tristan turned and began unbuttoning Michael's dress shirt. "Seriously, you'd think a whole group of intelligent men and women could come up with something better for Halloween than business casual."

"I guess," agreed Michael, laughing and fighting his way out of his clothes. "Look, I wanted to say again how sorry I am that Jeff was such a shit-heel."

"Just Jeff?" asked Tristan, his hands stopping on Michael's boxers. Michael was still toeing off his shoes so he could shed his trousers.

"No, Sparky, I have a very, very personal and detailed apology to make for my behavior, but on behalf of Jeff, because he's not likely to change, I'm just going to say sorry."

"I'll take it," said Tristan. "I liked Edward, his kid. My brothers would like him. I wish I could have gotten his e-mail address or something. He seemed so…isolated. I understand that half the year he stays with his mom in Denver?"

"You know more than I do, then. I just heard from Jeff that he'd gotten in trouble, smoking dope and hanging with a bad crowd. He got picked up once by the police for underage drinking." Michael, wearing only his boxers, sat next to Tristan on the makeshift bed. The fire warmed his skin, its glow throwing interesting shadows on the wall.

"It's sad, Michael," Tristan sighed. "The way his dad talked to him…"

"Maybe he earned it?" asked Michael. "Sometimes teenagers can be a trial even to parents that love them."

"I'd give Jeff the benefit of the doubt, but really, the way he talked to me? Did I earn that? I didn't do anything other than knock on his door," Tristan said, clenching his teeth. It was pretty clear he wasn't going to get over that feeling any time soon, he thought, surprised at how angry it made him. It wasn't that being disrespected was new to him, but being treated like that at a party based on his looks and perceived relationship with his date was. "He treated me like a rent-boy."

"He did," agreed Michael, who stretched out and watched him carefully.

"Am I likely to get that a lot?" he asked, thinking Michael would know what he was in for with his own friends.

"What, you mean, people treating you like arm candy? Probably. I think you're pretty." He batted his eyes.

"Michael," Tristan warned.

"No, really. I'm older, you're still in school, good-looking, and there's probably financial inequality. Yeah, you're a rent-boy all right." If Michael hadn't been smiling and trying to grab his balls when he said that, Tristan wouldn't have taken it as well.

"I'll be *your* rent-boy," said Tristan, straddling Michael. "I like being your arm candy." The way Michael was looking at him right then sent his blood thundering down to his cock. "I like how you look at me. I really, really like it." He ground his hips against Michael's for emphasis.

"Do you?" Michael asked. "Yes…oh…I guess you do." Michael bit his lip.

"I can make you want me." Tristan caught Michael's hands in his and held them over his head.

"Oh, yes, you most certainly can do that," said Michael thickly.

Tristan stretched out along Michael's body, moving against him. "Thought about you all week, which, really, I had midterms -- you could at least get out of my head when I'm busy."

"Sorry," said Michael, closing his eyes. "Probably."

"But I kept thinking about how you spilled your coffee at Borders when you were looking at me…and just how you were looking at me. It never fails to make me hot for you." Tristan was still holding his hands and licking and biting the base of his neck.

"Oh," moaned Michael as Tristan shifted both his hands into one and found his balls with the other.

"And, really, the brain cells I needed for midterms were so different than the ones that kept showing me naked pictures of you…and I did really well in all my classes, so I think that shows a certain mastery."

"Mastery," echoed Michael numbly as Tristan picked up the pace on his cock, stroking the whole length.

"What do you want, Michael?" asked Tristan, his cheeks burning and his eyes shining with need. "Can I taste you?"

"Um, yeah," he said, pulling his hand free to get a condom out from under the pillow for Tristan.

"I want to taste your skin, Michael. Hold on to that," he said against Michael's balls.

Michael's hands stroked his hair, feeling it sliding silkily along the skin of his hips and thighs, moving when Tristan moved. It was the most erotic sensation he'd ever felt.

"Love your hair, Tristan." He closed his eyes.

Suddenly Tristan was in his field of vision again, right in his face, smiling.

"Thanks for remembering to call me Tristan," he said brightly. "And by the way, we both know I couldn't hold your arms if you didn't let me, so how about bringing some riot cuffs home from work, okay?" Just like that, Michael felt his lover's mouth on his balls again, and he almost laughed. Almost, until Tristan took them into his mouth and made him moan instead.

"Oh, Tristan," he sighed as Tristan nuzzled him. "You know, I expected some amateur licking and a pretty girly blowjob."

Tristan stopped what he was doing and slapped Michael's dick with his hand.

"Ouch." Michael laughed. "Jeez, hear me out. There is no such thing as a bad blowjob, you know."

Tristan glared at him, waiting, his hand wrapped around Michael's dick to keep it busy while he listened to Michael's nonsense.

"Oh…" Michael reacted to the brush of Tristan's nail over his glans. "I never counted on your sheer unabashed interest in all things dick." Michael stroked his hair. "And this? I'll give you about forty years to stop."

Tristan muttered something under his breath and ducked his head back to Michael's cock, and by the time Tristan rolled the condom down on it, he'd seen and touched and tasted every part of him and had decided that he wanted to stroke Michael from the inside, as well as suck him.

"Lube?" He held his hand out, his head still between Michael's legs, sucking the inside of a thigh. He felt the lube drop into his hands. "'Kay, thanks," he said, returning to his task.

"Oh, yes, Tristan," he sighed, as Tristan's tongue flicked the sensitive slit at the tip of his cock, and then Tristan worked the bead on his tongue against it. "Oh, *there*, baby," he moaned again, arching, giving him access. "Oh, that's so…*shit*!" He jerked like a puppet every time the stud in Tristan's tongue ran up and down the length of his cock.

Tristan knew he didn't have any particular skill in this area, but he'd spent the week thinking about and listing the most exciting things he'd felt at Michael's hands and decided to try them all on him. What was it Michael had said about him, big air, big rush? Well, *hell yeah.* And Michael tasted so good -- at least he had before the latex -- his skin all salt and sweat and man that Tristan wanted to just devour him. He used his tongue piercing to tease him a little and discovered that Michael liked that a lot. *A whole lot.* Michael writhed, his moans becoming more frequent and his hips shifting. Tristan wanted to find that special place inside of Michael that would go *boom* up his spine while Tristan sucked his dick. Actually, that might be the sum total of his new plan, *the plan prime*, now that his old plan had changed his life the way it had.

Fingers plus mouth plus tongue piercing plus wild, unbridled enthusiasm, plus maybe a modicum of want-you-more-than-I-ever-the-hell-wanted-anyone-in-my-damn-life equals --

"*Tristan*!" shouted Michael, jerking off the futon in shock as he filled the latex inside Tristan's mouth. "Oh, damn, that was..."

Tristan slipped the latex off Michael's softening erection, the thought of what he'd done making him almost cream himself. Tristan couldn't help staying where he was, next to that slick, softening cock, taking in the smell of sex and Michael all at once.

"Oh," he moaned. "Gonna come just from watching how damn gorgeous you are. Okay if I...um..." He still had his fingers in Michael, stretching him, opening him.

"Yes," said Michael. "I...just...oh, *yes.*"

Tristan held out his hand for another condom, rolling this one quickly down on his throbbing flesh. He felt like he was going to tear at the seams, his cock was so hard. He looked down at Michael, the man all golden and rosy and waiting for him.

"Oh, Michael," he said, sliding his cock into Michael. "So tight," he sighed. "Never felt this…not like you…so hot."

"Yeah," sighed Michael, his cock hardening again, coming back to life between them. "Make me fly."

"Uhn…going to fly together," Tristan panted, giving him everything he had, holding Michael's knees in his forearms and bracing himself for long, hard strokes. "Going to make you give it up again," he said, hitting Michael's gland and causing him to tremble beneath him. He rocked into Michael, eyes closed, savoring the feeling for as long as he could. Sweat trickled down his back, and for a while, there was nothing but the movement, the moment, and the man with him.

"Tristan. Oh, shit, baby, you…only you."

"Me," agreed Tristan. "Yeah, only me." He felt a rush of heat between them as Michael came again. Michael jerked and shuddered in his arms as if taken by surprise by his orgasm. Tristan still took him with long, slow strokes until he felt his own balls tighten, and then he lost himself, pushing so hard into Michael he heard him gasp. He held himself there and spent, his whole body feeling like it siphoned from his dick.

"Uhn." His breath caught on the last waves of his orgasm, giving voice to his pleasure in noises he didn't recognize as coming from his own throat.

"Oh, that?" He fell limply into Michael's arms. "Was poetry."

Michael gasped as Tristan pulled out, removed the condom, and tied it off. Michael pulled him tight, the cum sliding between them getting sticky and sweaty and oh-so-slick. "Michael." Tristan laughed. "Guess what. I came."

"Tristan. Guess what, me too. You are so beautiful, did I mention that?" he asked.

He had, Tristan knew, mentioned that before. "Nope, never. Tell me all about it?" He preened, pleased with the dazed look on Michael's face.

"Just looking at you makes me hard," Michael said, stroking his hair. "And that's if you were bald."

"Oh, hell no," said Tristan.

"With the hair?" said Michael. "You're lethal."

"What, this hair?" Tristan teased, moving his head so it fell around them. "My same old boring hair?" He snapped his head and snaked it down Michael's chest and stomach until it tickled his balls.

"Somebody's going to need a shower," said Michael. "You're going to smell like me."

"Wish I could taste like you," said Tristan. "How could we lose the latex?"

Michael went dead silent. "It's not that simple."

"Well, can't we get tested or something?" He sat there happily contemplating what it would be like to feel Michael come down his throat.

"I'm clean," Michael said. "I get tested every six months, and there hasn't been anybody except you for a while."

"I see. Well, that leaves me, and while I practice safe sex, it's been more…how shall I say…recent and maybe indiscriminate. Okay, I see the problem. I could still get tested now and again in six months…"

"Um, yeah…you could." Michael remained silent.

"Oh…*oh*," said Tristan, realizing he was talking about an exclusive relationship. Duh. "I didn't think, how dumb. I was just problem solving out loud. It's not like I think we should be…" He turned to Michael. "I was just thinking in terms of getting the taste of latex out of my mouth. I'm…I…"

"It's okay," Michael said with a laugh. "Sometimes you think a little ahead of me."

"Yeah, oh, damn." Tristan was thinking hard. It was their second date, and he'd practically… *That clinches it,* he thought. *I'm a chick.* "I'm hungry," he said then, knowing that would derail the whole conversation, and Michael would go straight into foodie mode.

"I have just the thing to eat in front of the fire." said Michael, already rising to his feet. Tristan followed him, stopping behind him when he got to the fridge. Michael whipped around with a flourish, a large platter in his hands.

"Whoa," said Tristan, jumping back. "It's official, you're the master of the meat and cheese platter."

"Not just any meat and cheese platter," said Michael. "I got apples in Oak Glen, right off the trees."

"Oh, fresh apples?"

"Yep, and a pie that will make your toes curl."

"Oh," said Tristan again, wondering if Michael knew just how much his toes were curling already, just from seeing the man smile.

Michael put the platter down and picked up a colander of washed apples, both red and green, and a wicked, lethal-looking knife. He began expertly slicing the fruit into eighths, removing the seeds and stems until they were cut into neat wedges with the skin still on.

"Here, you carry this." He handed the platter to Tristan and went back to the fridge, opening it and then closing it again to lean against it, as if weighing something in his mind.

"You know, Sparky," he said, then quickly corrected himself. "Tristan. It's not like I have some big problem with you having a beer every now and then. Hell, I drank beer when I was your age."

"Michael, I…" began Tristan, but Michael stopped him.

"No, really, I trust you to drink responsibly. I shouldn't be such a hard ass. I know you probably drink with your friends... Maybe I've been a little too conscious of our age difference, and maybe I've been a shit about it."

"Michael, how old are you?" asked Tristan. "I don't believe you've mentioned it."

"I'll be twenty-eight on Valentine's Day," said Michael. "I'm almost ten years older than you."

"Can't argue the math."

"Does that make a difference to you?" asked Michael.

"No, not really. Except now I can take advantage of your dotage to wring you out for presents and money, like Anna Nicole Smith did to that billionaire guy," Tristan teased.

"Shut up," said Michael, going a little red.

"What, are you kidding? You worry about that sort of thing? Age?"

"Tristan, you can have anyone you want," said Michael. "You have no idea how desirable you are. I feel...honored to be the first."

Tristan put the platter down on the table behind him. He took in the man standing uncomfortably still in front of the fridge. "I don't want you to feel honored. I want you to feel like...good candy. Something I want all the time." Tristan advanced on Michael, taking his face between his palms. "Something I can't wait to get my hands and my mouth on."

"Sparky," sighed Michael against his lips. "Candy?"

"Mmmhmm. The best kind of candy, the kind you don't share." Tristan looked at him. "Unless you have to."

"*Oh.* I wouldn't say you had to worry about that."

"Michael?" Tristan ran his tongue across Michael's full lower lip and caught it carefully between his teeth.

"Hm?" said Michael, dazed, caught between Tristan and the cold metal fridge.

"You don't have to worry about that, either."

"Right now," qualified Michael.

"Right now," agreed Tristan. "But I can speak for the foreseeable future as well. I want to be your guy." Tristan buffeted him with a shoulder.

"You are my guy. Am I yours?"

"Mmmhmm. You're my guy. *My guy.*"

"I like that," said Michael. "Damn, the apples are going to turn brown." He looked at the food. "Do you want to eat?"

"Sure. I'm hungry."

"Okay, then let's eat. Can you get the pie out of the fridge?" asked Michael, going for the platter. "And the whipped cream?"

"Ooh, whipped cream. Now you've gone and made it official. You *are* my guy."

"Really. Listen, Sparky, if…I mean…would you like a beer?"

Tristan laughed. "That must have cost you." He held the pie with one hand and the can of whipped topping in the other. "But for your information, Officer Helmet, I don't drink…never have, really. I prefer speed to stupidity, so I never got into it. Think of me as having a high-octane brain. No alcohol necessary."

"But you asked me if I was going to offer you a beer last week."

"Yes, but I didn't say I'd accept it," said Tristan. "You hadn't offered me anything else yet, either. I just wanted something to drink. To be fair, I've been known to drink maybe one beer in an evening. Once or twice."

"Sparky," began Michael, but Tristan cut him off.

"And, yes, that means tonight we had our very first fight over nothing. Let that be a lesson to you." He winked and walked into the living room. “You can make it up to me by getting Edward’s e-mail address for me. I think he needs my brothers to befriend him and give him a safe place to vent. What do you think?”

Michael’s eyes followed him thoughtfully. “I think you are more than the sum of your parts.”

Tristan stuck his head around a corner and grinned. “But my parts? Wish you would get your parts in here. I have a can of whipped cream, and I’m not afraid to use it!”

Chapter Eleven

As he had on their first date, Michael found himself awake and watching as Tristan slept in the glow of the fire. Periodically, he added a log, keeping the room warm. Experimenting with touch, he found he barely had to ripple a light fingertip over his sleeping lover, and Tristan would move, twisting until he was melted into Michael's embrace. Stroking Tristan's cheek got Michael a sleepy kiss. Touching Tristan's back or sliding a hand down his spine earned Michael the satisfying squeeze of arms around him. And squeezing Tristan's ass got him a fully awake and erect boy-toy looking for love.

"Hey," said Tristan, pushing the hair out of his face as he climbed on top of Michael, rocking against him until they were both hard. Tristan grinned sleepily. "Ready or not…"

"Oh, *ready*," breathed Michael, kissing him. "I have never seen anything like you before."

"Like it?" said Tristan, flipping his hair. "Like what you see?"

"Oh, if you only knew," said Michael.

"I know." Tristan smiled. "The way you looked at me in the bookstore made me feel like a porn star."

"Sorry," said Michael.

Tristan ground his hips against Michael's so hard he gasped. "Look at me," said Tristan, nipping his lips. "Nothing, *nothing* has ever made me hot like having your eyes on me."

"Ooh, a little bossy boy-toy," sighed Michael happily.

"I'm going to make you squirm," said Tristan, teasing Michael's neck with his lips and teeth. "Going to make you beg." He caught Michael's balls with one hand, giving them the lightest squeeze. "Going to make you do me all night long -- hey, think I could ride you?"

"Right now?" asked Michael, wondering if Tristan was up to it.

"Yeah, then I could…" He whispered into Michael's ear. "…myself on your cock all I want."

"Holy crap. You are going to kill me dead."

"Yeah, probably. Just show me where the chalk is so I can draw a line around your body." Tristan laughed, lunging for the lube and a condom. "Here, get me ready. Okay?"

"Oh, um," said Michael, not sure what just happened. "All right." Somewhere in the back of his mind, he was remembering with fondness the sweetly hesitant boy he'd brought home the week before. Tristan twisted on top of Michael turning with a great show of effort so that his mouth could be on Michael's cock and Michael had the option of reciprocating. Michael opened the lube and found himself face to…butt…with Tristan's ass.

"I'll just…um…be here while you do that," Tristan said, and Michael felt something warm and slippery slide over his cock. Tristan nuzzled down into the creases between Michael's legs and body, his hair slipping and sliding on Michael's thighs.

"Oh, when you do that…I…" said Michael.

"Yeah?" hummed Tristan, around Michael's balls. He pulled Michael's knees up and dipped his head between his legs, slithering his tongue down the sensitive skin leading to Michael's hole. Tristan's tongue bead was going to make him crazy. Michael pressed a finger into Tristan's tight heat and was getting ready to insert another when he felt Tristan's tongue firmly invade him.

"Oh, shit!" He jumped, his pubic bone hitting Tristan's chin on the way up and snapping his teeth together.

"Whoa! Danger, Will Robinson," murmured Tristan, going back to tonguing his hole. "Does Michael like this? I think he does."

"Jeez, baby," said Michael, who slipped a third finger in and let Tristan rock on his hand, changing to two thumbs and brushing his gland with each in turn.

"I think…" said Tristan panting. "Oh, I want…" he moaned.

Michael withdrew his thumbs and took Tristan's hips with the intention of helping him turn around. Tristan shifted and turned again, this time more clumsily, his full, heavy cock banging Michael's chest and dripping on it as he positioned himself. He rolled a condom down Michael's dick with a practiced flick of his hands. "I need…Michael," he said, impaling himself in one swift motion, sucking in a lungful of air.

"*Oh*!" he gasped as he sat for a moment in shock. "Ooooh," he said again, more quietly, closing his eyes. He began, tentatively, to move.

Michael thought he'd never seen anything more awesome in his life. Tristan in the firelight, riding his cock, became the fire, the orange glow lighting his amazing straight, shiny red hair until it luminesced as if it were light itself. Michael could see the crimson stain of arousal creeping up Tristan's neck and staining his cheeks a dull red. He put his hands on Tristan's thighs, sliding them up to his hips, waiting, watching for the boy to start his ride. He felt Tristan's muscles relax around his cock, no longer squeezing the life out of him, but undulating, as if Tristan was testing out his own body, exploring the sensation without beginning to move.

It seemed an eternity passed in the hushed living room, the fire snapping and crackling the only sound besides their breathing, when Tristan began to move. He opened his eyes first, reaching out to touch Michael's face tentatively with what Michael privately thought of as his baby fingers. The sweetness of his touch made Michael want to close his eyes, to lean into the delicate embrace, but as soon as he did, Tristan gave his jaw a squeeze.

"Do *not* take your eyes off me, Michael," he commanded, and suddenly, Michael wanted very much to obey. The irony of a total newbie who could dominate him while he took it up the ass didn't go unnoticed. It simply sucked his brain out until he belonged to the boy, and if Tristan said jump, he would beg for the privilege of saying how high.

"Yes," he said hoarsely, clearing his throat. "Yes, Tristan."

Tristan moved then, using his strong thighs to lift himself off Michael and gravity to slam him back down a little, shocking the air right out of Michael's lungs in a *whoosh* that surprised him. "Going to take you there," said Tristan, now lifting the hair off his sweaty shoulders. "Take you wherever you want to go…"

"Yeah," choked Michael. "Hell yeah, baby, only you…" he panted, gripping Tristan's ass so hard he was sure to feel it the next day. It was as if Michael could taste him on the air, the smell of sex and skin and fresh apples teasing all his senses until his focus narrowed to the two of them, and nothing else existed.

"Only me…" whispered Tristan, dropping his hair. He slid his hands down his body, touching all the juicy parts on the way, and it drove Michael crazy. "When I touched myself this week, I pictured you," he said. "Your hands, your lips, your tongue. Touch me?" He put Michael's hands on his cock and held them there as he moved faster and faster, up and down, his tight asshole gripping and squeezing until Michael could hardly breathe.

Michael began to move his hands under Tristan's, pumping Tristan's cock, his hands gripping, pulling, and teasing the slit until Tristan writhed and clenched around him like a fist. He shifted

Tristan a little, making him gasp and shudder as he pushed his cock against Tristan's gland again and again and again.

"Baby," croaked Michael. "I'm going to... *Tristan*!"

He pumped Tristan's cock harder and felt it swell and harden like a stone in his hands, felt Tristan's balls pull up and his hole flutter as he shot jets of cum on Michael's chest and face. Michael followed him over the edge, yanking him down onto his cock until he was crushed beneath Tristan, moaning as he felt heat flood the latex, his body jerking and shuddering completely out of his control.

"Yesssss," hissed Tristan. "Yesssss...Michael...oh...*sweet*!" He reached for Michael, gathering him close.

Softening and slipping out of Tristan's body, Michael removed the condom and tied it off. He tossed it over his head somewhere, vaguely aware that it would probably be just *yuck* in the morning when he found it again. He couldn't stop touching Tristan, rubbing against him, stroking his back and his face and his cheeks. His hands roamed over the sweet body beside his, while Tristan just looked at him with honest blue eyes.

"Damn, Michael," Tristan whispered. "What happens to me when I'm with you?"

Michael smiled and ruffled Tristan's hair. "I have no clue," he said. "But I'm keeping you." Tristan licked a drip of cum off Michael's face and then kissed him. Michael tasted Tristan and apple and intimacy. He groaned and held him closer.

"Oh, keep me," moaned Tristan. "Please, *please*, keep me." He pressed hard against Michael's side, wrapping his arms around Michael's neck. "Never felt like that. Not ever."

"Me neither, never before you." It didn't matter if he said it or not, thought Michael, who didn't believe in playing lover's games anyway. "It's as if my whole life started at Borders last week when I looked into your eyes and thought...maybe."

"Yeah…maybe…" Tristan smiled. Michael kissed each of his eyes in turn and sighed. His Sparky was drifting, melting into him, and starting to breathe deeply and evenly.

"Love you," he whispered, when he was sure Tristan was sound asleep. "Love you so much, Sparky." He didn't play games, but maybe he'd hold on to that a little longer by himself. "Love you…"

Sighing, Michael drifted off to sleep himself.

* * *

The fire was cold, and Michael was alone on the futon when he awoke. He found the clock on the wall and discovered it was barely six in the morning. Somewhere in the house, water was running, and he got up to find the source of the noise. When he got to the bathroom, Tristan was just getting out of the shower. He looked so gorgeous standing there that for a minute Michael just sucked in a breath and stared at him. Michael handed him a large, fluffy towel.

"Hey, baby," said Michael, wrapping his arms around Tristan, who shyly covered his nudity. "What's up?"

Tristan tucked his head into Michael's neck. "Nothing," said Tristan, like a guilty grammar school kid. "Last night was pretty intense, huh?"

Michael's blood froze. "Hey…regrets?" He couldn't bear it if Tristan said yes. *Please, oh, please*, he thought, *don't say yes.*

"Oh, hell no, that was the best."

Michael breathed a sigh of relief. "Then what?" he asked, helping to fuzzle Tristan's long hair dry with the towel.

"It's like I have no idea who I am anymore," said Tristan. "Who the hell *was that*?"

"I don't know, but he's like…the porn fairy…and I'm not letting him get away." Michael grinned. "You are so hot, Tristan. Made me see stars."

"Liked that, did you?"

"I don't know. Maybe we'll have to try again. For reference, you know. Establish a control group."

"Oh, hey, I can do control," said Tristan. "Although before last night, I wouldn't have said…"

"Yeah…damn, baby." Michael sighed.

"You shower, and I'll make breakfast. You've got stuff to cook?"

"Of course. No running the water in the kitchen while I shower, though, or I'm the one that's going to get cooked."

"Gotcha. Never fear, if I forget, I'll just clarify some butter, in case you get boiled like a lobster."

"Um, that actually sounds…kind of hot," Michael said, thinking of being buttered.

"Fine, I'm on it." He left the bathroom, grinning at Michael's half-hard cock.

Michael turned on the water, wishing he could have showered with Tristan, but as he got in and the water pounded his slightly sore muscles, he thought a little "me" time was probably good for both of them. For a moment there, he'd thought Tristan regretted… It was amazing how one smile from Tristan could change how he felt about everything. He used a scrubby puff to soap up, liking the scrape and scratch of the nylon against his sensitive skin. After the night he'd had with Tristan, every cell in his body was awake and on fire.

Water ran over Michael's head, rinsing shampoo out of his hair. The little knots of tension in his body eased. In here with his private thoughts, he could acknowledge that he was a goner where Tristan was concerned. He was in love, deeply, for the first time.

As if fate were playing a sick joke, the water turned cold just as he admitted that to himself, and he cursed, turning it off. He toweled off, glad the mirrors were steamy so he couldn't see his face. In his room, Michael put on the casual clothes he reserved for Saturday mornings, adding an extra long-sleeved T-shirt for warmth, and went to find Tristan.

Tristan was in the well-lit kitchen, wearing an apron, oven mitts, boxer briefs, and a shameless smile. He was dancing to music from the small under-cabinet radio Michael kept for listening to the news. Toast popped in the toaster, and Tristan, still dancing, buttered it, slicing and arranging it on a plate. He didn't notice Michael standing in the doorway at first, and when he did, he stopped in his tracks, holding the butter knife like a shield.

"Hey, how long have you…" That gorgeous blush once again stained him.

"Long enough to see that the 'porn fairy' is in the hizzle."

"Oh." Tristan looked down.

"To date, this is my very best morning ever."

"Really?"

"Mmmhmm." Michael leaned against the doorframe to watch. "Yep, breakfast and a show."

"*Oh*." Tristan smoothed his hair back with the oven mitts. The little shit.

"Mmmhmm." Michael just waited.

"So." Tristan peeked into the oven and then slyly back over his shoulder at Michael, whose hot and hungry gaze was fastened on him like heavy-duty Velcro. "You like what you see?"

"Yes," said Michael. "I like it very much."

"What, this?" Tristan smoothed the oven mitts over his torso. "You like this?"

"Mmmhmm."

Tristan sort of worked it, grinding in his apron, running the oven mitts over his body. "This?"

"Yep," said Michael thickly. He was torn between laughter and bending Tristan over the kitchen table and showing him that bad boys get spanked. The oven timer beeped, and Tristan went to take out the food, whatever it was that he was cooking.

"Saved by the beep," said Tristan. "Voilà, an egg thingie."

"Oh, thank you," said Michael, taking in the baked omelet that Tristan was putting on the plate. "Can we revisit the show later?"

"Oh…um, sure," said Tristan, that damned adorable blush lighting him up like fire. "I liked that."

"Makes me hot, Sparky." Michael took a piece of toast and a kiss. "Lights me right up."

"Good. Me too." He cut the omelet into serving pieces. "I used the leftover ham." He handed Michael a bowl of cut-up apples.

"Mm, this is good," said Michael, wishing he could spend all his mornings like this. "After breakfast I need to water the backyard, and then I thought maybe you'd like to go for a ride."

"A ride?" Tristan's eyes went round. "Like on your cock again?"

Michael snorted. "No. A *ride*. Maybe out the canyon road and then to apple country? Get a little fresh air. I'm on shift tonight, but I have the morning, and then I'll need to nap before I go."

Tristan smiled. "That sounds nice. Can I help in the yard?"

"Nah, I have sprinklers. We can just…play," said Michael, who paused, the food in his mouth going unchewed for a minute. He swallowed hard. "Have I told you how much I love looking at you, Sparky?"

"If you did, you can still say it again." Tristan took Michael's hand and brought it to his lips. "Never hurts to clarify."

Michael pulled Tristan in for a kiss. "I *love* looking at you."

They finished their breakfast in silence, meeting each other's eyes and smiling like idiots.

Chapter Twelve

At eight a.m. Tristan and Michael wandered to the back to water. Like Michael, Tristan wore jeans and a long-sleeved shirt in the crisp morning air. He watched silently as Michael used a metal wand to spin the X-shaped sprinkler fixtures, turning on the water.

"It's already late October, so I don't have to do this very often," he said, nodding his head toward the yard. "I have a gardener who comes weekly to mow and keep things tidy; he does both yards -- mine and my mom's."

"Oh," said Tristan, looking around and spotting a basketball. Michael had a hoop permanently set into the cement on his side of the drive, the area between the two houses a perfect square of cement for a little one-on-one. "I think this is nice," he said. "A great find, two houses like this together."

"It originally belonged to a set of twins," said Michael, laughing. "I shit you not, these guys lived next door to each other and raised their families together. It seemed…cool. When I bought it, I thought it would be a great place for me and my mom."

"It's perfect -- private, but still connected," said Tristan. "Hey, let's move the cars and play b-ball while you water. How long does it take, anyway?"

"I let the sprinklers run for about a half-hour. I only do it twice a week so I soak it." He pulled his keys from the pocket of his jeans. "I'll move mine, and then you move yours, okay?"

"Okay," said Tristan, already getting into the driver's seat of his car. He watched Michael drive out between the two houses, making a mental note to back in next time like Michael did. If there *was* a next time… *Holy shit.* He parked his car in front of the house.

Michael was…everything Tristan had ever wanted. Everything he'd imagined, and some things he hadn't even known to believe in. How could he ever walk away not knowing if he was coming back, as he had so many times with Viper and the girls he'd dated? *I'll call you. Holy shit.* He saw Michael in his rearview mirror, confidently parking that huge truck of his behind Tristan's BMW, and hoped he could hang onto him. He got out of his car and joined Michael, smiling, listening as the man explained the shape these houses were in when he bought them.

"So I had to gut them completely, and that gave me all kinds of room for creativity," he was saying. "I had a blast putting in the moldings and the cabinets, even though it took me almost two years to do it in my off hours."

Tristan stopped in his tracks. "*You* did that?"

Michael looked back at him perplexed. "Yeah," he said evenly. "I did."

"Holy crap, that's some gorgeous woodwork. I thought it was original to the house. The leaf carvings on the mantle and the moldings are really, really beautiful."

Michael picked up the basketball, blushing like a kid. "Think so?"

"Yeah," said Tristan, crouching to play as Michael dribbled. "My dad and I used to tour historic homes. I just thought…" he said, going for the ball, which Michael effortlessly pulled out of his reach behind him, hooking it into the basket, swish, nothing but net.

"Me too," said Michael. "I like going through the places with a lot of carvings best, like the Queen Annes in old Corona on Main Street or by the circle in Orange. There's a lot there to admire, and the renovations are gorgeous." He snatched the ball away from Tristan again and hooked a shot, right in for two. "Hey, basketball's not your game, is it?"

"Nope." Tristan slammed the ball on the ground and dribbled it soccer style, going through Michael easily and playing him, making him come after the ball again and again until they both knew it was hopeless. He used the toe of one foot and the arch of the other to launch the ball in the air, hitting it with his head past Michael.

"Ow, you need a soccer ball. Note to self: Basketballs hurt." He rubbed the heel of his hand on his forehead.

"That's going to leave a mark," teased Michael.

Tristan jumped on him from behind like a monkey, wrapping his arms around Michael's neck and his legs around his waist. "I'll show you a mark." He laughed, his lips fastening on Michael's skin.

Michael staggered under Tristan's weight, walking like Frankenstein's monster to tease him a little. He turned when he heard his mother's voice and stood still, a little embarrassed.

"Hey, baby," said his mother, who stood on the back porch of her house in her pajamas and lit up a cigarette.

"Hey, Mama," replied Michael, as though he always walked around the yard with a redheaded boy on his back. "Did we wake you? Sorry."

"Nah, I was on my way up anyway." She took a big drag from her cigarette and exhaled slowly. A sweet, spicy fragrance filled the air.

"Mama, I thought you quit," said Michael, his voice tinged with exasperation.

"I did, honey, I quit smoking tobacco. This is a clove cigarette, smell." She blew out another puff. "See? All natural."

"Mama." He helped Tristan down. "A forest fire started by lightning is natural, but it's still not smart to breathe in the smoke."

"Oh, you. You won't be happy until I become a Republican," she said, good-naturedly, as though they had this argument every day.

"Well, that's not strictly true, either, is it?"

She grinned at him. "Who's your friend? I dated a boy with ginger hair like that once. He wanted to be a priest, until…"

"Whoa, TMI," said Michael. "This is Tristan."

"Hi, honey," Michael's mother said. "Call me Emma."

"Thanks." Tristan smiled back helplessly.

"I need your helmet, Mama. Can we borrow it?"

"Sure, baby." The tip of her cigarette sparked like a firework, almost catching her pajamas. She brushed off the ember.

"Um, Emma?" said Tristan, hesitantly. "I think you should know that those things spark a lot, the clove ones, you know? And, well, once one of my friends lit himself on fire and tried to douse himself with a vodka drink, and if we hadn't been playing beach volleyball at the time and rolled him in the sand, he'd have lost some body parts. Those things come from Indonesia, and they dry out…wow, *whoosh*, you know?" He mimed going up in flames.

"That's why I smoke them on the porch, honey; thanks for the tip, though," she said. "I like the way they smell. They remind me of the early days of the punk movement. I was like, the biggest Sex Pistols groupie, and --"

"The helmet, Mama?" said Michael, smiling.

"Oh, yeah, hey…sure." She left the burning cigarette on the porch railing and ran inside, coming out a few seconds later with a helmet emblazoned with stars and stripes like *Easy Rider*. "You need the bike too?"

"Sparky, do you have a valid motorcycle license?" Michael asked.

"Nope," said Tristan, rolling his eyes.

"Okay, no, Mama, thanks, though." He took the helmet from her and gave her a kiss on the cheek she leaned over the porch railing to claim.

"'Bye, baby, drive safe," she said.

"'Bye, Mama, you be careful." Michael turned off the sprinklers and locked the back door. He punched a code on the garage door, which rolled up to reveal an amazing woodworking bench, complete with all kinds of great tools, a weight bench, and a Harley Davidson Electra Glide Classic.

"Oh, shit," said Tristan, with an expression that could only be described as lust. "Toys," he sighed. "You have the best toys."

"Yep." Michael handed him the helmet and went toward the bike. "It's good to be me today."

"Oh," sighed Tristan. "It's red. Shiny and all chrome-y…I'm going to cream," said Tristan. "Seriously. Right here, right now."

"I have a rival."

"Oh, yeah. I…seriously, are you shitting me? You're going to take me for a ride on that?" He grabbed the front of Michael's shirt. "Don't play with me, man; my heart can't take it."

"Sure, baby," said Michael. "Really, let's ride." He looked at Tristan then, seeing the delight on his face. That he could put that happiness there made him feel amazing.

"Oh, with my legs around that and my arms around you, I think… Yep, I'm really going to cream."

"Get a grip, Sparky," Michael whispered, biting his neck. "My mama's still watching."

Tristan whipped his head around to look, but she was gone, and Michael was wheeling the huge bike out of the garage.

"Made you look," he said, taking his helmet off the handlebars and placing it on his head. "Come on, up you go." He helped Tristan onto the back seat of the bike.

Tristan was looking at all the pipes and touching the leather seat with reverent hands.

"Helmet," said Michael, sighing.

"Oh, yeah," Tristan said. "Wait a minute." He dug into his pocket and took out a rubber band, braiding his hair quickly at the back and securing it. "Here." He put on the helmet. "What do you think?"

"It'll do," said Michael, loudly so he could hear. "It gets cold; I have jackets." In anticipation of taking Tristan riding, he'd actually purchased a used motorcycle jacket that week in a boutique store on Harbor Boulevard that sold new and used clothes. It was a lucky find, because Michael thought he'd have to buy a new one, and while he would have done it, he didn't want it to look obviously new. This way he could just pretend he had it on his bike all the time just in case.

"Ooh, like leather?" asked Tristan, grabbing the front of Michael's shirt. "You mean I can be your hot leather boy-toy?"

"Um, well." It was Michael's turn to blush. "If you want to look at it that way."

"Bring it on!" He held out his hands. "Gimme."

Michael laughed and tried to kiss his lips despite the helmets. Which didn't work, exactly. He pulled out the jacket and got his own. "Here."

"Oh, it's great, I feel tingly." He put on the jacket, slipping his hands in the pockets. "Oh, there's something in here." He pulled out an ancient, desiccated condom, which had evidently been used. "Ick. Not so tingly anymore. Somebody must have left in a hurry."

Michael took it from him, not moving a single facial muscle because, really, what could he say? He took it to the big black trash bin next to the garage. When he came back he said merely, "Long story," and cursed himself for not checking the pockets.

"Oh," said Tristan, biting his lip.

"Anything else in there?" said Michael, hoping that was it, but seriously, what kind of a person saves a damn condom?

Tristan checked the rest of the pockets and came up empty. "That's it, boss, your last boy just left you a sweet reminder, I guess. I promise to leave cash or something for the next guy so it's not so traumatic." He'd intended it as a joke, but seeing Michael's face, he knew it fell flat. He wondered if Michael had cared about the boy who left the condom, and oddly, that caused an alien aching sensation in his chest.

"You're my last boy, Tristan," muttered Michael, getting on the bike.

Tristan could say nothing in reply, the thunder of the motorcycle preempting any further conversation. As the unfamiliar forward momentum of the bike altered his balance, Tristan found his hand rests and held on, the sensation of riding along behind Michael heady and exciting. He found he loved the feel of the wind as it caught at his clothes and tugged his hair loose from his braid.

That tiny frisson of fear that jerked and yanked at his stomach as the bike leaned this way and that made his heart pound like great sex, and he had Michael, who was great sex personified, to hold on to if he wanted to. He wanted to throw his arms in the air and shout for joy as they took the Carbon Canyon road out toward the 71 Freeway and Norco, the winding, twisting two-lane road an undulating playground where cars and other bikers buzzed around for a Saturday drive.

After a while, Michael dropped down the 71 Freeway east toward Riverside and traveled for a while to the apple country, out by Yucaipa where he'd purchased the apples and the pie the day before. About two hours later they came to rest, finding a parking space in front of a picturesque little tourist destination with a definite apple motif.

Tristan's legs shook when he got off the bike, and he held on to Michael, laughing and talking as he removed his helmet. He latched it onto the seat in back and removed his jacket. "I can't believe we actually did that. It was so awesome. That was the best ever," he gushed.

Michael shoved the jackets into the hard bags and locked them in. "Let's get some lunch, Sparky, I could use some coffee."

"Me too." Tristan looked around. Several other bikes dotted the parking lot, but none could compare with Michael's. "Your bike is so gorgeous. How long have you had it?"

"This one? About three years." Michael led him across a wooden sidewalk of sorts to the end of the row and a restaurant called Apple Annie's. He told the hostess his name and how many, and they walked back outside, prepared to wait. Everything about being here with Michael was magical for Tristan. The motorcycle ride gave him an adrenaline rush. Michael looked gorgeous and watched him with a kind of slow, burning sensuality that made Tristan's hair tingle. The air smelled like mountain and pie and coffee.

They made their way through the crowd of people who were waiting for a table. Most were families or seniors traveling together. He saw kids with their faces painted and balloon animals and people milling around with purchases from the rustic little shops or fresh-baked pies.

"This is great," said Tristan. "I came here with my folks as a kid, but I only barely remember it."

"I came here a lot with my mother when I was younger. She used to bike with a club, and I'd ride with her." He seemed to be imagining it; his eyes were closed, and he had a sweet smile on his lips.

"That sounds like fun. I liked your mom. She's..." Tristan searched for the word.

"Yes, she is, isn't she?" said Michael dryly. "She's always been good to me, though, and I like her more and more as I get older. What's your mom like?"

"A mom," said Tristan. "Really a great mom, but mom-like. Smart, funny, serious, loving. She had this hierarchy of stuff, you know, God and family first, education second, music and sports third. Nothing could get in the way of those things. When my dad died, she had to go back to work. It bothers her, I know, that she can't be home for every little thing. It's taken some of the sparkle out of her." He looked away. "I stayed home so I could help, but she still has to go to all the parent-teacher stuff, the recitals, and the soccer games. No substitute for moms, I guess. I help haul people around, and when I can be, I'm there when they get home from school."

Michael smiled. "I'll bet your mom has no idea that you worry about her as much as you do."

"Nope, she'd box me up and mail me to Stanford if she knew I got in. I don't dare let her know I think about any of this, or she'd have me gone in a second." He rested his elbows on his knees. "My youngest brother is a freshman in high school, so by the time he's out, I'll be nearly twenty-five. I'm planning on a graduate degree anyway, and like I said, free room and board doesn't suck."

Michael just gazed at him, perfectly relaxed with his hands clasped between his knees. "See what I mean?" he asked quietly.

"So very *shiny*." He looked at Tristan with something Tristan couldn't quite define in his eyes, yet he soaked it up like a sponge.

"Michael?" said a deep, rich voice from behind him. "Hey! How the hell are you?" Another man in full-on bike leathers held out a hand to shake. "Haven't seen you. Where've you been?"

Michael looked up at the newcomer coolly. "Around. Sparky, this is Ron, a friend from my mom's riding club. Ron, meet Sparky." Tristan couldn't understand the exchange, or why Michael's behavior changed, but he held his hand out and Ron shook it heartily.

"Sparky, eh? I guess the hair has something to do with that." He turned his attention back to Michael. "I've missed seeing you around," he said quietly. "Don't you ride with your mom anymore?"

"Sometimes," said Michael, again vaguely. "Lately I've been doing a lot of remodeling on an apartment building."

"Oh, hard work," said Ron, and for some reason, the way he said *hard* set an alarm off in Tristan's head. He looked at Ron closely. Ron was a very attractive man, with salt-and-pepper hair and dark brown eyes. He had a craggy, lined face, but not in a bad way. He looked like a cowboy from the movies, except in biker clothing. He was watching Michael intently, like a bird of prey. It seemed to be making Michael uneasy.

"Nothing wrong with work," said Tristan, seeking to ease the tension. "Michael does some great cabinetry, really first rate."

"I know," said Ron. "I taught him all about working with…wood."

"Ron," warned Michael.

"Michael here," he said to Tristan, "didn't know the first thing about wood when I met him." There was something about the way he said it that made Tristan squidgy. Nothing overt, but if this man had been speaking to either of his brothers, Tristan would have shut the innuendos down immediately. "The thing is, he didn't seem to realize that when you work with *good* wood, sometimes you gotta really work it, you've gotta master it."

Tristan blinked up at the man, appalled. Nothing was veiled there, and something Michael had said the first time they had talked clicked into place. *Something about people who don't care about using you.* Was this the man that had made Michael feel that way? He looked like a normal guy, but the hand he currently had on Michael's shoulder, while it looked perfectly benign, tensed in an attempt to squeeze Michael painfully.

Oh, hell no, you do not *do that,* thought Tristan angrily.

"The thing with wood" -- Tristan reached over and removed Ron's hand from Michael's shoulder -- "is that as it ages, if it's properly cured, it gets stronger. But if it's brittle and weak, it's best to discard it entirely in favor of newer and greener wood. Wouldn't you agree, Michael?" he asked, his eyebrows raised expectantly.

"Oh, yes," said Michael, visibly relieved, the twinkle coming back to his eye. "Green wood is good and strong. Makes you *want* to work with it. Makes you proud when you get it in shape and can take a good, long look at it."

"Yep. Michael here has been using exclusively green wood for his latest projects, and they've been phenomenally successful. Astounding, really."

"Yes, sir. I'd never go back to old wood. It's so...dry." He looked at Ron pointedly, and Tristan assumed there was a story there he wouldn't want to hear if his life depended on it.

"Yeah," said Ron, making a "tch" noise, like a pop can opening. "Well, I guess I'll be seeing you and *Sparky* around sometime."

"Yeah." Michael held out his hand to shake. "Sure, see you."

Tristan shook Ron's hand when it was his turn. Ron turned and left, walking around the corner where they couldn't see him any more.

"Awkward," said Michael, who didn't look at Tristan. "Not exactly how I wanted to spend my day with you."

"Then don't let him ruin it. Look at me," said Tristan.

Michael looked at him.

"Oh, good, that's better."

"What?"

"What, what?"

"Didn't you want me to look at you so you could lecture me?"

"No, I just wanted you to look at me because it makes me hot," sighed Tristan.

Michael started laughing. "You are one of a kind. New wood, old wood, I thought I'd die."

Tristan narrowed his eyes. "Well, no one is going to hurt you on *my* watch."

Chapter Thirteen

Michael pulled the Harley back into his garage at around three in the afternoon, tired and dusty from riding, but happy.

"That was the coolest thing! I could just get on that and go with you forever," Tristan said. "Do you ever take it on road trips?"

"Sure, all the time. Not long ones since I was a kid, but to Vegas and sometimes New Mexico. I'll tell you, though, sometimes you miss the truck, especially in an electrical storm when you're in the desert, and you're the tallest thing out there."

"Oh, yeah, I guess that would be a little intimidating."

"Yeah, but it's gorgeous," said Michael. "Hey, Sparky, I need to work tonight, so…"

"Oh, I see. Maybe I'll just get my stuff and go."

"No, I…" Michael bit his lip. "I wondered if you'd like to take a nap with me. I mean, wow, how exciting, right? Taking a nap. But I need to sleep a bit, and I…don't want you to go just yet."

"No, well…I don't want to go, either." Tristan held his hand out for Michael. "A nap would be great. I'm tired from the ride anyway."

"Okay," said Michael. "Okay." Together they walked to the house, and Tristan thought he'd never make it to the bed he was so tired. He stripped down to his shorts, as did Michael, and they slid between the sheets together, this time in Michael's bedroom.

Tristan tried to remember the last time he'd gotten into bed with anyone when sex wasn't the major motivating factor.

"Hey, you know what?" he asked. "I've never just slept with someone, for sleep, you know?"

"Really? Why else would you sleep with someone if not for sleep?"

"For sex? Duh."

"Yeah, but then you're not sleeping." Michael tucked him in under his arm, spooning up to him. "When you sleep, you're not having sex, are you?"

"Well, no, but I've never just gone to sleep with someone," said Tristan, turning to look.

"And alas, this still remains the case, even though it's what you're supposed to be doing right now," Michael reminded him.

"Oh, all right," Tristan growled. "I just wanted you to know that everything I'm doing with you seems sort of new and lovely and wonderful, that's all, don't mind me…"

"Hush, love, and I'll blow you later," said Michael.

Tristan made himself silent as the grave and woke up two hours later, blissfully aware of a condom on his cock followed by a mouth that could suck the Starship Enterprise into hyperspace.

"Oh," he moaned, his back arching and his hips undulating without his informed consent. "You…baby…go…" he said. Swallowed literally by sensation. He stroked Michael's soft blond hair, knowing by its dampness that the man had already showered.

"Oh, no fair, you got all wet without me," he sighed. Michael merely nodded and continued to suck Tristan's cock, sneaking a lubed-up finger into his ass.

"Oh, Michael," said Tristan, slightly sore from the night before but still so needy. "Way to wake up…oh…*so good.* We need to invent alarm clocks that do this…"

Michael tried not to laugh because it was ruining his rhythm. He loved this. His boy smelled so good…soft red curls and sweat and sex and man; Michael closed his eyes and used his tongue to tease and excite his lover, feeling Tristan's pulse against his lips. Soon Tristan gripped Michael's hair and started taking his mouth, mindlessly jerking until his balls tightened against Michael's hands, and groaning, he shot hard into the latex. He held Michael's head there as he came, muttering something unintelligible, until Michael gently disengaged the hands from his hair and removed his mouth and then the condom. Despite his resolve to play safe, Michael couldn't stop himself from tasting, flicking his tongue over the slit in the tip of Tristan's cock. He laved Tristan's balls and kissed his inner thighs, rising up and crawling toward the head of the bed where Tristan lay panting.

"Hey, Tristan," said Michael, grinning. His lips looked fuller and darker and so delicious.

"Hey, Michael," said Tristan, hooking a hand behind his head to bring him in for a kiss.

"I've got to change and go." Michael stroked the side of his face again. "I overslept, and I'm running a little late."

"No time for a little quid pro quo?" asked Tristan, pulling him close.

"Love to, but I can't. Next time, I'm counting on it." He smiled.

"Next time?" asked Tristan. "Okay." He smiled back. In fact, it occurred to him that they were both smiling like stupid people. "We're smiling." He stated the obvious.

"You make me smile, Sparky, even in the weirdest, non-smiling kind of moments." Tristan grinned, eyeing the man's twitching cock.

"Thank you for today; it was awesome."

Michael responded with a quick kiss before he rose from the bed. "I'll be ready in twenty, and then I'll have to leave."

"Oh," said Tristan. "Oh, okay." He got up from the bed too, his legs still a little wobbly. "I'll get my stuff, and you can see me out." Tristan started dressing in the same clothes he'd worn for their ride. He placed his folded-up costume carefully in the duffel and made sure he didn't leave socks or underwear lying around because, ick, he'd rather Michael remember his ass than his dirty laundry.

"I…um…well," said Michael, not quite looking at him, "could meet you sometime, down by UCI for lunch or something."

"Sure," said Tristan. "I'd like that." He found himself right next to Michael. He couldn't help it; he was gravitationally predisposed to lean into Michael's embrace.

"Can you make coffee while I dress?" Michael asked. "I could take a travel mug to work."

"Sure. I could use a cup anyway. I'll put my stuff by the door and get right on it. You go do what you need to do."

"Okay." He sighed. "I wonder why being together seems so natural and parting is awkward as hell. I wish I didn't have to go," he added.

"Oh, me too," said Tristan, launching himself at the surprised Michael. "Isn't that dumb? I just don't want to…"

"I know," said Michael kissing him. "Me neither. I can't figure out why…"

"Kiss me more," said Tristan.

"*Shit*," said Michael, pulling away. "Work, work, work, work, work, stupid…*stupid* work." He marched himself down the hall and slammed the bathroom door.

Tristan laughed on his way into the kitchen, saying, "School, school, school…stupid school." He found the coffee and managed the coffeemaker, getting a cup for himself. When Michael came out in his uniform, Tristan stopped in his tracks.

"Officer Helmet," he said on a sigh. He didn't know why it was such a shock, seeing Michael fully dressed in his uniform, armed, and remote. It wasn't exactly the first time he'd seen it. It *was* the first time he wanted to cuff the man and use him like an inflatable doll. Oh, hot, hot, hot.

"This okay?" said Michael. "Does it bring bad memories? Feel like running?"

"Oh, not exactly. Officer Truax. Michael." Tristan walked up and ran a hand over the chest pockets of the uniform, carefully touching the badge. "I'm never going to look at cops the same way again."

"You'd better not look at *other* cops the way you're looking at me." He took the travel mug, and together they walked the short distance to the front door. "They really will think you're a rent-boy."

As Tristan neared the door he thought of everything he wanted to say to Michael, except he had no time and didn't know where to begin. He turned around suddenly. "I like your texts. That's really nice, you know? Sometimes when people say they'll call they don't…or well…I didn't when I said it to girls and now…I just wanted to say I like it when you text me." His heart beat as though he'd run a marathon.

Michael smiled.

"I wish I'd thought of it that way when…I may have hurt some people." Tristan tried to smile when he said that, but the thought of pain he may have caused in the past didn't make him feel much like smiling. Tristan wished now he'd had more empathy. He'd always held lightly to the girls he dated. He was going to have a hard time holding Michael that way.

Michael appeared to think about that for a while. "I'll keep in touch, Sparky."

Tristan gave him a radiant smile. "Me too, if that's okay with you."

"Of course it's okay," said Michael, kissing him senseless and then setting the house alarm. A high-pitched whistle sounded, and they walked out the front door into the fading light. Daylight savings was still in effect, and there was a little residual twilight. "I have to close the door, or the alarm will go off," he said, close to Tristan's ear, and Tristan realized he was standing in the way.

"Oh." He moved. "I guess I'll be seeing you," he said, walking down the porch steps to his car. "Um, sometime soon, I hope."

"Yeah, you can count on it, Sparky."

Tristan got into his car and began the drive back to his home. Cinderella's carriage was turning back into a pumpkin, and the real world intruded on his thoughts. He found himself fretting about homework he hadn't even given a thought to for the whole day and worrying about his family. While he was with Michael, the world receded, and all that existed was the two of them.

He got home at about six in the evening; the sky was darkening, and the air was getting crisp. The first thing he did was call his friend Jonathon to tell him he wouldn't be up for poker. He had to talk to his family -- had to do it now when he was riding the high of being with Michael, before doubt and uncertainty made him wait, made him think of hiding his truth from his family. Truth was truth. This wasn't going to go away.

When he entered he could hear his brothers, Devon and Randy, arguing at the top of their lungs about who should clean their room. His sister had on her iPod and was sitting at the kitchen table with her laptop, pretending to do her homework but probably instant messaging her friends. His mother was sitting at the computer in the kitchen where she did the bills and caught up with her own e-mails.

"Randy, Devon, feel like a run?" he called. His brother Randy stuck his head out of his bedroom door.

"At the park?" he asked. Randy was the one who enjoyed running at the park, because of the people walking their dogs. He could make friends with a dog in seconds, and it would remember him for a lifetime. Devon thought dogs were okay, but didn't have the same affinity for them. Fortunately, he wasn't too picky about where they ran.

"Sure, if you want. I'll talk to Mom and you talk to Devon," said Tristan.

"Okay," said Randy. He stopped shouting at his brother long enough to get his attention and start another fight, this one about where to go jogging.

"Mom," said Tristan, getting a glass of milk from the fridge. "I thought I'd take the boys to run at Craig Park; is that okay?"

His mother was preoccupied, cursing under her breath at their Internet service, which was always slow in the evening. "Damn it! This always happens on Saturday night. This is going to take me hours at this rate."

"What is it?" he asked, coming around to see.

"Just bills, honey, nothing big, it just takes forever. Yeah, running sounds good. They've been at it since four. Maybe you could run them down for me a little." She took off her reading glasses and smiled. He looked at her for a minute, realizing he hadn't really *seen* her for a while. Her blue eyes, so like his own, seemed more tired than he remembered, and her red hair seemed whiter around the temples. It wasn't exactly that she was getting old; she just looked like she was changing into someone more muted than the woman he'd known growing up. He knew his father's death had been hard on her, but hadn't noticed exactly when it had washed her color away. She patted his hand with a freckled one very like his own, and he laughed.

"I really am your mini-me, aren't I?" he said, giving her hand a squeeze back. "Sometimes I forget. I'll get the boys, and we'll be back by…seven-thirty or so, okay?"

"Sure, fine…take your phone." She went back to her bills.

As Tristan left the room, he looked back at her. When had she gotten so small? He had decided on his way home from Michael's to tell her the truth about himself, but now it gnawed at him. Not knowing how she'd take it was worrisome. He didn't much care and couldn't change what others thought, but he agonized over how it would affect those he loved.

"Mom, when I get back, I'd like to talk to you for a bit; maybe we could go for coffee?" he said, hoping she didn't get too wrapped up in anticipating what it could be about.

She sat silently contemplating him. "Okay, but first tell me, does it have anything to do with immediate physical danger or possible jail time?" she asked, her typical response to make a joke.

"Nope, neither." He smiled.

Reassured, she went back to her bills. "Sure, coffee, but you're buying."

"Right." He was able to round his brothers up in less than fifteen minutes, almost a house record, and they were off to the park.

Jogging with his brothers was something Tristan did almost every weekday until Halloween, when the park hours changed, and the gates closed at six. It was always exhilarating to run in the park after dark. Smiling, he imagined that was how wolves felt, running in a pack, and realized that the boys were his pack. He said a silent prayer that they'd have big, happy families, and he could run with nieces and nephews some day. Lily gave no indication of even being interested in any boy who wasn't about to starve himself to death over the injustice of life. Tristan despaired of her ever choosing someone healthy enough to procreate.

While jogging along the peaceful paths with his brothers, Tristan divested his mind of everything but what he wanted to tell his family and how he was going to do it. There was no doubt in his mind; he couldn't live a lie. That he wasn't scared down to his nuts to tell his mom he was gay reflected, he thought, her loving acceptance of him for most of his life, even when he probably didn't deserve it at all. Tristan was afraid it would shock and sadden her, but for the most part, he didn't think it would change their relationship. Strain it for a while, maybe, but fundamentally, his family was solid, and they would all stand behind him.

Hoping he wasn't naive and stupid, Tristan jogged on. He thought telling his brothers might be as hard as any part of the whole ordeal. They were just old enough to really understand what being gay meant, and it would probably gross them out completely. Lily would think it romantic, but be angry that he didn't have a vampire lover or something cool like that. He ran along with them, stopping to greet every dog along the way, and hid his laughter when Devon complained about it holding them up. Randy, to teach him a lesson, simply stopped to chat with each dog until Devon was tapping his foot in agitation, and both Randy and the dogs were laughing at him.

To prevent bloodshed, Tristan argued for crossing the park and going directly to the car instead of taking the roundabout way. He was tired, both physically and emotionally, and a little sore, his muscles reacting to both his exuberant new love life and the long motorcycle ride. The three of them got to the car sweating and happy, ready to crank up the radio and drive through Jack-In-The-Box for shakes. Tristan bought one for each of his brothers and picked up an Oreo shake for Lily. He wanted a latte, so he decided to wait till he was out with his mom.

They pulled into the driveway around eight o'clock, the boys jumping right out and racing to the house with their shakes. Tristan took Lily's to her.

"Here, Lily, I brought you a shake. You and the boys can stay here. Mom and I are going out for coffee, okay?"

Lily raised her eyebrows. "You and Mom are going out?" She had an incredulous look on her face. "Since when do you take Mom out for coffee on a Saturday night? Isn't this, like, the night you get laid or something?"

"Very funny."

"Really, what have you done that you need to talk to Mom about it in a public place?" Her eyes were wide. He knew her imagination was in overdrive.

"Well, if you promise not to tell her," he said, looking around as though he were going to confide.

"Shit, I knew it was big… What's up?"

"I have to ask her if I can dig a big hole in the garage floor, under where the car goes, you know?"

"No way. Really?"

"Yeah, I have to have a place for my vampire lover's coffin and the earth to surround it, you know?" he said. "So the sunlight can't get in."

"Oh, you're an asshole." She grabbed her shake and tore the paper off the straw.

Their mother came into the room. "Such language," she said. "I wish you'd think about how it makes you sound."

"Sorry." Lily slunk behind their mother to stick her tongue out.

"We'll be back soon, honey. Keep the boys from burning the house down, okay?" Lily acknowledged that she'd try.

Tristan opened the car door for his mom and closed it after she got in. When he got into the driver's seat, she watched him in that careful way she had, studying him in order to brace herself. "You realize you're scaring me right now," she said, giving him the opportunity to put her at ease. He knew he should do it, but found he had nothing flip to say.

"I know," said Tristan. "I just thought it would be good if we talked, and I...didn't want the boys or Lily to interrupt." He pulled out of the driveway and headed the short distance to the strip mall. It seemed strange to use his dad's car, especially to take his mom places in the passenger seat. He felt...so inadequate to step into the shoes his father had left behind.

"Is this about school? Are you in trouble?" she asked finally.

"No, Mom, I'm really not in trouble, I promise." He looked at her again out of the corner of his eye. She was forty-two, still young, still attractive, and still mourning the death of her husband two years before. Tristan's father had been talking to her on the phone, just connecting, asking her about dinner plans, when an aneurism in his brain had ended his life. She was young enough to date again, marry again, and conceivably to have more children. She had a friend who'd had a child at forty-four. Whether she wanted to or not, she had never allowed her children to even imagine she entertained such thoughts, and for that, Tristan was shamefully grateful. He knew he should be urging her to consider getting out again, but the comfort of the familiar had enticed him into maintaining the status quo. And now what he was going to tell her would change everything.

At Starbuck's they got in line and ordered lattes from the cashier, waiting patiently for the barista to prepare them. When at last they sat down, Tristan found he wasn't at all as brave as he thought.

"Okay, Tris, I'm here and I've waited. I've gone through everything in my mind from unplanned pregnancy to ecoterrorist. Please tell me what's up before I tear all my hair out," she begged. "Please, Tristan… Spill it."

Chapter Fourteen

Tristan's fingers picked at the little cardboard circle around his cup that served to keep his fingers from getting burned. "I'm in love," he said finally, knowing that was just an appetizer at the honesty buffet. His mom blew out a breath.

"That's it?" she asked. "Wow, I thought… Oh, man, I thought it was going to be something awful." She laughed nervously. "Love. That's good, right?"

"Well," he began. "Yes. I think so…yes."

"You don't sound so sure. Is it unrequited?" she asked. "Such an old-fashioned term. Is it mutual, do you think?"

"Um, yeah, maybe… It hasn't really gone that far. We've only been out twice. It's been really sudden. For me, anyway."

"Ah," she said, taking a sip of her coffee. "That's hard, isn't it? This is the first time for you… Despite your rather strenuous efforts in the area of…romance."

"Yeah." He looked down at his coffee cup.

She watched him some more. "Why aren't we at home having this conversation?"

"Well…that's really not all there is to it. It's complicated." He felt it was to his credit that he met her eyes squarely. "It's different than what you might think."

He could see her trying to imagine the possibilities. "You know, if she's a different race or religion or something, those things don't matter as much as they used to. If two people love and respect each other, most things can be considered details." She touched his hand with hers. "Is it one of the girls from school?"

"It isn't a girl," he said.

His mother stared at him. "Is it a woman?" she asked, turning her coffee around in her hands, nervously now, as if her heart was telling her brain not to listen.

"No," he said, waiting.

"Oh. I'm going out on a limb here and assuming it's a human?" she asked, searching for a joke.

"Yes. It's a man."

She deflated. Sort of just slumped over her coffee with her lips pursed, thinking hard. "You're not punking me?"

"I wish I were." He still watched her struggle with the dawning realization, his eyes glittering now with unshed tears. "It's a guy. I'm in love with a guy."

"Okaaaaay," she said slowly, and he could tell she was slipping into crisis mode, like when Randy had fallen and broken his arm, and she had marshaled all their resources to have him at the emergency room in twenty minutes flat. "You know, sometimes, it can feel like love when it's just kind of situational."

"I'm in love with a guy," said Tristan implacably. "I promise you, I wouldn't bring this to you if I didn't think it was a done deal."

"Oh," she sighed. "*Oh.*" Her blue eyes, so very much like his, were watering a little. She exhaled in a long, slow sigh. "How come I've gone to sleep every night for five years with a prayer on my lips that you wouldn't impregnate half the girls in the neighborhood by morning?" She leaned in to hiss for emphasis. "You've been a pretty determined hetero until now!"

"I know," he said. "I know that I've swung like a gate, and it may seem strange. I've always liked girls. I mean, I don't dislike them, and they're pretty determined as well. What's not to like? It's just that ever since I was a kid, it was like… See Dick… See Dick run… See Tristan push Jane and run after Dick." He sighed. "I hardly admitted it to myself, but it didn't go away. It's not going to."

"Well, shit," said his mother, taking another drink of her coffee. "How do you know, I mean, how does anyone know they're gay? Lots of people have relationships with people of the same sex, and not everyone who does that is gay. Some say it was a mistake, or an adventure. How do you know?"

Tristan thought about that for a long time. "Mom, remember when we were watching that U2 *Rattle and Hum* DVD, and you and Dad kept saying that you'd seen the concert, and the DVD couldn't compare to watching the band live?"

"Yeah," she said carefully.

"Well, that's what it's like. It's like the difference between watching the symphony on a small-screen television versus watching it live at the Hollywood Bowl. I can't explain it any better than that. I've never been in love before. I don't know if it's even mutual, but if it is… Oh, damn, Mom, it's really, *really* right."

"And it's not just about sex?" she asked. "Do you know the difference?"

He shrugged and looked away. "I think so; who the hell really knows? There's an over fifty percent divorce rate in this country. He's a kind person, a good man. His mom's a trip. He's…special. If Lily brought him home, you'd be on your knees thanking God."

"If he's everything you say and he loves you and you love him? I'll be on my knees thanking God anyway. Don't think that I'd ask you to throw that away just because it doesn't fit my preconceived notion of what is right for you. It's just hard, you know?" She wiped a tear off her cheek. "It changes all the plans I had for you."

"I gotta tell you, it's not that easy for me, either," said Tristan, laughing a little.

"Then why do it, why put yourself through that? You've been perfectly happy to nail every girl who gave you the opportunity for five years." His eyes widened at her frank talk. "Like I didn't know, Tris. Why can't you find a girl who's special?"

"It's not that simple. I'm not certain I could. Sure, I had sex," he said, loudly enough that his mother cringed, and he lowered his voice. "But what I want is what you and Dad had. I want to love someone and build a life with that person, and I couldn't do that with *any* girl I've ever been with. I'm just made differently, I think. I never knew I could feel this way. I know I couldn't go back. It wouldn't be fair to the girls or to me."

Tristan's mother pursed her lips. "Jeez, what will we tell the boys? I hope you know it's bad enough not having your dad around to talk sex to them, but now? I have no idea what to say to them about --"

"I know," Tristan interrupted. "I thought about that tonight while we were jogging. I think they'll hate me for a while. Lily will probably think it's cool, as long as I bring home some poetry-spouting faerie prince. Not going to happen, by the way. I know I kind of jumped in with both feet. This guy, Michael, he's older…"

"How much older?"

"He'll be twenty-eight on Valentine's Day," said Tristan, smiling. "He's so nice, it would make your teeth ache. He bought a duplex with twin houses, and his mom lives in one, and he lives in the other, and she comes out on the porch in the morning to smoke clove cigarettes. Of course, he's all like, 'I thought you were quitting' cranky with her, you know? I'm gushing like a little girl, aren't I?"

"I think," she said carefully, "if you're certain this is who you are, you should invite both of them for Thanksgiving…maybe."

"Maybe," he concurred, finally attempting to drink his coffee.

"And, yes, you're gushing. What does he do for a living?" said his mother.

Tristan almost spit his coffee out. Almost. "He's…a police officer," he sighed, putting his head in his hands so his mother couldn't see his face. "Kind of puts a whole new spin on sticking it to the Man."

Julia's own hands flew to her face, the blush building there like a forest fire. Tristan peeked through his fingers, but couldn't tell whether she was laughing or crying. He thought, after a while, maybe a little of both.

They drank the rest of their coffee in silence. Tristan sprang for a decadent chocolate pastry, sharing it with her wordlessly. Just before they left, she said simply, "If you're sure, we'll have to have a family talk. I don't want your brothers and sister stuck with questions that you or I haven't answered in person to their satisfaction."

"I can do that. I wish I…"

"Never mind, Tris, you did right to tell me," she said. "If I'm half the mother I've been pretending to be all these years, I'll be ready to march in my first gay pride parade any minute now."

"Holy crap, you'll be marching alone. I hate that kind of stuff," said Tristan, leaving the Starbuck's and getting out his keys. "You know, Michael's the one that gave me that ticket for not wearing a helmet."

"Oh, no, he did not!" said his mother, appalled. "Well…you should definitely ask him for your money back." She grinned.

Tristan felt himself smile. He felt hopeful for the first time since they'd started to talk.

"I'm glad you trusted me with this, Tris. I hope -- I mean, *I know* you're being safe, right?"

"With Officer Helmet?" he asked. "You can count on it."

"Good to know, baby," she sighed, getting into the car. "Good to know."

* * *

Sitting between Randy and Lily in church the next day, Tristan listened to the minister's sermon on the true spirit of the upcoming holidays. He looked at his siblings, who were yawning after the late night they'd had. Each of them had taken the news that their brother was gay relatively well. They'd had lots of questions and made lots of yuck faces, but really, it had gone remarkably well. He knew how lucky he was to have a family that was loving and supportive, even if they felt a little shell-shocked. It put his mind at ease, and after church, he had a ton of homework he could get to with a fairly focused brain.

Tristan jumped a little when his phone vibrated in his pocket. Pulling it out, he saw he had a text from Michael and blushed like a kid. His mother caught the look and raised her eyebrows. He grinned and looked to see what the text said.

Hey, Sparky. R U in church? it read.

Tristan looked around. Thumbing, *Hey, Michael, yep.*

Michael's next text made him smile. *E-mail addy for Edward is NotNeddie@hotmail.com. I told Jeff he was wrong about you.*

Thank you, Tristan texted back.

I forgot 2 tell you I love U, came the next, and Tristan put a hand over his mouth. He dipped his head and cleared his throat, sinking lower when someone nearby gave him a hard stare.

Me 2, I love you 2, he texted back, shamelessly ignoring his mother's glare.

Can I get an AMEN? Michael sent, making him smile.

Amen, sent Tristan, sighing. Oh, yeah, Thanksgiving would be fun.

Chapter Fifteen

In chemistry class, Tristan's professor was a tall, thin, angular woman who claimed that the Santa Ana winds gave her energy. Today she had an abundance of it, giving her lecture in an exuberant monotone, which she occasionally abandoned for staccato bursts of emphatic laughter. Three girls in the front row were clutching their hearts when Tristan's phone vibrated to let him know he had a text message.

Have time 2 meet 4 lunch? asked Michael.

What time? Tristan texted back carefully. Texting in class was strictly déclassé, but not entirely forbidden. Still he didn't want his professor to connect his face with any rude behavior; in case his grade hovered a little, it was always better to be on the teacher's nice, rather than naughty list.

About 1? Michael sent.

Okay, sent Tristan.

Pick U up? sent Michael.

Meet me at Johnny Rocket's in The District at Tustin Legacy? texted Tristan.

By the old airship hangars? sent Michael.

Yes, said Tristan.

K, TTYL, texted Michael.

K, L, texted Tristan.

* * *

At one o'clock, Michael was waiting for Tristan outside Johnny Rocket's. He looked at his watch again. It wasn't that he was nervous that Tristan wouldn't show, he thought, but he was actually anxious to see him. It seemed like weeks since he'd ridden with Tristan out to Oak Glen, even though it had only been three days. They'd kept up a pretty regular text conversation. Michael had sent him the "I love you" text on Sunday; the thought still made him blush like a kid. It was like he was passing notes in school. Michael just couldn't get his mind off Tristan going toe to toe with Ron, removing his hand, and letting him know there was a new guy on the scene. He kept thinking of the words, *No one is going to hurt you on my watch.* They had opened something inside his heart that had been closed a long, long time. It was a done deal. Tristan owned him.

Minutes later, Michael saw the small cream-colored BMW pull into a parking space, and Tristan climbed out. He wore drawstring pants that rode really low on his waist and a hooded T-shirt with a design that looked like a tattoo on it. Michael could see a tantalizing strip of ivory skin between the two and wondered if meeting Tristan in public was such a good idea. He was getting hard already, and the boy was still half a block away.

"Hey, Michael," said Tristan, smiling when he reached the place where Michael waited.

"Hey, Sparky." Michael buffeted Tristan with his shoulder, but he wished he were touching with his hands.

Tristan lowered his eyes, and a delicate blush stained his cheeks. "I'm glad you called."

"They should have a table waiting; I gave them our name."

"Good thinking," said Tristan, following Michael into the restaurant. "I'm hungry."

"Me too," said Michael. They followed the hostess to a booth and sat down. "What's new in Sparky's world?"

"I had chemistry today. The professor acted like she was on speed. It was entertaining," said Tristan.

"Oh?" asked Michael. "I would have liked to see that. My chemistry professor was a tiny little man with frizzy gray hair who spoke with a Polish accent. It was like listening to the Pope, the last one. John Paul."

Tristan smiled. He took a deep breath. "I told my mother about us. Had a talk with the family."

"What?" asked Michael, leaning forward. He was concerned. "Are you okay?"

"Yeah, I decided I wanted to tell her before anything else happened. I told her on Saturday night. I…we had a family talk after I told her. Everyone took it better than I thought. I don't know what that means. They want you and your mom to come for Thanksgiving. That gives you a month to run screaming." Tristan didn't look up.

"Yeah, it does. Sparky, do you think I'm going anywhere?"

"No."

"Burgers, fries, and shakes? Or do you want something different?"

"I'll have half of whatever you're having." Tristan smiled, picking up his foot and sitting on it. "And a chocolate shake."

"Okay." Michel flagged down their waiter. He ordered for both of them and turned back to Tristan. "How did your mom really respond when you told her you were gay?"

"I don't think she believed me at first. She asked if I was punking her." He smiled. "I *have* given her reason to believe that I like girls fine in the last few years."

"Sparky, maybe..." Michael searched for the right words. "Maybe that's something you should consider. I don't know a lot of gay men who have had as much experience as you on the other side of the street. My heart wouldn't be in it quite so..."

"Are you kidding me?" snapped Tristan. "Are you trying to talk me out of being gay? Because if you are, so help me, I will make you sorry you brought me to this restaurant by showing you just how damn gay I am."

"Tristan, really." Michael held his hands up. "I didn't mean to upset you. I just thought it was something to think about."

"At fourteen I was a walking hormone," said Tristan. "And for some reason every girl at the skate park wanted a piece of that. I liked it, *sure*, what's not to like?" A couple at a nearby table stopped their conversation to gawk at Tristan, who was turning red.

"Tristan, I'm so sorry," said Michael, urging calm. "It's just that I don't understand you as well as I would like to."

"It's not rocket science," said Tristan, leaning over to speak more quietly. "I was a horny kid who took whatever was offered. But when I decided to choose, I chose *you*." He picked up his napkin and placed it on his lap when their server brought out their drinks.

Michael was still feeling argumentative. "Not really. Actually, I kind of forced the issue, and you were backed into a corner."

"Michael," said Tristan, clearly holding on to his patience by a thread. "I chased your truck down my street on a skateboard. My decision was made then. *I chose you*."

"I'm glad," said Michael thickly. "Really, really glad."

"Me too. Next time we have this discussion let's do it in bed, though. I think it will take more time to convince you, and it would be a hell of a lot more fun." He smiled. The server brought them their lunch and an extra plate for sharing. They ate slowly and quietly, making quality eye contact. Michael smiled around his straw and tossed his napkin on the table when they were finished.

"You want to walk a little? I have until about three," he said. "It's starting to get crazy; tomorrow's Halloween, we're all working, and there still won't be enough of us."

"Oh, yeah, I love Halloween, but it must be hard on you and *the brethren*," said Tristan. "I never thought about it that way."

"It's just a natural law; whenever everybody parties, people do stupid stuff, get drunk, and get in accidents. Lots of DUIs. Sometimes kids get hurt. It's not very much fun for me anymore." Michael left money on the table to cover the bill plus a generous tip, and he rose, waiting for Tristan to precede him.

"I guess," said Tristan. "I guess you can tell I like Halloween.

"Yeah, and come to think of it, taking you out of those Samurai pants didn't suck." Michael smiled. They walked out into the sunshine, into the warm wind that was kicking up around them. "Shit, this wind always means fire danger too." He sighed.

"Do you think that now that I'm gay I should dress differently?" he asked, trying to distract Michael a little.

"What? Do I dress differently?"

"No, but I'm thinking you can't because you have that totally conservative job. I'm in school, you know? I could work it a little while I'm still young." He had a teasing light in his eye that Michael found adorable. "I kind of need a queer eye for the queer guy, don't I?"

Michael looked him over and sighed. "You do fine, Sparky. You're edible as it is."

"Oh," said Tristan, coloring a little. "Well, now that you bring that up, Officer Truax, can you tell me how much trouble I could get in if I were to…say…suck you off in your truck?"

Michael, to his credit, kept walking. "More trouble than I'd like, Sparky. I'm not one of those guys who gets off on risky sex." After a while he muttered, "Much."

"Hey," said Tristan. "I heard that." He grinned at Michael, raising his eyebrows, and lifted his foot to tap Michael's ass from behind with the heel, like they were kids.

"I just can't, Tristan," said Michael. "I couldn't."

"Okay." Tristan was only mildly disappointed. "I just thought..."

Michael smiled. "No, it's nice. Here, I wanted to give you this," he said, holding out an envelope. He handed it to Tristan and stepped back.

"What is it?"

"It's the key to my house," said Michael. "And the alarm codes. You could stop by sometimes. If I wasn't there, you could maybe wait."

Tristan broke into a radiant smile. "Hey! You trust me with your beautiful house?" he asked.

"Sure. You like my house, you'll take good care of it."

"Of course I will. This is the nicest thing." Tristan bit his lip.

"I'm, um, usually off on Friday during the day until Saturday night. It's quiet, and you might like to do your homework there sometimes." Michael sighed, feeling like an idiot. "Anyway, I'll get you a copy of my schedule, and you can come and go as you please, okay? I'll be working a couple double shifts in the next few weeks."

"This is a big thing, isn't it?" said Tristan, looking at him. "It's like...we're a couple."

"Aren't we?" Michael turned to him. "Aren't you my guy? You said you were."

"I am," said Tristan. "But aren't you going to want to drop-kick my ass into the gutter if I'm around too much?"

Michael laughed. "I don't think it will come to that." He kept walking. Tristan ran forward to face him.

"You really meant it, didn't you; it wasn't just a goofy text."

"Meant what?" said Michael quietly

"That you love me. You meant that, didn't you?"

"Yeah, did you?"

"Yes. I told my family I'd fallen in love with you. That was Saturday. Just so you know."

"Before I told you?" Michael smiled.

"Yep," said Tristan. They began walking again.

"Ha, ha," said Michael in a singsong voice. "You said it first." He chuckled to himself as Tristan followed after him.

"Also just so you know, I knew you loved me all along," said Tristan. "And by the way, my mother says you should pay us back for that ticket now that I'm your ass slut."

Chapter Sixteen

Finishing up his shift on Halloween, Michael eyed the fog rolling in and figured that while visibility wasn't good, it was plenty safe to drive. It had been a hell of a night, and he was anxious to wash his tension down the drain and sleep. He had probably made a difference in someone's life, although he wasn't exactly sure whose, and he pulled his truck into his driveway exhausted, parking it in its usual place. It had been three days since he'd given Tristan the keys, and he wondered if it was too soon for a key exchange. Maybe Tristan didn't want to use them; maybe he wasn't ready. It made Michael a little sad, but he figured he'd wait until Tristan decided to talk to him about it.

As soon as he walked in the door he noticed that the alarm wasn't on, and he could smell a fire going. He smiled. He hoped it wasn't a burglar, because he didn't have his weapon drawn as he walked into the living room. Tristan had a candle going that smelled just like a pumpkin pie and was asleep on the futon in front of the fire.

Michael leaned over him, trying to decide whether he should shower first or wake Tristan and see if he'd like to take a bath. He stroked along the side of Tristan's face with a finger. "Hey, Sparky."

"Hey," said Tristan sleepily, his face coming up from the pillow with little sheet wrinkles on it. "It's about time you got home."

"Miss me?" Michael asked, content to gaze at him.

"Yes." Tristan sat up. He took a long, hard look at Michael, concern in his eyes. "Bad night?"

"Kind of," said Michael. "No fatalities, thank God. A kid was hit by a car while crossing the street. That one was touch and go. I think he'll make it. I hope he will. It was a mess." He could still hear the kid's mother screaming.

"Oh, baby," said Tristan, reaching out. He held Michael, running his hands in his hair. "What can I do?"

"You're doing it. I've never been happier to see anyone in my life." He sighed. "Take a bath with me?"

"Sure." Tristan got up from the futon and followed him. "I parked down the street. I was trying to surprise you." He blew out the candle on the way to the bath.

Michael smiled. "I'm glad, except you have to watch out when you surprise police officers, Sparky. I saw the alarm was turned off and guessed it was you, but I didn't see your car. I could have come in here with my weapon drawn."

"Not a good beginning," agreed Tristan. "Note to self: Never surprise an armed man."

Michael turned on the water and added something that smelled like herbs. "I'm going to go put my stuff away," he said, leaving the bathroom for a minute.

Michael left Tristan where he was, enjoying the sound of his boy humming from the other room while he put his weapon away. When he re-entered the steamy room, Tristan had the candles lit and was just slipping into the tub.

"Now that's therapy." Tristan had put his hair up in a rubber band and for some reason, it appealed to Michael that way. Parts of it floated around his face like feathers.

"What are you looking at?" teased Tristan.

"I can't figure out…" began Michael. "No, it's nothing."

"What? You can't just say something like that and leave it hanging," said Tristan, as Michael got in behind him. He laid his head on Michael's shoulder.

"I was just thinking that you set a standard for masculine beauty."

"Wow," said Tristan, going still.

"But it's weird, because you do all these things" -- he flipped Tristan's ponytail -- "that I think of as feminine. It's not something I've ever gone for before."

"Really? What's your usual type?"

"I don't know that I've had a particular type," Michael said, but knew he was lying even as he said it. *Biker* wasn't his type actually, but it seemed to typify the men he'd dated. He was positive they mostly chose him and not the other way around. Plus there was that whole proximity thing. He biked with his mom on his time off, and that's where he met guys.

"I don't think I do, either. I mean, I didn't start out with the idea of a type. I was going for willing. Maybe able. Maybe even just breathing."

"Thanks, Sparky, high praise indeed," said Michael dryly. He was looking at the candles as he stirred the water with his hand.

"Okay, I was going to say that if I had a type, you'd be it, but now you've gone and ruined the moment." He smiled and kissed Michael's neck where he could reach it. "You know how I feel about you."

Michael smiled. "I know."

"I'm going to soak as long as you need to, and then I'm going to be your sex slave until seven-thirty, when I have to leave to get the boys to school. Let me know what you need, okay?" he sighed, pulling Michael's arms around him. They sat like that for a long time, the water lapping against them, the quiet cocooning them in warmth.

"Sometimes I need someone to tell me what I need," said Michael very quietly, as though he were going way out on a limb. He held Tristan while he thought this over.

"I see," said Tristan.

"I wonder if you do." Michael stroked him from his chest to his balls.

"Sometimes you need to give up control."

"Yes," hissed Michael, feeling stupid. Feeling like he was giving this baby- handed boy the security code to his soul. "Yes. Sometimes. I like to be the one who..."

"I see."

Michael said nothing. He just continued to stroke Tristan's torso thoughtfully, as though he had all the time in the world.

"And I don't exactly fit the profile of the guy who can take you there." Tristan sighed.

"It's not that I need to go anywhere," said Michael brusquely. "Forget I said anything about it. I just..."

Tristan turned in Michael's arms, the water in the tub swirling around him, his cock and balls bobbing as they came to rest against Michael's. Michael gasped at the sudden sensation, and the grinding that Tristan was doing against him had him hard in an instant.

"But make no mistake, Michael. I can and will take you where you need to go *and* protect you when you get there." He took Michael's lips in a punishing kiss that left no doubt that he could fulfill his promise.

Michael had trouble catching his breath.

Tristan pulled the plug on the water, and it started down the drain. "Oh, damn, it's like you said the secret word or something." He rubbed against Michael, holding him tightly, keeping him still.

"What do I get?" asked Michael between panting breaths.

"What do you think?" Tristan rose from the tub and handed him a towel. "Blow out the candles and meet me in the living room," he added, sauntering from the room naked. Michael briefly worried about getting what you wished for and creating monsters and things like that. Then he dried off quickly, blew out the candles, and followed his boy.

Telling Tristan about that secret part of him was only natural, especially after seeing Ron again, but Tristan thinking he had to be a guy like Ron somehow just didn't feel right. He thought he ought to clarify when he found Tristan on his knees adding more wood to the fire. Tristan looked so…damn. He was closing the chain curtain when he turned back to look at Michael. Once again the fire gave the illusion that Tristan was lit from within. Or maybe he just was. Probably he just was.

Michael kneeled on the futon, just looking at Tristan, holding himself still and quiet. "Hey there, Tristan."

Tristan didn't move. "Hey there."

Oh, thought Michael, *a serious Tristan. Lucky, lucky me.*

Tristan came to him then, sort of slid into him, his red hair draping down over his shoulders, teasing the skin on Michael's thighs as he pushed his face into Michael's groin. He hummed against Michael's balls, the vibration of his lips making Michael weak. Michael started to take Tristan's hair in his hands.

"Put your hands behind your back." He waited until Michael complied. "Don't move your hands unless I tell you to."

"Yes," acknowledged Michael. He had no idea what to expect from Tristan, didn't know if he played games.

"Spread your legs and let me see you."

"Yes," said Michael. He complied, allowing the towel to drop and his legs to spread wide, leaving his cock and balls and a hint of the skin behind them exposed.

"Oh, my," said Tristan. "Such a beautiful man." He looked at Michael, from the top of his head to his knees on the ground and repeated, "A beautiful man." He smiled, returning to Michael's balls, licking and caressing them, holding one in his mouth, then the other, as Michael squirmed. He licked up the long vein under Michael's shaft and captured the head in his mouth, stroking the tip and its small slit while he cupped Michael's balls with his hand. He took his mouth away long enough to put a condom on Michael's cock.

Michael knelt with his hands behind his back, allowing Tristan to touch him and to play. He wasn't certain how long he would be able to sit motionless like that. Tristan's mouth was hot, and his tongue was doing such good, good things. He gripped his own wrists with the opposite hands and held on. Tristan was now licking his fingers, spreading him wider to have access to his ass. Michael closed his eyes as he felt the invasion, but as soon as it came and he began to melt into it, it disappeared.

"Keep your eyes open. Hands behind your back," Tristan reminded him. "And eyes on me. Can you do that?"

"Yes," said Michael, his breath hitching.

"Is there something you want?" asked Tristan.

"Yes."

"What is it?" asked Tristan, hands and mouth completely still now, waiting.

"Suck me."

"Suck you, what?" said Tristan, *the little shit.*

"Suck me, *please.*" The throbbing in Michael's dick echoed all over his body and into his head.

Tristan went back to his cock, wrapping his lips around the head and using his tongue piercing to punish the slit in the tip. The bead rubbed on the head and under the crown, two places he'd discovered Michael liked to feel the pinch and push of the metal against his flesh. While Michael watched his every move, he left his cock and lubed his fingers, slipping them into Michael's tight hole, one at a time, as he fondled Michael's balls with his mouth. He curved his fingers and searched for the sweet spot, and when Michael jumped, still keeping his hands behind his back, Tristan returned his mouth to Michael's cock and swallowed it.

Michael was sweating, his eyes wide open, as Tristan took his cock. Any time he began to look like he was going to close his eyes more than just to blink moisture back into them, Tristan stopped everything he was doing, leaving Michael crazy and desperate. Tristan continued to tease him, taking him to the brink and backing off, sometimes leaving his cock completely to lick a drop of sweat from Michael's chest. Once he bit Michael's nipple hard, and Michael almost came then and there.

After what seemed like an eternity, Michael watched, eyes wide, as Tristan's head bobbed up and down, feeling the beginnings of his orgasm deep in his balls and the base of his spine as he tightened up and shot, filling the latex in Tristan's mouth. Tristan kept sucking until Michael was relaxed and flaccid in his mouth, and then he removed the condom and tied it off, tossing it in the general direction of the trash.

Without saying a word, Tristan rose up behind him and pushed Michael down on all fours. He continued to finger Michael's hole while he opened another condom packet with his teeth, slipping it on his cock one-handed. He removed his fingers and took Michael's ass in both hands, squeezing hard. "I want to give you what you need, Michael," said Tristan, positioning himself. "What do you want?"

"Your cock," said Michael. "Please."

"Uhn," groaned Tristan as he eased himself in. "So hot…"

Michael cried out as Tristan grasped his shoulder and held him down. Tristan slid out, then in again, hard and fast, the rhythm changing a little as he shifted to find the place that would send Michael flying. "Going to give you everything, Michael," he said, hitting the sweet spot over and over again as Michael keened below him. Michael was getting hard again, and Tristan captured his cock as he held Michael's head down with the other, pumping his cock into him hard and fast. "Come on, baby," he murmured into Michael's back. "You've gotta give it up again; I'm waiting for you."

"Yes," said Michael, grinding his teeth, his heart pounding and his body flying. "*Yes.*" He bit his lip. Tristan was holding him down hard; he couldn't move. Tristan's thrusts pushed Michael, literally pounding him into the futon as he reached toward something he could hardly imagine. He held his breath and let himself go completely as he felt his body go wild beneath Tristan's, his balls drawing up tight. His cock slipped through Tristan's fist, and the friction burned so good and so bad and too much. After a while he just soared, flying beneath Tristan, part of him. Safe. Loved. Home.

Tristan's body began its inexorable slide into orgasm, his fluid motions becoming jerky as his cock took over and his brain shut down. He thought he might be affecting the rotation of the earth, slamming into Michael's ass so hard, but he couldn't make himself stop.

"Come on, baby." He tried to hold back. "Give it up." He was moving on sheer instinct and primitive self-gratification, his cock pounding Michael's hole, the long thrusts slapping his balls against Michael's ass. "Come on, baby," he said, as he suddenly felt wet heat splash from Michael's cock onto his hand. He jerked one last time, sending his cock so far into Michael's ass he didn't know where it could possibly be; he just knew he shot buckets into the latex, pushing and grinding until all his spasms subsided, and his breathing began to return to normal.

Tristan pulled off the condom and tied it, tossing it to the side with the other one. When he turned to look, Michael was still face down, his ass in the air a little. "Hey, where'd you go?" he said, running a hand up Michael's back into his hair. "Michael?" he murmured into his ear.

Michael said nothing, just hid his face in the pillow and stayed there, his shoulders tense from the awkward way he had his hands bunched under it.

"Come here, baby." Tristan gathered Michael close. "Come here," he crooned to the man as he settled in beneath him. "Talk to me."

Michael didn't say anything for a long time. He just rested his head on Tristan's chest, his lover's arms around him.

"That was good, Tristan," said Michael, finally, as Tristan continued to stroke his hair. "Really, really good."

"You were good, Michael," said Tristan.

"If you say, 'good boy,' I'll slap the shit out of you," said Michael, lazily licking the sweat off Tristan's chest to take the sting out of his words.

"Okay," said Tristan sleepily. "Boundaries are helpful." He curled around Michael and held him, drifting off to sleep. His phone was set to go off at six-thirty, theoretically enough time for a quickie and to get Randy and Devon to school on time. He sighed, holding Michael close.

"Love you," said Michael, catching a ribbon of Tristan's hair and holding it to his face like a blanket.

"Love you," sighed Tristan.

"Best Halloween ever," said Michael.

"Me too." Tristan fell asleep a few seconds later with a smile on his face.

Chapter Seventeen

Michael parked the squad car in front of his mother's house and let himself in the front door with his key. He had a minute and decided to let her know about the chimney cleaner appointment in person, intending to write it on her white board calendar so she wouldn't forget.

"Mama?" he called, hearing voices in the kitchen. "Mama, I let myself in. I wanted to tell you about --" Michael stopped when he saw Ron in his mother's kitchen with his large hands wrapped around a coffee mug.

"Hey, baby," said his mother, automatically coming for a kiss, then getting another mug from the open shelving along the wall of the kitchen. "Have time for a cup of coffee?"

"Sure. Yeah, I'd like that." He took a seat at the kitchen table. "Ron," he acknowledged the man's presence.

"Ron stopped by to say hi and to ask if we were going on the Thanksgiving ride to Taos." Michael watched his mother as she poured him a cup of coffee, bringing the sugar and creamer to the table with it and setting it before him.

"Still drinking your coffee like a little girl?"

"Yep," said Michael, loading it up. "I like it chunky."

"So, boy, are you coming to Taos? Should be a good ride. Some of the guys are going, and Elizabeth's going, Emma; you two always got along."

"What do you think?" asked Emma, looking at Michael.

"I wanted to talk to you about that, Mama. Tristan's family invited us for dinner on Thanksgiving. I think it's important to him." He looked at his mother, knowing that she'd do whatever he wanted.

"Well, that's fine, then. It looks like we're busy that weekend, Ron. Maybe next time." She sipped her coffee and smiled.

"Tristan?"

"Yeah, you remember, the guy I was with when I saw you at Apple Annie's," said Michael, although he knew perfectly well that Ron remembered. In fact, he thought that was probably why Ron was here with his mother now.

"Oh, yeah, the Boy Scout with the red hair." Ron looked at his coffee. "I'm surprised at you. What is he…thirteen? And you a cop and all."

Michael pursed his lips. "He's legal," he said. To his mother, he added, "I'm thinking we should teach him to ride."

She smiled back at him, a knowing look in her eyes. "I'm thinking he likes riding behind you."

"Him?" Ron snorted. "He needs a sidecar." He looked at Michael, a serious question on his rugged face: *What do you see in him*? "Or a pet carrier."

"Hey, don't disrespect the redhead," growled Michael. "You'll be seeing him around a lot."

"Yeah, until you need a real man."

"Ron." Emma shot Ron a warning look.

"Don't worry, Mama. I know a real man when I see one," said Michael. "Even though they're scarce on the ground these days." He got up. "I just came by to tell you the chimney cleaner is going to come by Thursday between eight and ten a.m." He took the dry-erase marker down and wrote the appointment on her calendar. "And he's doing both houses, so be here to let him in, okay? I'll be working a double shift like today."

"Sure, baby," said Emma, leaning her cheek out for a kiss.

"Thanks for the coffee," he said. "Nice seeing you, Ron." As he left the house, he found himself surprised that he meant it. Ron was a nice guy, if a little rough around the edges. He'd been there for his mom and him, had taught him woodworking and carpentry when he was young, and had revealed that he wanted to teach him something else entirely when he came of age. That Ron was a dominant man had appealed to Michael in the first few months of their new relationship, but he was too young then and too naive to see that Ron's playfully sadistic bent was entirely unacceptable to him. It had been confusing and painful, and left him feeling defective for a time.

Thankfully, Emma had caught on and put a stop to the whole thing, explaining to him that it was okay for two people to have kinks, but they had to match or it was abusive. She and Ron had remained cautious friends, and Ron had backed off Michael immediately, apologizing for any harm he'd caused and explaining that he'd enjoyed consensual BDSM relationships and thought that's what Michael wanted too. Michael, for his part, opted out, backing away from the whole thing without ever sorting it out in his heart or his mind.

Tristan, it seemed, understood implicitly. Michael got back in his squad car and took off, making the turns he needed to get back out to Harbor Boulevard. Tristan had given him precisely what he needed by holding him down and screwing him into the futon, controlling him utterly without stripping him of his dignity or hurting him physically. Which made him more than a man in Michael's book; it made him a damn hero.

Michael shook his head. He took his phone out at an intersection and checked it for messages. He didn't have any, but decided to text Tristan anyway, accepting his invitation to

Thanksgiving dinner on behalf of himself and his mother. Michael was nervous about meeting Tristan's family, but philosophical. Children and dogs usually liked him. He cooked and was handy, so moms probably would too. If not, he'd just kidnap Tristan in the middle of the night and that would be that, because no way in hell was he giving him up.

Tristan was in an impromptu study group when he got Michael's text message. He smiled to himself and took some ribbing from the guys about his red cheeks. He wondered what would happen if he just told them the truth, that the chick they thought he was dating was a guy. He went back to his books, smiling sadly. Chances were they'd distance themselves from him, not because they didn't like him or because he'd changed, but because they'd be embarrassed by the mental images they had of him and his lover. Sometimes even he just froze up, unable to comprehend the things he'd done.

"Earth to Tristan," said one of them, and he looked up.

"Hm, what?" he asked.

"I asked if you're doing anything special for Thanksgiving, or going out of town. Some of us are going to try to go to Vegas and see the Blue Man Group."

"Oh, we're having guests for dinner Thanksgiving, and we always do the holiday as a family. I'd like to go to Vegas, though," he said, thinking of going on the back of Michael's bike. "That would be cool."

"Yeah," said Jonathon. "Michelle can't get home for Thanksgiving. We tried that last year, and between the weather, the traffic, and all the other people traveling, she spent more time in airports than she did with her family. She has a friend in New York, and she's going to have Thanksgiving there. We've scheduled phone sex for midnight on the twenty-seventh." He sounded resigned.

"How romantic and spontaneous of you," said Tristan, laughing.

"By midnight I would be in a food coma if I were going to my grandmother's," said Daniel. "But she's going to my aunt's in Arizona, and my mom doesn't feel like doing it this year."

"I know this will shock you, but Thanksgiving isn't really a traditional Pakistani holiday," said P.K., who had been assimilated into their group the week before when they'd seen him coming out of Diho Bakery with his arms full of veggie buns. "I can't exactly spend it with my family, who're on another continent, so…"

"Damn," said Tristan, realizing how glad he was that he had his family and Michael. "You guys are pathetic."

Jonathon smiled. "Well, we can't all be the Ass Master."

"Excuse me?" said Tristan. "What did you just say?"

"You know what I mean. It seems like you're getting texts every five seconds in class and blushing like a fool. You come to school all marked." He held his hand over his heart. "Makes us proud, dude."

"I have no idea what you're talking about."

"It's the hair and the blush. Every time that white skin of his lights up, women fall like bird shit from the sky," P.K. said. "I blush, but you cannot see it as well."

"I don't blush," said Jonathon. "But you might have something there. Let's all try to blush in unison, shall we?"

"Would you all just shut the hell up?" said Tristan, who was trying to control the flush on his face and just making it worse.

"Look, there he goes," said Daniel. "Do you suppose we could just get contact mojo from that?"

"I doubt it very much," said P.K. seriously. "I think it is his very whiteness that comes into play. I wonder if that's why the sun never set on the British Empire during the time of Queen Victoria. The glow from Tristan's very pale skin makes me want to experiment."

"Perhaps we could just use it to annex the physics department," said Daniel.

"You sicken me," said Tristan returning to his books.

"Well, I must say, Tristan, that's harsh," said Daniel, laughing. "We only want to share in your glory."

"I doubt that," said Tristan. "I doubt that very much." He thought of using his tongue piercing to tease Michael's ass open. Once again, *damn it*, he felt the skin of his face heat.

"Look at him," said P.K. "Oh, someday, at least, I hope you'll write epic poetry about this." He shook his head, going back to the study guide. "For posterity."

"Of course I will," said Tristan. "I'll hardly be able to help myself."

After the group dispersed to move on to their next class, Tristan headed to philosophy, thinking hard. He wondered if he should tell his friends he was gay just so if they found out later they wouldn't think he'd been lying to them all this time. Recently the thought had been plaguing him that it was rather inauthentic to keep letting them think he had some sort of harem. He was no nearer to coming to an answer when he got a phone call. He checked caller ID and found it was from his brother.

"Randy," said Tristan.

"No, Devon. I'm using Randy's phone."

"Okay, Devon, what's up?"

"Psych, it's really Randy."

"Randy," Tristan warned. "I don't care who it is; *what is up*?"

"I'm just calling to tell you that Edward got permission from his dad to meet us at the park to go jogging tonight."

"Hey, that's cool. How'd you manage that?"

"Mom talked to him. She told him you were the only deviant in the family as far as we knew, and I guess he accepted it."

Tristan pursed his lips. "Very funny."

"Yes, well, he said he'd withhold judgment. He's hoping we'll be there to watch your every move. You know, so we can insure little Neddie's virtue stays intact."

"How were you getting to the park again?"

"C'mon, Tristan. Lighten up, bro."

"All right, *bro*, I'll see you when I get home. Get your homework done and tell Mom I said thanks for talking to Jeff, okay? And I'll be home by four so we can run before the park closes. Tell Edward to expect us around four-thirty."

"Okay." Randy hung up.

By four-thirty, Edward was waiting for them in front of the gates at the entrance of the regional park. He was dressed all in black, loose shorts and a T-shirt, and had a hoodie wrapped around his waist. His black hair and nails rebelled against his pale skin. Tristan, Randy, and Devon joined him.

"Hey, Tristan," said Edward, coming forward shyly. Tristan thought it was amazing that his brothers got this kid out from behind his computer at all, much less to go for a run. He looked like he expected the sun to kill him like a vampire.

"Hey, Edward. These two" -- he indicated Randy and Devon -- "are my brothers. The one in red is Randy. He's the one who has to stop and pet all the dogs when we run. The other one is Devon. He's the one who will complain about it."

"Hi," said Edward, still uncertain, as the four of them took off at an easy pace. Tristan pushed a little ways ahead in order to give them a chance to talk to one another. As he'd suspected, they had a lot in common, and even though Edward's dyed dark hair and black nails put them off at first, soon they were laughing together, although probably the joke was on him. He'd introduced Edward and his brothers over the Internet, and the three of them had messaged each other for a week or so, finding they had, among other things, music in common and a deep and abiding passion for manga, anime, and fan fiction.

Tristan ran along, listening to the sounds of their laughter. Edward sounded younger to his ears than he had the night of the party, and Tristan knew he hadn't been wrong about Edward and his brothers. They were definitely going to get along. They rounded the bend and were jogging down into the low-lying area by the baseball diamonds when Randy spotted a dog that he knew and ran toward it. All three of them went, although Devon hung back on principle, and Edward seemed to be wary of dogs. The smallish woman the dog had on his leash seemed to be wary of Edward, as well, and Tristan hid his laughter.

"Dogs love Randy," said Devon, explaining the attraction to Edward. "He seems to think on their level, and they can sense that."

"Unlike Devon," quipped Randy. "Who rarely thinks at all and bores them."

It wasn't going to be Devon's night at all, Tristan thought. Just about every dog they'd ever seen was in the park, and those that weren't were probably on their way. One after another, Randy stopped and greeted the dogs and the owners, until Devon was jogging in place enraged, and Edward and Tristan were laughing out loud. Randy was tearing across the grass with someone's Jack Russell terrier on a leash when Tristan heard a shriek from behind him. He turned his attention away for a moment to see a small woman controlling a Saint Bernard on a short leash and turned back to see Randy on the ground, and the laughter died on his lips.

"Randy!" he shouted, running toward his brother, who was on his back, clutching his ankle and cursing.

"There's a hole," said Edward, looking at the ground where Randy had tripped. "Oh, man, you must have stepped in just the wrong place."

"Randy," said Devon. "Is it broken?"

"How the hell should I know?" said Randy, through his teeth. The terrier's owner came over to take her dog.

"Randy," she said, worried. "I'm so sorry, should I call someone? Can I do anything?" She was tiny and frail, like the dog, Tristan noted absently, and had a plastic bag of poop over her wrist like a purse.

"Thank, you," Tristan said. "I'm sure it's going to be fine. It could've happened to anyone. I wonder if they play ball here -- it's dangerous." He looked around at the uneven ground.

"I feel just awful," she said.

"Don't worry," said Randy, and Tristan thought he was saying it more to the dog than its owner. He was still cradling the dog, petting its fur as it licked at his hands. Eventually, the woman moved on, and Randy waved good-bye.

"It's going to be all right," Tristan said. He made Randy stretch out on the grass and went to his knees to examine the injured foot.

Randy grimaced. "You sound like Mom."

"I could sound like worse people." He looked at Randy's ankle, which was already swelling.

"I think you should stay right here -- don't move. I'm going to bring the car." The curious Saint Bernard was on his way over, pulling his reluctant owner with him. "The biggest problem I foresee is getting you away from all these dogs." Randy already had a whitish tightness around his mouth, and in the dying light,

Tristan could see the sweat beading on his forehead. Tristan pulled off his sweatshirt and helped Randy put it on over his head.

"It hurts, Tristan," said Randy, who sounded very much like he had when he was a really small child, and Tristan felt his stomach clench.

"I know, bro, hang in there. I'm going to be back quickly, okay? I'll call Mom, but I think she'll tell me to take you to emergency. We can drop Edward home on the way." He looked at Devon, who nodded at him and sat on the grass next to his brother.

"I can walk, or call my dad --" Edward began, but Tristan cut him off.

"No, it's on the way." Tristan took off, calling over his shoulder, "Besides, if your dad thought I was a flake before, just think what he'd say if I left you in the park alone after dark." He took off running, his thumb already pressing the speed dial for his mom.

Tristan was in the emergency waiting room, reading the *Newsweek* he'd picked at random from a stack of torn and outdated magazines. Randy was in the emergency room, waiting to be taken to radiology. It was already taking longer than he thought it would, but he wasn't surprised. The last time Randy had been in emergency, when he'd broken an arm rollerblading, he'd been in the ER for hours. Tristan's mother asked him to drop Devon at the house and take Randy to the hospital. Eventually she would meet them there, but she was stuck in traffic. He noticed the sign that said ##No Cell Phones.## The automatic doors opened with a swish as he returned to the parking lot, dialing Michael's number, knowing that at this time of day he'd likely get only voicemail.

"Hey, Michael," said Tristan, scanning the parking lot for his mother's car. "It's me, Tristan. I just wanted to let you know there was an accident, and it looks like Randy might have a broken ankle. I'm at St. Jude Medical Center, and I'll be turning my cell phone off. As soon as I'm done here, I'll call you, okay?" He hung up and went to his car for his backpack, lugging it in with the intention of getting some work done. He was writing the outline for a paper on rationalism and empiricism for philosophy when a body hurled itself at him and pulled him up into a hard hug.

"Crap," said Michael. "Sparky, are you all right?"

Chapter Eighteen

It probably didn't go unnoticed by Michael that Tristan's mouth hung open in surprise. Michael shifted from foot to foot, his nervous agitation flooding out through every pore. He looked around, realizing he'd just manhandled someone in public while in uniform.

"Why wouldn't I be all right?" asked Tristan. He put his work aside carefully and gave Michael his full attention.

"You called and said there'd been an accident...you were at the hospital...Randy might have a broken ankle." Michael took a seat beside him. "I'm glad you weren't hurt," he said. "How's your car?"

Understanding dawned. "No, hey...whoa. Baby," said Tristan quietly, leaning toward Michael to talk in a low voice. "No. It wasn't that kind of accident." Michael's shoulders visibly relaxed. "I'm sorry I didn't make that clear. *Randy* had an accident. He fell. He stepped in a hole at the park and wrenched his ankle."

"Oh," said Michael. "*Oh.*"

"I'm sorry."

"No, it's cool. I guess I overreacted."

"I guess," said Tristan. They sat side by side staring at the information desk. Neither one looked at the other for a long time.

"I'm going to have to get rational when it comes to you, or I'm going to make a complete ass out of myself."

"Could be," said Tristan, not so secretly delighted.

"Unless I already have."

"That too." Tristan grinned like an idiot.

"Stop that, will you?" said Michael angrily. "In case you hadn't noticed, *scooter*, I practically had a heart attack thinking you were in some kind of accident. That doesn't make me the most capable civil servant."

"I will not be *scootered* by anyone," said Tristan. "I happened to have left a perfectly clear message on your voicemail. I'm not the one at fault here."

Michael rubbed his face, all the fight gone out of him. "It's my fault, I know it," he sighed. "In my job I don't always see the best that life has to offer. I think I worry a lot."

"It's not a fault to care. I'm sorry I said it like that," said Tristan. "I love you. If something happened to you, I'd bust my ass to get there. You know that, don't you?"

"Yeah," said Michael. "Yeah." He smiled.

"Do you want to know what?" Tristan asked. "I have ICE numbers on my phone. Why don't I change them so that if anything does happen, you get a call too?" He pulled his phone out and turned it on, earning a look from the woman at the information desk. "Let's go outside."

"Okay," said Michael, following him.

Once outside, they walked companionably. "Here, in my 'in case of emergency' data, I'll write 'call both,' okay? And I'll tell my mom to call you right away if anything… You know." He added Michael's cell number to his mother's, which was already programmed in.

Michael pulled out his own phone, doing the same. "I'll mention it to my mom as well, and program your number into her cell phone. You do the same with your mom's, okay?" said Michael, looking relieved.

"Feeling better?" asked Tristan, seeing Michael smile. Really the man was delicious. "I guess I can't kiss you. I could eat you up right now."

It was Michael's turn to blush. "Yeah, I really don't do that. Love you, though."

"Me too. I'm going to help Randy and Mom out, and then I'm on the hook for a whole ton of homework."

"Guess I won't be seeing you."

"Guess not, sorry. Till tomorrow, at least."

"Oh," said Michael. "I'll try to last that long." He stood there, at war with himself. Tristan saw his discomfort and butted Michael's shoulder with his own.

"You know what? My friend has phone sex with his girlfriend because she's at NYU; I thought it sounded like fun, call me later? Midnight?"

"If I'm still awake -- I'm covering a shift for someone, and I'm likely to be pretty tired tonight."

"I won't wake you; if you don't call, we'll make it another night." He grinned. "Good thing I don't share a room, huh?"

"Yeah," said Michael climbing into his cruiser. "Sparky?"

"Yeah?"

"Are you feeling everything I'm doing to you in my head?" he asked, looking around to make sure no one was close enough to hear.

"Yep, and I'm about to embarrass us both." Tristan acknowledged his half hard cock.

"Yeah." Michael smiled. "See you; glad you're okay."

"Love you," said Tristan again, meaning it, letting it shine in his eyes.

"Love you," said Michael, backing out and driving away.

* * *

It was eleven when Tristan heard his mother and Randy return from the hospital carrying what smelled like burgers in greasy paper bags.

"Not broken." Randy grinned, waving one crutch around. "Just badly sprained and I have to stay off of it." Tristan saw it still looked swollen. "I'm going to eat in my room, okay? I want to lie down."

"Just remember to haul the trash out when you're done. I don't want critters." She rummaged and removed a burger, handing him the rest.

"You mean besides Devon?"

"Yeah," she said.

Tristan followed his mom into the living room.

"How about you, did you eat?" she asked, holding her food out to him.

"Yes, thanks, I got burgers for Lily, Devon, and me on the way back from the ER. You know what? I want to put Michael's phone number on your cell contacts. He worries too much. Apparently I didn't make it clear I wasn't part of Randy's accident. You should have seen him. He came to the hospital thinking I was hurt."

"Worried?"

"Yeah. He's rather overprotective. I think that's why he's a cop." Tristan sighed. "I put him with my ICE numbers, and I told him I'd give you his cell so you could call him in case anything happens to me."

"Yeah? That's kind of…well…nice, I guess," said his mother.

"He does see the worst kinds of things on the job. He said a kid got hit by a car on Halloween. I think that kind of thing takes its toll."

"How does that make you feel?"

"What do you mean?" Tristan came in to take a seat opposite her.

"Michael has a dangerous job. He probably sees things every day that people shouldn't have to see. Have you thought about how that's going to affect you?"

Tristan couldn't say that he had given that any thought. "Yeah…but…Michael -- he chases kids on skateboards and stuff. Gives tickets for safety violations. He's not really that kind of cop, you know?"

"Is that what he told you?"

"Well, not in so many words…but I can't see him going all *NYPD Blue*, you know? Chasing street thugs and mob guys down Harbor Boulevard." He couldn't really see it, but did that mean it didn't happen?

"Have you thought about how you'd feel if you got a phone call about him?" she asked quietly.

"Okay, this is going somewhere, isn't it?"

"I guess so, yeah," sighed his mother, unwrapping her burger. "I was just thinking about today." He stared at her for a second and then realized with a kind of horror that it would have been his father's birthday.

"Oh, shit. I'm sorry. I forgot." He rubbed a frustrated hand over his face.

"The date is not that important, Tris. I was just thinking, though, about your dad and losing him like that. I keep going back to that moment, the last thing we said…"

Tristan got up and balanced on the arm of the chair she sat in, wrapping an arm around her. *When had she gotten so small?* "Mom --" he began, but she cut him off.

"Hear me out, Tris, I really need to say this. I was with your dad for twenty years, and I probably shouldn't feel like I was cheated. But I do. Every day I think I'm going to get better, and every day something else reminds me that it can't ever get better. I didn't walk into that with open eyes. I married an architect. There was no indication, ever, that he wouldn't live to be a hundred. And one day we were just talking…"

"I'm sorry, Mom." A huge, hard lump burned in Tristan's throat.

"If you keep dating a cop, you have to go in with your eyes open. You can't fool yourself about this. If you really love Michael, you need to cherish every second you have with him." She grabbed the box of Kleenex that was on the end table and yanked out several of them, covering her whole face, which seemed to dissolve before his eyes.

"That's just not because he's a cop, though, is it?"

"No."

"It's good advice." He hugged her hard, knowing she'd probably spent the day needing it.

"My phone's on the counter in the kitchen, and there's ice cream for dessert." She sniffed loudly and went back to her food.

"They're coming for Thanksgiving," said Tristan, hesitating and then rising from the arm of the chair.

"Good, it will be nice to meet them."

Whatever she really thought about Tristan's choices, Tristan thought, she'd keep quiet until she saw for herself. She was that kind of mom. He worried his tongue bead a little as he got himself a small bowl of ice cream. He could see himself standing in this very same kitchen with his father, working the microwave for popcorn or trading stories at the end of the school day.

It made him a little sick to think that he'd forgotten his father's birthday. It had taken months after his father's death before he could enter the house without expecting to see his face at the desk in his office, waiting to ask him how his day had gone. He imagined sitting in Michael's kitchen, so alive with everything that was so quintessentially Michael in it, and knowing he'd never see Michael come through the door again.

Suddenly, he didn't feel much like eating.

* * *

Michael slept as soon as his head hit the pillow, and he dreamed of his boy. He dreamed the hospital was an impossible drive away, and when he got there, his Sparky was gone. He woke up sweating at four a.m. and realized he hadn't called Tristan at midnight. *Shit.* He was covering a shift again on Thursday, but he could sleep as much as he wanted today, and he needed it. He hoped Tristan didn't take it personally. He rolled over and went back to sleep. This time, he dreamed of Tristan making his body fly.

Chapter Nineteen

The two weeks before Thanksgiving sped by in what seemed like a second for Tristan. His homework load ground him down to nothing, yet he and Michael shared quiet, intimate moments in Michael's house that still made him tremble with erotic aftershocks whenever he thought about them.

Thanksgiving Day turned out to be one of those cool but sunny California days when cooking a turkey and making a ton of side dishes appeals not at all. Tristan was trying to take it seriously, peeling potatoes and roasting squash, but his heart wasn't in it, for more reasons than one. Randy and Devon had been tiptoeing around the house being quiet, a sure sign something big and nasty was up, and Lily went into hysterics the minute Tristan and his mother had removed the bag o' guts from the turkey.

"Honestly, I don't see how you can stand near that thing much less eat it," she wailed, holding her nose. "It was once a *living thing*."

"More for us," said their mom, taking the high road.

"It's disgusting. I can't stand to be in the same room." She turned her back on them.

"Yet I notice," said Tristan, "that you aren't forgoing the pleasure of toasting those Pop-Tarts in here on principle. Don't they taste good cold?"

"You? Shut up," she said, still with her back toward him. "I take it we're meeting Mr. Magic and his mother tonight?"

"Yes, and Edward's coming too," said Tristan evenly, wrestling the bird out of the sink into the roasting pan. The girl had a point; this was really pretty nasty. "And I would change my tone if I were you. Michael is bringing something meatless especially for you. He wanted to try out a dish that a friend of his told him about. He won't say what it is."

"Well, that's nice," said Julia. "Isn't it, Lily?" She looked at her over her glasses, and Lily agreed reluctantly.

"Yes, it's nice." She took her Pop-Tarts and fled.

"How long do you think the whole vegan thing will last?" asked Tristan.

"Well, vegan will probably last until she discovers that butter and cream are what make mashed potatoes taste good, and vegetarian will last until she meets a cool guy and sees him eating breakfast sausage. That's the way it was for me anyway. Did I ever tell you I was a vegetarian until I met your dad?"

"No way. Really?"

"We went to Denny's after our first -- well, for breakfast." She blushed, and Tristan laughed.

"Can't hide it, can you? I never knew it was such a big deal until lately. I light up like a forest fire when I think of Michael. My friends give me all kinds of crap."

"You've told your friends?"

"Well..." He couldn't look her in the eye. "My friends think I have a girlfriend."

"That must be an uncomfortable place to be, Tris."

"I know. I can't decide whether I should just..."

"I never told my mom I was sleeping with your dad before we got married. I know it's not much of a comparison, but at the time I tried to tell myself it was private. Really, I was just afraid she'd kill me. I guess that made me uncomfortable too. I knew she wouldn't approve."

"My friends are not going to get it at all," Tristan agreed, sighing. "I don't think I'm ashamed of it; I tell myself I'm not."

His mother said nothing, waiting for him to finish his thought.

His voice caught a little. "I guess I must be a little, though, huh?"

"Not necessarily, Tristan. You told me; you told your family. I know you told us because we love you and you could count on that. You're not so sure of your friends. No harm, no foul. Don't always second-guess yourself. You have a fully functioning moral compass."

"And no filters." He thought about telling his friends what he did with Michael and went up in a fury of color. "Damn, I'm turning red again."

"Get used to it; it doesn't seem to go away," she sighed.

"Mom?" said Tristan. "Don't you ever want to…well…hasn't any guy ever asked you out since Dad died?"

"No. I probably don't give off an approachable vibe. I'm not interested." She stuck the probe sensor into the turkey's thigh and attached it to the thermometer.

"Really?"

"Really," she said. "For now anyway. I don't want anyone to come into what I have here. I don't want anything new. If it happens, I'm not averse to it, but I really don't want to change anything. For now anyway." She rubbed her hands together as if to say, *That's that.*

"Oh," said Tristan, reaching for what he wanted to say. "I've been feeling more than a little altered lately."

"Hey," she said, turning around with a concerned look on her face. "I don't want you to think you can't go forward. It's true I don't like change, but if you move on, move out, or whatever because you've found something special, I'll deal. Of course, it's going to be hard for me, but I know that someday you'll want something of your own. You know I want that too, right?"

"Sure, I know that," he said. "I *know* that. I'm not ready for anything yet, though, so you're stuck with me. For now anyway."

"Every mom should be stuck with a guy like you, Tris," she murmured as she shoved the roasting pan in the oven.

By the time Tristan checked out the table for the twelfth time to see whether all the places were set properly, it was almost time for their guests to arrive. Family holiday OCD kicked in, making him a nervous wreck. He was obsessively checking the food, the table, the house, and his siblings, who resented it. His mom was laughing at him behind a mask of motherly concern.

The doorbell finally rang, and he answered it, smiling shyly at Michael and inviting him in. "Hey, Michael."

"Hey, Sparky." Michael leaned in to kiss him lightly on the lips, establishing the privilege before Tristan gave it any thought.

"Hello, Mrs. Truax," Tristan murmured, the usual guilty crimson staining his cheeks and betraying his thoughts.

"Call me Emma," she said, handing over a casserole. "Here's my contribution to dinner, such as it is. Michael's is probably much better."

"Thank you," said Tristan. "I'm sure it's great."

"Um," said Julia. "I guess I'd better introduce myself." She held out her hand. "I'm Julia Phillips, Tristan's mom, and this is Lily, my daughter." She pushed Lily forward, giving Emma a pleasant smile. "And those" -- she indicated the two boys who sat on the couch in the living room playing a video game -- "are

Randy and Devon, my younger sons. Devon is the one on the right." Devon took a minute out to wave.

"Come in and make yourselves at home," said Tristan, noticing Michael was carrying some sort of hot pack for food. "Michael, come with me, I'll show you where to put that." He led Michael into the kitchen.

Michael casually glanced around the house. "This is nice. I've always liked this neighborhood. The trees overhang the streets." He put his package down on the counter. "This will probably stay warm until dinnertime, so you don't need to worry about it. It's totally meat-free, and if I do say so myself, probably tastes better than the vinyl bag I brought it in."

Tristan put Emma's casserole down. "Do I need to heat this?" he asked, lifting foil and looking under to see the food inside.

"Yeah, probably. That's Mom's famous sweet potato, tropical fruit, nut, and marshmallow bake. Just when you thought it was safe," he sighed.

"I heard that, Michael," said Emma from the living room.

"No offense, Mom, but dessert is supposed to come after the meal," said Michael.

"Who says?" asked Emma. "Anyway, I eat it, and you did too before you went and got all epicurious on us."

"Just because you *can* put everything into a casserole doesn't mean you *should*."

"I have been making that since before you were born, and you remain unharmed."

"Yeah, but who knows, if you hadn't made it, maybe I'd have turned out straight," he teased, coming up behind her and kissing her cheek lightly. Randy and Devon gaped at them.

"Lily," said Julia. "Maybe you could put on some music for us?" She looked at Devon and Randy, who exchanged excited glances.

"We could choose the music," Devon said, smiling.

"No, thank you," said Julia. "I'd rather Thanksgiving come and go without screaming EMO music or techno dance tunes. Lily will play what she knows I want to hear."

"Or maybe the boys would like show tunes?" asked Lily sweetly. "I think I have some Barbara Streisand…" Michael chuckled lightly, but Tristan flushed.

"Lily," her mother warned.

"Oh, all right, what good is having a gay brother if I can't make fun of him?"

"You just wish the last ten guys who asked you out were as hot as Michael," said Tristan.

"Oh, hey," said Michael, flushing.

"This is like Thanksgiving on Jerry Springer," said Emma, smiling. "Cool."

Randy and Devon looked at each other and smirked. "Maybe it's time to start getting dinner on," said Julia.

"Sure, that sounds great," said Emma. "Can I help you in the kitchen?"

Tristan led Michael out to the backyard, thinking it might be the only place they could talk without being stared at. "I feel like a panda on a first date at the zoo." He rubbed his face with both hands.

"It's new. They'll get used to it." Michael put a hand on Tristan's shoulder, cupping it and giving it a reassuring squeeze. "You didn't think this would be a slam dunk, did you?"

"I don't see how it could be. But still, I just want everyone to go back to looking at me normally, and not like I'm about to…"

"Tell them something shocking that in a million years they never imagined? Something that would change how they saw you overnight?"

"Okay, you're right; they have reason to be twitchy." Absently, Tristan stroked Michael's arm.

"Put yourself in their shoes. Say Lily brings home an older woman."

"Oh, just yuck," said Tristan.

Michael raised his eyebrows.

"Okay, you've made your point, and I'm scarred for life." Tristan heard the doorbell ring and started for the house with Michael right behind him, meeting Edward, wearing his usual all black, at the door. "Hey, Edward," he greeted him warmly.

"Hello," said Julia coming out from the kitchen. "I'm so glad you could make it."

"Thanks so much for inviting me. Really, why did you?" he said, waving to his ride. He looked around at everyone. "It's not like you even know me."

"We always like to have a crowd." She indicated Edward should enter the living room. "Have a seat; we're getting dinner ready now."

"The excruciating staring-at-each-other part won't last long, I promise, and then we can eat. Edward, can I get you something to drink?" said Tristan.

"Water would be great," Edward replied, looking Tristan's family over. "Dude!" Edward said, staring shamelessly at a mark beneath Tristan's left ear.

"What?" asked Tristan.

Edward pointed to his neck.

"Oh." Tristan's face caught fire. "Thanks a lot, Mr. Hoover."

"What did you call me?" asked Michael. Edward suddenly seemed to find the video game Devon and Randy played fascinating.

Devon spared Edward a glance. "Get used to it," he said. "One minute, hot chicks are coming through this house like it's Grand Central Station, which kind of rocked for us, you know? And the next, he's Officer Helmet's boy-toy." He shook his head and went back to his game.

Randy chimed in, "Never going to get used to it, and I miss Viper the goth chick."

"Me too," sighed Devon. "She was going to show me a spell to make my enemies itch in uncomfortable places."

"Devon," said Julia sharply. "It's time to come to the table. Rock paper scissors Randy for grace."

The boys played three times, each time ending in a draw. The fourth time Randy won. "Gotcha," he said, waving his paper hand around. "Paper always wins in the end."

"Like you actually wanted to say the prayer," said Devon.

"Actually, I did," said Randy, with a grin. When everyone was seated at the table, they joined hands.

"Dear Lord," began Randy, who paused for long enough that Tristan sneaked an eye open to look at him. His saw his mother's cheek twitch with what he thought might be apprehension. "We are so grateful to be gathered here today with our family, and the family of our brother's homosexual boyfriend, and our new little goth friend who has a gay dad, whatever the heck *that* is all about. We'd like to say we're grateful this year for condoms, lube, and Ellen Degeneres, and for those guys on *Queer Eye*..."

"Randall Evan Phillips!" his mother shouted.

Chapter Twenty

Michael and Tristan sat companionably on the roof of Tristan's house as they waited for Devon and Randy to plug in the Christmas lights they'd tacked into place. Tristan was pleased, because with the four of them working on it, they'd completed it in record time and had even added a little extra panache, thanks to Michael's creative use of the existing light fixtures and a couple of extra extension cords.

The sky was a rich auburn, puffy with ribbons of clouds that he thought looked like a painted backdrop in a film. Tristan was enjoying the silence between himself and Michael. He wanted to sit like this, completely content to watch the darkening sky paint different colors on his lover's light hair forever.

Dinner went well, once everyone realized that Randy and Devon were going to do everything they could to mess it up. Then, oddly enough, it became the Randy and Devon comedy show, and it was hard to say who laughed the most. They were merciless in their humor, and no one was exempt. Even Michael's vegetarian dish came under their scrutiny when Lily prodded it for the first time.

"What is this?" she asked, not too rudely, looking at Michael.

"It's a meat substitute."

"Like tofurkey? I have a lot of friends who are eating tofurkey today."

"Well, yes, but since we were already having turkey, I thought I'd try something with a tofu substitute for duck instead."

"Oh," said Lily. "It's actually very good."

"Um, you know," said Randy. "If tofu turkey is tofurkey, then this would be…"

"Tofuck," said Devon. "Definitely."

"Ah, yup," said Randy. "This would definitely be tofuck."

"Tofuck á l'orange," said Emma, shamelessly. "Isn't that what it is? With the orange sauce?" She looked at Michael keenly.

"You people are heartless," said Lily throwing her napkin on the table. She glared at her brothers. "Shame on you, you're like…barbarians. I'm getting myself some juice."

"Oh, shoot," sighed Emma after she'd gone. "I'm probably sorry."

Michael laughed into his napkin. "I didn't go to a lot of trouble."

"I should go talk to her," said Julia, swirling another glass of chardonnay. "But to be honest, I can't seem to dredge up the sincerity." She and Emma burst out laughing.

"Honey, we have to get you a motorcycle," said Emma.

"If she gets one, I get one too," said Randy.

"Me too. I'm not riding in anyone's bitch seat," said Devon.

Tristan colored faintly. "That's hardly a nice thing to call…"

"Ha!" said Devon. "That's where *you* ride, isn't it?"

"What did I tell you?" said Randy. "You owe me five bucks."

"Of course, he rides behind Michael," said Devon. "Where do you expect him to ride; he doesn't have a motorcycle license. That doesn't make him Michael's bitch."

"Devon!" his mother hissed. "You watch your language."

"Sorry, Mom," he said, with an exaggerated look of innocence that everyone at the table knew to be wary of. "But really, Michael, between you and Tristan, which one of you *is* the girl?"

"Jeez, what do they teach in school these days?" said Emma, disgusted. "Neither one of them is a girl, Devon, that's why it's called homosexuality, 'homo' from the Greek word meaning same."

"Greek…" said Randy. "Figures.

"No, it's just a prefix," said Julia. "It's like homophone and homogenize."

"What's a homophone?" asked Randy.

"That's easy," said Devon. "That's what Michael uses to call Tristan."

"Are you finished?" asked Julia in a deadly voice. "Because I am."

Lily entered the room at that exact moment with her eyes all red from crying. "So am I. I can't believe you're being so hateful. I, for one, will support Tristan in his new lifestyle, even if he is a total jerk."

"I'm a what?" asked Tristan.

"I think it's romantic," she said, mostly to Edward. "Cursed to live their lives in the shadows, to be together only under the cover of darkness…hiding their love from the sunlight."

"They're gay, honey," said Emma. "Not vampires."

"Oh, but wouldn't it be cool if we were gay vampires?" said Michael, obviously enjoying himself more and more by the minute.

"Oh," moaned Julia, almost accidentally. "Okay. I just had a Brad Pitt and Tom Cruise moment."

"Yeah," said Lily. "But better. There's definitely more chemistry right here at the dinner table than in that whole movie."

"You got that right," said Julia, her face washing red like her son's. "May I be struck dead for even thinking such a thought."

"This is so freaking weird," said Devon.

"But the food is good," replied Randy. "Although I can't bring myself to eat anything called tofuck, can you?"

"Nope," said Devon, looking at Michael. "No can do, buddy. Sorry."

They both gazed contritely at Michael, who gave up and laughed.

"Okay, you *men* get to put up the Christmas lights, and then maybe" -- said Julia, giving them the evil eye -- "maybe I'll allow you to eat dessert."

"Okay," said Tristan, anxious to be out of there. "Michael?"

"Sure," said Michael. "I'm going to put ours up tomorrow. You going to help me?" He gave Tristan a look that said, *You'd better.*

"Sure," said Tristan.

Michael looked at Randy and Devon, then at Julia, and winked. "I don't suppose your mom lets you do this yet? Are they old enough to help out?"

"Of course we can. Right, Mom?" Devon gave her a pleading look. Julia looked like she wanted to high-five Michael.

"I guess…as long as you're careful," she said.

"I will be," said Devon. "Hey, Tristan, Mom said I could help." He ran out the door, leaving Tristan and Randy staring after him.

"That idiot has no idea he's just been played." Randy walked out after Devon.

Tristan met Michael's eyes and sighed. He went after his brothers, consciously delighted as he imagined Michael's hot gaze behind him, fastening on his ass.

Michael took Tristan's hand in his. "Thanks for today, Sparky. Your family is crazy."

"Yeah, well, about that," said Tristan, turning red even without the sun's setting glow. "I'm sorry. They're really just trying to adjust."

"What are you sorry for? I've found kids living on the streets whose family just tossed them out like so much garbage for being gay. I'm delighted all I had to do was field a few probing questions over dinner. Although I don't expect we've seen the last of that."

"Probably not," agreed Tristan. "You're right, though, good-natured teasing is better than anger or silence." The lights came on, and Tristan held his hand up for a high five. "Looks great; thanks for all your help."

"My pleasure," said Michael. "I'm sorry I have to work tonight. It's probably pretty quiet right now, but on my shift people will be starting to drive home with a little too much holiday cheer in them. Plus, I want to check the park, see if Mary's out tonight. It's going to get cold, even though it was warm today."

"Who's Mary?"

"That's right, I haven't told you about my gang," said Michael. "Mary is one of my homeless people. Sometimes she sleeps in the park. I try to talk them into going to the shelter when it's really cold. They can be…recalcitrant."

"Why?" Tristan asked. "Doesn't it get cold in the park this time of year?"

"Some of my guys aren't rational anymore," said Michael quietly. "They think they can take care of themselves, and they don't like people trying to tell them what to do. Sometimes they're off meds they should be taking."

"But if it gets too cold, don't they stand a good chance of getting hypothermia?"

"Yes," said Michael grimly. "So that's why I try to find them if they're in the park on a night like tonight. As soon as the sun goes down, the temperature goes down with it, and I just feel better when I get the chance to check things out."

"You're my hero, did you know that?"

"Thank you, Tristan," he said thickly. "You don't think I'm a hyper-vigilant pain in the ass?"

"No. I think you're one of the good guys."

"I'll have to go in a few minutes; my shift gets out there before the drunks and sleepers hit the road," said Michael.

"Could be another bad night," said Tristan. "Michael, do you see things on the job that you don't tell me about? Bad things?"

Michael looked at Tristan for a long time in the dying light. "There's some stuff I don't tell you, if that's what you mean. No point in carrying it home, is there?"

"Yeah, but you carry it, don't you?"

"Yes."

"I guess I always thought your job was, you know, chasing down upper middle-class white kids like me who were violating safety laws."

"Really?" asked Michael. "That's what you thought? I wish my mom thought that. She sees me doing the road show of *Serpico* every night."

"What's the truth, Michael?"

"We live in a dangerous world, Sparky." Michael put his arms around Tristan. "People hurt each other, they want things they can't have, they steal, they lie...they kill. At the best of times, I get to run after a fast kid who needs to put on a helmet. At the worst… I don't bring that home."

"But you do."

"Yes. I do," said Michael. "But not to you. Where's this coming from?"

"The other day was my dad's birthday." Tristan wondered if Michael would understand. "I lost the most important man in my life two years ago. I don't know…"

He heard the boys come out with Julia and Emma. "I think we'd better go down."

"Wait, Sparky," said Michael, concerned. "What did you mean?"

"Look," Randy was saying. "I'll bet that's the fastest we ever put up the lights."

"It's awesome," said Edward, looking up.

Michael took the opportunity to brush Tristan's lips with his, deepening the kiss when Tristan sank into it. "We'll talk later," he whispered against Tristan's lips. Tristan nodded.

"Yeah," said Devon. "And ours is the only house on the block that has gay guys kissing on the roof. Won't we be the envy of the whole neighborhood?"

"I'll go down first, and then you can arrest me for fratricide when you get there, 'kay?" said Tristan, heading down the ladder, rung by careful rung.

"Take your time," said Michael. "I'm not on duty yet."

Chapter Twenty-One

Tristan and Lily were putting the finishing touches on the glassware as they replaced it in the china hutch in the dining room. They worked in relative silence, since Devon and Randy were sound asleep in the living room a few feet away. Julia was in the kitchen, trying to figure out how to squeeze thirty days' worth of leftovers into one relatively small refrigerator.

"I thought Michael was nice," said Lily tentatively. "He doesn't seem like the Officer Helmet you always complained about."

"I've made my peace with Officer Helmet," said Tristan lightly, putting in the last of the white wine glasses and getting started on the china.

"He's younger than I thought," she said. "I mean, you know, to be a cop and all."

"Yeah," said Tristan. "He's only twenty-seven."

"And he said he went to school at CSUF?" asked Lily.

"He majored in communications," said Tristan.

"Why on earth did he become a cop?"

"I don't know. He said that's what he wanted to do."

"But…"

"But what?"

"The hours are long, and people use you for target practice. That's what."

"Lily!" said Tristan.

"I guess Fullerton isn't so bad, though. Not like L.A."

"I'm sure Fullerton is nowhere near as bad as L.A."

"Hey, I didn't mean anything by it, I just…"

"Michael is smart and strong, and he plays it safe." He threw down the towel.

"I'm sure he does."

"And it's not like anyone is perfectly safe, is it?"

"Tristan, what's…?"

"I have to go." Tristan said good-bye to his mother and caught up his keys. "I have my cell, if you need anything."

"Mom," said Lily. "When I'm Tristan's age can I spend the night with my boyfriend too?"

"Oh, hell no, honey," said Julia, giving Tristan a hard stare. "Tristan's ship sailed a long time ago. Yours? Isn't going to get out of the harbor. Ever."

Tristan practically ran out the door before he could be subjected to Lily's eruption. He could hear her as he ran toward his car. Good thing he'd placed a change of clothes and a toiletry kit in the back earlier. He started the car, listening to the engine rev as the cool night air sank into his skin.

Tristan started the short drive across town, still dazed by his good fortune. Michael loved him. They'd kissed on the roof. Their families had met, and it hadn't sucked. He drove down Chapman carefully, thinking the last thing he needed was to get a ticket from one of Michael's coworkers, or worse, Michael himself. The man would never let him live it down. He pulled into Michael's driveway and could tell that Emma was still up watching television. The blue light glowed from her windows, and she frankly had it on way too loud. She was watching a ball game, or the highlights of one, because he could hear marching bands and cheering every so often as he walked to the front door of Michael's house.

As soon as Tristan entered, he turned off the alarm using the code Michael had given him. He switched on lights, feeling a little easier in his mind every time he did it. As he came to this house more often, usually in the night without Michael, he became more comfortable and familiar with it. It seemed less like someone else's home and more like a place he belonged. The first time he came here to surprise Michael, he'd hardly dared to heat up water for tea. Lately, Michael had taken to leaving things around that made him feel welcome, a note here, a photograph there. Things that made the place seem more like theirs, rather than simply Michael's.

Today, in plain sight, was a note from Michael, welcoming him home and telling him there was pie in the fridge if he wanted it. Earlier in the day he'd told his mother he wasn't ready for something like this, but that wasn't strictly true. He was torn by his love for Michael and the love he felt for his family. He felt that his mom still needed him to be there for her. At least the next day he didn't have to drive his brothers to school, so that meant a whole lot of snuggling and whatever else came to mind.

The heavy futon made a dragging sound on the floor as Tristan tugged it into place in front of the fireplace. It wasn't long before he lit a fire, added another log, and had the chill off the room.

This close to the college and downtown, Tristan could hear the emergency vehicles racing up and down busy Harbor Boulevard. He found himself holding his breath, waiting for sirens to get closer or farther away. He had to tell himself to breathe again, even if it was Michael's siren, and even if Michael's job was a dangerous one, because it wasn't helping Michael any for Tristan to be lying in front of the fireplace holding his breath.

On nights when fear churned in his stomach, he tried to remember that a policeman's job was dangerous, and an architect could die talking on the phone to his wife. He worried that loving his family and Michael as much as he realized he did and thinking about it consciously was going to make him a nervous wreck. He drifted off into the first beginnings of an uneasy sleep, realizing that if anything, happiness was a damned double-edged sword.

* * *

Driving his patrol car up Harbor by Hillcrest Park, Michael gave a last look around to see if any of the homeless people he knew were camped out there. It was chilly out -- he could see his breath, and when all was said and done, he hoped most of the folks he was looking for would have tried the shelter on a night like this. Ever since he'd taken this job, he'd had a particular affinity for the small, constantly changing group of homeless men and women that regularly wound up in Hillcrest Park. Mostly they were just lost, damaged people who didn't have anywhere else to go. Recently, he'd had a talk with some of them, and they'd agreed that they needed to be indoors when the temperature got cool like this. One of the older women, Mary, came from San Francisco and always laughed at the idea of what she called "LA cold." Even if the climate was temperate, he reminded her, there were things out there worse than the cold. Better to be safe. It was one of the things he charged himself with, checking on these people. His gang.

Michael didn't see anyone in the usual places, so he hoped they'd all had a nice meal and a good night's sleep, and started back to the station. He looked forward to seeing Sparky, knowing that when he got home there would be a fire, and his boy would be waiting for him.

Something about that made his heart so full and warm he was afraid to trust it. He knew they hadn't been together very long, but already he'd placed his heart and his home completely in Tristan's freckly young hands. He'd taken to leaving little notes and trinkets around for his boy to find. When he rattled around the house alone, he always knew Tristan was just a short drive away and that any moment he'd arrive and make the house *feel* like a home again. He wanted Tristan to move in permanently, but knew just from talking to him that he wasn't ready yet. His own family needed him. No way would he be comfortable abandoning his mother, even for love. And that conversation on the roof… What had brought that on?

Finishing up his paperwork, Michael said a tired goodnight to his friends. Some of them were just going on shift, and they laughed at how bleary-eyed he looked. He headed for his truck, his Tristan, and his home. His head felt like lead, but his heart was light.

* * *

Tristan felt rather than heard when Michael came through the door. The flames danced in the fireplace, and the cool air blew across his skin. He turned, still a little dozy- feeling as he lifted his arms for Michael to come to him. Michael didn't hesitate, dropping onto the futon beside Tristan, his weapon stored safely in a case in the closet, the only part of the uniform he'd removed.

"Michael," said Tristan, pushing hard into his embrace. "Missed you," he sighed, still waking up.

"Me too. I thought about you the whole night. Thought about this. Scoot over," he said, getting under the covers.

"You still have your shoes on?" asked Tristan, feeling them next to his feet. "Come here." He sat up and began to remove Michael's shirt, carefully helping to slide it off Michael's shoulders, holding him up and giving his neck a good kiss while he was at it. "Let me get those shoes," he added, slipping down to untie the laces. "Here."

"Sparky," said Michael tiredly. "You're so warm."

"Going to warm you up in a minute, Michael," said Tristan, who was working to unzip Michael's trousers and slide them off his body. "Once you're all undressed, we can share body heat."

"Sounds good," said Michael. "I've been up for about thirty-six hours, Sparky. I need to sleep."

"Okay, baby, whatever you need." Tristan removed Michael's undershirt and scooted on top of him as Michael toed off his socks. "Go to sleep."

"Have to," said Michael. "But I'll be dreaming about loving you later."

"Okay, later," said Tristan. "There's plenty of time later."

"Later. Did I tell you I love you yet?" said Michael, oozing into sleep muscle by muscle.

"Nope," said Tristan. "Not yet."

"I love you," said Michael, his breathing becoming deep and even. "So much."

"Me too," said Tristan. "I love you, Michael." Tristan lay on Michael until he felt his body warm up and then moved to the side, away from the fireplace, so that Michael was right next to it. He wrapped his arms around his lover possessively and then his legs for good measure, and fell into a dreamless sleep beside him.

* * *

Several hours later when Michael woke up, it was to find an amorous, sleeping Tristan rocking against him. "Oh," said Tristan, as he pushed his erection hard against Michael's. "So good," he sighed. He nuzzled into Michael's neck, setting little smoldering fires on his skin as his lower half plunged Michael into instant erotic overdrive.

"Hey," said Michael, finding Tristan's mouth and opening it, waking him with a thrusting tongue. "Wait for me."

Tristan, for his part, didn't care who started it or how, he only knew that Michael was playing, and he was on fire. "Oh." He smiled against skin. "Glad you're awake."

"Come here," said Michael, rolling Tristan onto his back. "I want inside you."

"Yeah. Sweet," said Tristan. "Yeah." He tasted Michael's lips and reached up to find a bottle of lube and a condom under the pillow.

"How?" asked Michael softly in Tristan's ear.

"Surprise me," said Tristan, laughing. He nipped at Michael's jaw sharply, more than ready to be with him. "I want you so much." Tristan gasped as Michael's lube-slicked finger entered him, playing with him gently for a time. Just as suddenly, it left him empty and needing. He tried to move back toward that hand.

"Turn over," said Michael rolling him. When Tristan complied, the fingers came back, two this time, stroking him from the inside. "So hot for you," said Michael. "You're so beautiful when I do this."

"All for you," gasped Tristan as Michael hit his gland.

"Yes," said Michael. He pushed in a third finger, and Tristan closed his eyes and bit his lip. "Like that?" he asked.

"Yes," hissed Tristan. "Feels good." He writhed under Michael's hand, his head down, his hips up. He felt Michael's hand leave him to put on a condom, and the head of his cock took its place. "Oh," breathed Tristan, sucking in a deep breath. "Oh, so good."

"Yeah," said Michael, sliding in hard, all the way to his balls. He kissed Tristan's back, arching to push into him with everything he had, then placed an arm around Tristan's chest and lifted him, pulling him up and against his own, letting Tristan ride his cock from a position straddling Michael, with his back to Michael's chest.

"*Oh*! Shit," said Tristan, as the new position drove Michael's cock so deeply into him he seemed to feel it everywhere. "I can feel you…your heartbeat," he moaned, his head falling back onto Michael's shoulder. "It's like I'm part of you."

"Uhn…you are, baby," said Michael, kissing Tristan's neck where it lay exposed in front of him. "Surprise."

Biting his lip to keep from crying out, Tristan lifted his arm and took hold of Michael's head. He held him close, while Michael bit and licked his neck. Michael moved inside him, and he thought he would expire from the pleasure of it.

"Shit," said Tristan, his own strong legs absorbing the shock of Michael's determined thrusts. "Oh, Michael! *Shit*," he said again, as he melted into the arms surrounding him, holding him fast while Michael's cock pumped in and out of him harder and deeper and faster still. He understood what Michael meant now when he said "make me fly." Tristan was beyond his body, soaring.

"Hm?" said Michael into his neck, seemingly lost to speech as he grasped Tristan's cock with one hand and began to pump it too. Waves of pleasure shot through Tristan's body like sound.

"I'm all full," moaned Tristan, who was so stimulated that his body didn't feel like his own any more. "Oh, *harder*," he begged.

Michael pistoned into Tristan's body like a machine, crushing him in his arms. Tristan made low moaning sounds, his cock gliding through Michael's slick fingers. He cried out and shot hard, his whole body spasming out of control until Michael came as well, pulling Tristan in close and pushing himself into Tristan's heat as deeply as Tristan could take him. Tristan trembled when he felt the jerk of Michael's release inside him, and it flooded him with warmth.

Michael and Tristan stayed joined, kneeling, until everything around them stopped whirling and spinning, and it was just the two of them again loving each other.

"I think you severed my spine," moaned Tristan, falling forward with Michael still in him and holding on from behind.

Tristan hissed as Michael withdrew and pulled off the condom, tying it and tossing it. He put his nose in Tristan's hair and inhaled. "You smell like Thanksgiving and man and fire and sex." He sighed. "Jelly legs?" he asked.

"The worst," said Tristan. "Or the best, I don't know which yet."

"The difference is always how much you need to pee." Michael laughed.

"Well, I do," whined Tristan. "And how I'm going to get there remains a mystery."

"I'm going; why don't we try the buddy system? I'll help you up."

"I'm serious," said Tristan as Michael righted him, and he began the trek to the bathroom on the shakiest legs of his life. "Wobbly."

"I've got you, love." Michael held him firm, and Tristan leaned into him, walking the short distance with him. "Bath?" he asked while Tristan was relieving himself.

"Yes." Tristan plunked himself down on the thin lip of the tub. "I'd love a bath. As long as there's some of that herb-y stuff and you in it."

Michael turned the water on. He sat down next to Tristan and pulled him in for a kiss.

"Wow. I'm going to feel you next week." He put his head on Michael's shoulder. "Not that next week I won't want to feel you again. Or an hour from now."

Michael slid his hand into Tristan's hair behind his neck. "I always want you," he said, kissing him. He took the bottle of herb-scented oil, added it, and then went around the bathroom lighting candles.

Tristan climbed in and rested his back against the tub, rippling the water around with his hands. "I get to hold you this time, your tub, my rules." He smiled an invitation.

Michael slipped into the water and slid between his legs. "Cold night last night," he said. "I was worried about Mary and her friends."

"The homeless lady you told me about?" asked Tristan.

"Yeah, but I think they must have gone to a shelter," said Michael. "I didn't see them. I hope they did."

"You know, when you mentioned that you'd seen kids thrown out by their parents, I thought, how can someone be so..." Tristan slid a hand over Michael's chest, and he kissed the nape of his neck. "I think I'm very lucky."

"I think you are too. No matter how goofy they were acting, your brothers were still being your brothers. Your mom may be shocked, but she's dealing. And your sister? She can't wait to sew us those ruffly poet shirts."

"You got that right." Tristan smiled. "Maybe we could get our picture taken as vampire demon lovers and give that to her for Christmas."

"Sweet! We could get those contacts that make your eyes red. Except your eyes are the most perfect shade of blue. They still go straight to my dick."

"Wrong," said Tristan. "*Your* eyes are the most perfect shade of blue. But it's true that when you're around my eyes go straight to your dick."

"Love you." Michael turned to kiss Tristan.

"Love you too," said Tristan, bent on discovering other things that could go straight to Michael's dick, like his hands and his mouth.

Chapter Twenty-Two

By the early afternoon, Tristan was finding new things to fascinate him about Michael's body, having licked and sucked his way to his toes. Michael lay spent, relaxed, his hands behind his head, watching Tristan play like a puppy over every part of his skin.

"It is good to be me, Sparky," he sighed, as Tristan nipped his ankle.

"Mm," said Tristan. "Tattooed skin tastes just like chicken." He licked around the band tattoo on Michael's leg, his tongue lavishing the simple design with special attention. "Love this, love the way you look inked."

"Hm, what? Oh." Michael stiffened and pulled away a little. "That was a stupid whim."

"Yeah? Don't you like it still? I love it. I think it's hot. I wanted to lick it in Borders when I first saw it." Tristan licked over the design again, sending a frisson of something erotic and hot through Michael.

"It's not that." Michael pulled away. "I just... Sometimes I don't like the memory of getting it."

"Really. Did it hurt that bad?" Tristan slid up Michael's body.

"It hurt, but...I got it because someone wanted to mark me, and it just isn't the best memory," he sighed, running a hand over Tristan's hair. "Such beautiful hair."

"Tell me."

"Tell you what?"

"Michael," Tristan growled. "There's a story behind that tattoo, and I want to hear it. Please?" Tristan kissed Michael, catching his lower lip between his teeth and teasing him with his eyes. "Come on, baby, tell me." He smiled.

"I'm still not sure what the story is. I was going out with Ron when I was young, younger than you." He preempted Tristan's outraged snort. "I was legal, only…just barely."

"Hm. I'll bet you were just a baby."

"Well, yeah, I guess. In terms of relationships? Yeah." He tried to think back to what he felt, the confusion, the fear, and also the love. "I thought I loved him. He was good to my mom and me. He'd been a friend for a long time."

"At least he waited. He did wait, didn't he? Till you were of age?"

"Yeah. He never made a move till I was old enough…but maybe I just wasn't." He bit his lip, thinking hard. "Anyway, he wanted the ink to symbolize ownership, I guess. Ron is into BDSM and Master/slave relationships. He liked doing scenes. He could make it seem so exciting. He liked things rough and kinky, but he never got it about me. I didn't want to be hurt. I didn't want to be degraded. I took it all so seriously. I didn't mind being controlled; I just didn't want the pain. I still don't see how that could be a game." He lifted his ankle and turned it, looking at the simple tribal design around it. "It confused him as much as it confused me, and to this day, I think he wonders what happened."

"That's sad," said Tristan. "His loss, Michael. You know I get it, right?"

"What do you get?" Michael wrapped his arms around Tristan and kissed his temple.

"Well, it's about safety, isn't it? I don't think you'd want to be really *controlled* by someone. You just need a safe place to *give up* control for a while. Maybe with someone you trust who won't hurt you. That's not a Master/slave thing, that's just…what lovers do. Right?"

"Oh, Sparky," said Michael softly. "You have a very special heart, do you know that?"

Tristan responded by licking a long line up his jaw and kissing him sweetly. "Just common sense," he mumbled into Michael's lips.

"Not common at all, love," said Michael. "Hey!" He sat up suddenly.

"What?"

"Come with me," he said, getting off the futon with enough energy to make Tristan fall back in a heap.

"Where?" Tristan pushed the hair out of his eyes. "I thought we were going to spend the day in bed?"

"No, I have to do something first, come on." Michael was already walking back to the bedroom to dress.

"Oh, hey, well…all right." Tristan fumbled off of the floor and looked for his duffel. "Let me get dressed."

In minutes, Michael came from his bedroom dressed casually, with his hair combed and smiling a minty fresh smile. "Ready?"

Tristan was hopping into his drawstring pants. "Uh, no, I gotta brush my teeth and comb my hair." He headed for the bathroom, muttering, "Like some damned morning person when you wake up."

"Come on. We've got to go see Meghan."

"Who's Meghan?" asked Tristan as he finished up in the bathroom and followed Michael to his truck. "Does this Meghan come with coffee?" He got into the passenger seat as Michael was already firing up the engine.

"Of course. Maybe even food. We'll see." The truck was moving before Tristan had even settled back against the seat.

They pulled into a parking lot in the downtown area of Fullerton, behind some of the newer, trendier restaurants, and got out of the truck. Michael seemed to know where he was going, and Tristan followed along, certain that coffee would be forthcoming eventually. They walked along Harbor Boulevard a ways until Michael led him into a boutique-looking place called "I.N.KD."

"Hey," said Tristan, looking around at all the pictures on the walls of people showing off body art. "Michael?" He looked around at the mostly empty place. Apparently people didn't get tattoos much the day after Thanksgiving.

A man came out from behind a curtain in back, and as soon as he saw Michael, he smiled and walked faster. "Officer Mikey!" he cried as he took Michael's hand and clapped him on the back. "What can I do for you today?"

"Sparky, this is Jim; he owns this place." Michael returned the handshake and gave Jim a hug.

"Pleased to meet you," said Tristan.

"Likewise," said Jim. "You're here in your civilian clothes, what's up?"

"Is Meghan here?" asked Michael, looking around. "I need her to touch me up."

Jim raised his eyebrows. "Yeah, she's getting coffee. You thinking of getting inked again?"

"I just want to change my band a little," said Michael.

They stood there in silence, Tristan looking at the design boards on the wall.

"See anything you like, Sparky?" said Jim.

Tristan looked at Michael then, his cheeks pinking up. "Oh, yeah," he smiled shyly.

Jim barked a laugh. "You're trouble."

"You got that right," said Michael, smiling.

The door chimed, and a woman came in carrying two coffees. Tristan thought she looked like a younger, darker version of Michael's mother. They both had an otherworldly vibe that, in Emma, took the form of mismatched bohemian clothing and layers of jangling jewelry. On Meghan, it manifested itself in ink. All over her body, from her head to her toes, she had tattoos.

"Meghan, you have a visitor," Jim said, taking his coffee and returning behind the curtain.

"Michael!" she said, coming over to give Michael an extraordinary, full-body hug. "Hi, baby." She stepped back and put her coffee to her lips, taking a sip, cursing softly when it burned her.

"Hi, Meghan, I need my band touched up," Michael said, smiling.

"Something fading?" she asked, looking down at his ankle, which was bare.

"No," he said, in such an odd way that Tristan looked up to see what was on his face. "It's not that. I just want to put something over it."

"You mean change the whole design?" she asked.

"No, just add a name. I want you to put a name over it and make it part of the design. Can you do that?" asked Michael.

"Sure," she said. "Let's do it." She looked Tristan over, giving him a dimpled smile that said she was curious, but not going to ask.

"Good, do you have time now?" Michael asked.

"Sure." She motioned him to a table. While they worked out what he wanted, Tristan looked over the various types of tattoos and piercings available. It was true he had a tongue piercing, but he'd never cared much for the other kinds. He thought of his tongue as a kind of secret weapon now, knowing how Michael responded to being teased by it, and he got an erotic thrill every time he used it to pleasure him. He'd thought about tattoos, though, and especially after seeing Michael's, he'd considered getting one like it. Tristan didn't want it to be something that reminded Michael of his time with Ron though, and he wondered what Michael was going to do to his tattoo, now that he was here.

"Sparky?" said Michael, pulling his wallet out. "Do you mind going to the bakery around the corner on Commonwealth and getting us some coffee and something to eat?"

"No, of course not. I'll go." Tristan collected the cash and gave Michael a squeeze on the shoulder. "Do you want anything in particular?"

"Amuse yourself," said Michael, smiling. "This might take a while."

"Okay," said Tristan, leaving the small shop. He walked down the busy street, looking in the windows, painted now with snowmen and wreaths and all kinds of holiday designs.

Tristan had been on this street a thousand times, but everything seemed new this day and a little too shiny. He'd been screwed so completely he could still feel it. His legs rang with little shocks as he put one foot in front of the other, and the light of day seemed overly bright. The traffic moved a little too fast for him. He found things he normally took for granted confusing, as every cell in his body vibrated with an electric sexual energy that he was afraid spilled out of him and bled into the street. He found it frightening to take in the whole of his life at once and had the absurd urge to run back…to reconnect with Michael…to touch him as though he were the only true and safe thing in the world.

Someone was trying to get his attention. "Hey, did you want something?" asked the girl behind the bakery counter.

"Hm, what?" Tristan said, startled out of his thoughts. "Yes, oh. Yes, I'd like two large coffees and some of the cheese Danish, please. And two cinnamon rolls." He paid as if on autopilot and gathered his coffees and the bag of pastries. The idea of going back into that boutique where Michael was having jets of ink drilled into his skin didn't appeal, but he squared his shoulders and started back, because strangely, he was beginning to panic. Something about even the air crackling around him seemed foreign and different and fundamentally changed as he made his way back to I.N.KD.

If his breathing remained deep and even, Tristan found he could keep calm, even in the face of the disorientation. Michael was safety. Michael was equilibrium. Michael was home. He focused on Michael as he walked back into I.N.KD and saw the man getting work done on his ankle. Tristan sat beside him, and something on his face must have given away his unease, because Michael looked at him with concern.

"Something wrong?" he asked. He watched as Tristan put sugar and creamer in both coffees, adding quite a lot more to the one he handed over with a smile.

"No," said Tristan. "Well, I was feeling…different. Like I've seen everything before, but it felt more vivid today. I don't know." He looked around the small shop and spoke softly in Michael's ear. "I just felt like I had to get back to you or nothing would make sense anymore." He breathed a sigh of relief. "Stupid, huh?"

"No," said Michael. "I know that feeling." He put his arm around Tristan's shoulders and brought him close enough to whisper, "Like the whole world's changed, and there's only one person in it."

"And if you can't get to that person and touch them, it will all swallow you whole. Never felt that before," Tristan whispered, looking down at his hands. "Never felt a lot of things before." He sipped his coffee, idly picking at a cheese Danish.

"I'd say I'm sorry, but I'm not," said Michael, brushing the hair out of Tristan's eyes. "Not sorry at all. I'm keeping you, love."

Chapter Twenty-Three

Whatever he expected to find on Michael's ankle as Meghan finished up her work, placed a bandage on the site, and gave Michael aftercare instructions, he did not expect to see his given name, Tristan. A little padlock attached to the open part of the "a," making the whole band seem more like a manacle than ever. And that definitely violated the don't-do-anything-to-make-me-cry-in-public rule Tristan thought he'd firmly established.

Michael laughed as Tristan blinked back tears. "I thought probably" -- Tristan swallowed hard -- "probably you'd put Sparky."

"Sparky's not your name," said Michael gently. "It's just something dumb I call you, like love, or baby. Names are powerful juju."

"I know that; why do you think I asked you to say my name when we make love?" Tristan realized belatedly that they were walking down a busy street together. His head swiveled side to side.

"Don't worry about it." Michael waited for him to catch up. "Don't worry about watching your tongue every minute of every day."

"I'm sorry," said Tristan. "There's something about today, Michael. I feel slow and stupid. Maybe I'm coming down with something."

Michael laughed. "Yeah, a bad case of 'I came out to my whole family on Thanksgiving and now what?'"

"You really think that's it?" asked Tristan. "Like buyer's remorse?"

"What do you think? You've been edgy since we came out this afternoon. Nothing's different. It's just you and me."

"I know. I know that, but…"

"Cards on the table, but maybe I should have asked you before I got your name inked on my ankle," said Michael, turning to him. "Am I still your guy?" He looked into Tristan's clear blue eyes. Tristan thought he saw him flinch a little.

"Yes," said Tristan in a rush of breath. "Yes, yes, yes." He reached out for Michael's arm. "Don't be stupid. Yes." They continued walking, shoulders pressed together.

"Then what? Tell me so I can understand. I don't think I've ever seen you this uncertain about anything." He used his remote to unlock his truck, then gingerly got into the driver's side while Tristan got in the passenger door. "Crap, I forgot this stings."

"I don't know what it is. This morning…you rocked my world, Michael. I've never, ever been *screwed* like that." Tristan put his face in his hands.

"Oh," said Michael, his cheeks catching fire. "*Oh.*" Michael started the truck and edged it out into traffic. They drove along familiar streets for a while in silence.

Tristan tried to explain himself again. "It may seem like we've been together for a while, and we've made love a lot, in different ways. But what we did this morning…just…damn, baby," said Tristan shaking his head.

"Damn good, or damn bad?" said Michael.

"Just *damn*, Michael," said Tristan. "I was…completely out of myself."

"You lost control," said Michael suddenly.

"Yeah. But I would have given it up willingly. It wasn't a bad thing. Just a scary new thing." He peeked at Michael's face.

"Should I just not…"

"No," said Tristan firmly. "You were awesome. I didn't know it could be like that, is all. I should have. I hoped. But I didn't know it could be like that between *us*. I love your gentleness. I love your generosity. But, Michael, I swear when you held me like that and…just damn."

"It's okay that way, sometimes, don't you think?" He pulled into the driveway and parked behind Tristan's car.

"Yes," said Tristan. "Yes, it is. It's a part of you that I never saw before, and it unleashed something deep inside me that I didn't know was there. It scared me."

"I see," said Michael.

"It opened something up I can't close." Tristan got out of the truck, followed Michael to the small back porch, and waited while he unlocked the door. He preceded Michael into the kitchen, automatically going to the stove to make tea. He looked up to see Michael leaning against the wall, staring at him.

"There's something you don't understand," Michael said, so softly Tristan barely heard it over the hiss of the gas from the stove.

"What?" asked Tristan, going to him, leaning into him against the wall. He pressed his forehead to Michael's, enjoying the contact.

"The minute I met you, from the first moment I laid eyes on you, I felt the very same way." Michael took Tristan into his arms for a deep kiss. He brushed Tristan's hair aside and cupped his face between his hands, taking his mouth. "I didn't mean to frighten you; I just wanted to love you," he said, pulling him close.

"Have you been holding back?" Tristan whispered.

"Yes," said Michael, color flooding his face. "A little."

"Don't." Tristan calmly walked to the stove and turned it off. "Just don't." He left the kitchen, heading for the living room and their bed by the fire.

Michael followed him.

When he got to the living room, Tristan wasted no time shucking off his clothes and starting a fire in the fireplace, crawling into the bed to watch Michael take off his clothes piece by piece.

"You're awesome, Michael," said Tristan, appreciating the show.

Michael smiled in the dim light. He kneeled on the futon, sliding to recline next to Tristan. When his face was inches away, he stroked the silky red hair back off Tristan's face. "When we first..." He seemed to be choosing his words with care. "When you came here with me from Borders, I didn't want to overwhelm you. I had the feeling that maybe you thought you could just change partners and dance."

"What?"

"Remember all that stupid talk about different holes?" Michael's lips twitched. "Just whose holes were you thinking of?"

"Well," said Tristan. "*Oh.*"

"See? I wasn't sure you wanted to...well...give up, you know, control. And it's been established that I do. Sometimes."

"Yeah," said Tristan. "But not this morning."

"No, not this morning."

"That was hot." Tristan sighed and turned to him. "I liked that. A lot."

"Yeah?" Michael ran his hand over Tristan's firm abs. "What did you like?"

"Mm," said Tristan, molding himself to Michael. "Everything."

"Tristan?"

"Hm?"

Michael looked at him with blue eyes lit by the firelight. "Want to play?"

"Yes," said Tristan, without thinking. "Absolutely.

Michael smiled and left the futon, going to the other room. When he returned, he had an old-fashioned glass filled with an amber liquid.

"What's that?" Tristan asked as Michael lay down beside him again. He rolled Tristan onto his back.

"Whiskey." Michael held the crystal tumbler, not drinking from it.

"Okay."

"Put your hands over your head," said Michael, putting the drink down to fold one of Tristan's hands over the other as if he were going to catch a ball. Tristan's arms were bent at the elbows, his hands cupped above his head.

Tristan smiled. "What are you up to?"

"Just stay there." Michael placed the tumbler in his hands. "And whatever you do, don't spill any, okay?"

"Okay," said Tristan, the heavy glass resting on his open palms on the floor. "I won't."

"No matter what I do." Michael pinched his nipple in a hard, not unpleasant way, and followed it up with a lick of his slick tongue.

"*Oh.*" Tristan suddenly realized that holding the drink still might take some concentration.

Michael slid over Tristan, slipping his body between Tristan's legs. He held himself up on his elbows as he took his time kissing

Tristan in a slow, sensuous dance of tongues and teeth and lips that trailed down to Tristan's neck and found the hollow at the base of his throat.

"I can feel your pulse beat against my lips," said Michael, nipping at the skin there, sliding his unshaven cheek along it and abrading it a little with his beard. "Love the flavor of you," said Michael. "You taste red."

"Red?" said Tristan, holding the glass in his hands still, feeling the liquor warm from the heat of his palms.

"Mmmhmm. Or maybe pink. Tasty," whispered Michael, working his way down to Tristan's nipples, lavishing attention on first one and then the other, until they stood out in stiff, warm peaks on Tristan's chest.

"Oh." Tristan bit his lip and concentrated on keeping the glass upright as his hands began to shake.

"Yeah." Michael kissed a burning path past the taut muscles on Tristan's chest to his abs. Michael tongued his navel thoroughly, while Tristan struggled, his muscles clenched to stay focused on his task. "Don't spill my drink, Sparky," he warned.

"Tristan," he gasped, his arms trembling. "Call me Tristan."

"Tristan," whispered Michael. He deliberately worked his way down Tristan's body, teasing first his cock, then his balls, and then his hole with a slick tongue, mounting an all-out assault on Tristan's senses, looking to melt the glass in his hands and catch the liquor in it on fire.

"Michael," breathed Tristan, gripping the glass like it held the cure for cancer. "I..."

"Shh," said Michael. "I need you."

"Take what you need. Not going to spill it." Tristan bit his lip on a grin as he issued the challenge, dissolving into a moan as Michael put his mouth on his cock.

Michael hummed a little as he swallowed Tristan's cock, working it with the muscles in the back of this throat. He cupped Tristan's balls in his hand and squeezed lightly, just enough to make him jump.

"You're sure of that?" he asked, licking his fingers and pushing into Tristan's tight, puckered channel with two of them, just hard enough to be forceful, to get Tristan's attention.

"Mm," said Tristan, meaning to say "yes," but incapable of forming the words. He writhed under Michael's assault, his hips moving, the muscles in his back arching all out of his control, but he held the glass in his hands still by sheer force of will.

Sliding further down on the futon, Michael searched for and found a condom and lube, tossed carelessly in the bedding earlier. He nudged Tristan's legs as far apart as they would go, rolling the condom down his aching cock. "Want you so much," he said, lifting Tristan's knees to expose him completely. He bent down once more to lap at Tristan's hole, now relaxing a little for him as he thrust his tongue deep.

"*Damn*," cried Tristan, the contents of the glass he held sloshing dangerously around, a drop sliding to his cupped hands.

"Don't spill," commanded Michael as he pushed two lubed fingers into Tristan, making him pant between thrusts to hold onto the glass. He searched for and found Tristan's sweet spot, hitting it, making Tristan jerk and clench his teeth.

"Not going to." Tristan's every cell was rippling with the erotic, electric shocks generated by Michael's talented fingers.

Michael slid his arms under Tristan's knees, bringing his legs up like a pair of suspenders, one at a time, to his strong shoulders as he took what he needed, entering Tristan with a strong thrust of his cock.

"Feels so good, baby," he sighed when he was in balls deep and rocking in slow circles, not moving yet. He got a shuddering sigh from Tristan, who breathed deeply and accommodated his body, his arms going rigid above his head.

Fully joined like that, Michael kissed Tristan hard and deep. A man's kiss. A plundering kiss that left no doubt that Michael knew he would get what he wanted from Tristan's body with the ease of long practice.

"Michael," breathed Tristan in awe as Michael moved within him.

"*Come on, baby,*" said Michael, burying his face in Tristan's neck, his ear pressed to Tristan's throat. Tristan made inarticulate moaning sounds in time with his thrusts. Air, rushing through a human voice box, just going somewhere with no one to control it. Michael pressed his whole body into Tristan's, mindless now with pleasure, their mutual passion mounting as he pushed deeper and deeper still.

Suddenly Tristan stiffened beneath him, his body going rigid as he shot a ribbon of cum between them. The heat and the clenching of Tristan's ass pushed Michael into his own release. He lifted his head, arched his back, and slammed one last time into Tristan's channel, the gush of hot fluid filling the latex.

Tristan could still feel Michael straining inside him, felt his release and the pulse beat of his cock as he came. "Love you."

"Tristan," moaned Michael. "Tristan. Love. Mine."

"Yes," hissed Tristan, still holding the glass. "Yours, *yes. Yours, Michael.*" Still joined, Michael removed the glass from Tristan's trembling hands and took a long, slow sip, covering Tristan's mouth to share it with him. They kissed around the alcohol, and when it was gone from their mouths, they kept kissing until Michael softened, and his cock slid out of Tristan's body, and Michael had to put the drink down and leave Tristan's lips to slide off and discard the condom. He took another drink and shared it with Tristan again, jetting the fluid into his mouth with a push of his lips.

Tristan lapped at him languidly, his lips and tongue hungry to taste Michael's, the warm, whiskey-flavored kisses they shared the only thing that mattered. He felt the alcohol to his toes, the warmth spreading throughout his body as Michael's cum had warmed his core even through the latex. He was unused to even beer, and as the tingling feeling made its way around his limbs, he clung to Michael, whose solid body anchored him to the world. He was still mumbling as he drifted off to sleep.

"So…" said Tristan. "Much. Love you so much."

Chapter Twenty-Four

It was a cold damned night as Michael got back into his cruiser after a routine traffic stop. The winds were high and icy as the southland was gripped by some of the coldest temperatures on record for LA. Arctic air whipped his exposed skin and chapped his cheeks. He'd already seen several downed trees, one of which had caught power lines, shutting off the electricity to Jeff Clayton's upscale hilltop neighborhood. Jeff had already called him twice on his cell, worried about his tropical fish. *Well, shit, can't have fish in danger.*

Fortunately, even though Christmas was only two weeks away, there were few people on the road this weekday night at four a.m. Bars had seemed more deserted than usual, and he hadn't gotten many calls that didn't have to do with the wind and the weather. Maybe people were smart enough and cold enough to stay inside. Which didn't reassure him at all, considering that if his guys from the park weren't in the shelter, somebody could die tonight. He circled around on Brea Boulevard, making the left on Harbor to run by the park. Hopefully, he wouldn't find anyone there, and he could finish up his shift by chasing down more tree branches and frightened homeowners. Maybe he'd even go home and get his generator for Jeff, to keep the fish alive.

Making a careful drive by Hillcrest Park, he couldn't tell if anyone was there, but the wind was wreaking havoc, kicking up dirt and debris and some rather large branches. He parked in the lot on the bottom terrace of the multi-level park, noting that the lights appeared to still be on in the surrounding areas. He got out his flashlight and took the path to the area behind the bathrooms, where he knew he would most likely find anyone who was squatting there.

At first he saw what he thought was a trash bag, slumped against the side of the building, in the small area that provided privacy on the way in and out of the women's restroom. Thinking it was trash somebody dumped, he almost walked past the dark shape, but realizing the small protected entryway was an adequate windbreak, he checked closer to see if the strange shadow was more than the bundle of rags it looked like.

Michael shone his flashlight into the confined space. The pile of rags scuttled sideways and backward, like a startled spider. Something about the dirty silver hair captured Michael's attention.

"Mary?" he asked. "Mary…it's me, Michael."

"Don't know you," muttered Mary. She cringed back from him in fear. "Mary don't know you."

"Mary," Michael tried again gently, not making any sudden movements. "Mary, it's me. Michael. Officer Truax. We talk sometimes. Do you remember?"

"Mary don't know you."

Michael trained the flashlight over her body, wondering where her coat was, her blankets. She didn't have her usual things with her, and he was worried. Then he caught sight of a dark stain on the ground near her leg and saw that her sweatpants were torn and possibly bloodied.

"Mary, are you hurt?" he asked. "Did something happen?"

"Mary don't," she said. "Mary don't know you, and you've gotta *back off*." She barked this last. She didn't look at him directly; her eyes moved in wild patterns over the concrete at his feet. This wasn't normal, and it alarmed Michael as much as the wound she'd apparently sustained.

"Mary," he said quietly. "Where are your things?"

This appeared to be the wrong thing to say, because all of a sudden Mary drew herself up to her full height and screeched at him. "They was taken!" she shouted. "They took my shit!"

"Mary," Michael said again in the voice he used on charging dogs and frightened children, but before he could say anything further, she seemed to explode into action.

"Don't!" she screamed. "Don't you hurt me! Don't you touch me!" She was tearing at her hair, and silver ribbons of it were floating around her, caught by the wind.

Michael backed away immediately. He touched the radio on his shoulder to ask for immediate assistance and requested paramedics. He saw, now that Mary had stepped into the pool of light cast by a street lamp, that she was bruised all over her face and arms, and that the leg of her sweatpants wasn't the only thing torn and bloody. She'd been attacked, he surmised grimly. He racked his brain for something to say that would calm her.

"Mary," he said. "Please. It's Officer Truax. Some of the kids call me Officer Helmet. Remember we talked about what to do when it's cold?"

He waited, but she just stood staring at him wildly, frozen, having stopped tugging her hair.

"I'm here to help you, Mary. I'm going to find you a nice, warm place where you'll be safe. Okay?"

"Not going to be safe," Mary wailed, heartbroken. It hurt Michael somewhere deep inside to hear it. "Not ever going to be safe anymore."

"Mary," he tried again. "It's okay. We can go someplace safe." He took a cautious step forward, then another. "Remember me? You always tease me that I get too cold?"

"No…Mary don't know you." It was more like a whimper.

"Come on," said Michael. "It's okay. It's going to be all right."

"Can't be all right no more. I lost all my stuff," said Mary. "Can't live without my stuff. Gonna die without my stuff, sure as shit."

"No, Mary, we'll get your stuff," said Michael, taking another cautious step. "Hey, you know what? Maybe we can shop for new stuff. I could get you some new stuff, Mary." He didn't like the way her dark eyes looked like they were swallowed by the whites. It reminded him of spooked horses. Michael was two feet from her when a second patrol car and the paramedics, with their lights flashing, pulled up, and all hell broke loose.

"*No*!" screamed Mary wildly. "*No*! Not going. Mary don't know you!"

"Mary," said Michael, putting his hands out where she could see them, holding his flashlight in the least threatening way possible.

"No," she said, lunging for him. "Don't touch me, can't touch! Don't hurt!" She was on him in a second, close enough to for him to see the fresh bruises and lacerations on her face, her split lip. "No! Can't again. Not again!" Her hand lashed out at him and he thought she pushed him back, but when he looked down he saw he had some sort of shiny metal thing sticking out of him above his utility belt on the right side.

"Mary?" he asked stupidly, as she put her hands over her mouth, her eyes wide. "Mary, it's me, Officer Truax. Michael." He put his hand up and felt the warmth and wetness on his uniform, vaguely wondering what could make his hand warm on such a cold night.

"Can't go," she said sadly, so quietly he wondered if he'd really heard it. Her eyes widened in sudden recognition. "Michael?"

The young officer from the other patrol car heard Mary ranting and quickened his pace, coming around the building fast.

"Shit," he muttered, drawing his weapon. "Freeze!" He crouched into position, his gun trained on Mary, who stood in the pool of light, hysterical again and ranting. Her ragged clothing swirled around her, her arms raised to gather them.

"*No*!" shouted Michael, wondering why his voice seemed so far away. "Don't hurt her!" But she had launched herself at the other police officer, and it was too late. By the time Michael slumped to the ground, Mary was dead.

* * *

As always on windy days, Tristan's chemistry professor was talking in an excited, somewhat agitated cadence that burst and sputtered like she was experiencing occasional power surges. Tristan expected that at any minute she would arc and spark like a transformer blowing. He was taking notes off and on and spinning his pencil in his hand like a rotor when a noise alerted him to an incoming text message. It was his mother. *Call me 911 Emergency immediately 911.* He grabbed up his things and bumbled them out the door of the classroom where he dropped his pack on the ground and called his mother. He listened numbly as she told him what she knew, then jerked his bag over his shoulder and ran the distance to the parking lot. His heart raced, his mind a blank, and all he could think of was the first few words of the Lord's Prayer. "Our Father, who art in heaven…"

To be fair, Tristan thought on the excruciatingly slow drive to Fullerton, he had always known two words could change the world. I'm pregnant. You're fired. *It's war.* When his mother said, "It's Michael," Tristan felt his whole world crumble beneath his feet like the overpriced real estate under the Laguna Canyon homes that slid down the muddy hills each year. "It's Michael" meant everything and nothing. It meant the difference between what he wanted and never wanting again; it meant his life. Michael *was* his life.

The thought couldn't come to Tristan straight on that Michael had been injured on the job. It seemed he had to come to it obliquely, from odd angles. *St. Jude Medical Center is a good hospital and Michael is strong. Journalists exaggerate, hyping stories for effect. Christmas is only two weeks away and Tristan still hadn't had the time to decide what would be an appropriate gift.* He could barely perceive the inevitable truth: Michael was in the hospital, in surgery, in serious condition, prognosis unknown.

Tristan tried Emma's cell phone time and again, but it went straight through to voicemail. By the time Tristan got off the 91 Freeway going north on Harbor, his teeth were chattering. He went through all the motions at the hospital, parking in the appropriate lot, finding his way in, going to the registration desk, finding the right place to ask about Michael. He gathered his courage.

"I'm here…" he began, swallowing hard. "I'm here for Michael Truax. I…is Officer Truax all right?" He looked around the waiting room and saw a uniformed police officer pacing and two others talking quietly.

"I'm sorry, are you a relative of the patient?" asked the woman behind the desk kindly.

"No, I…uh…I'm a friend. I'm Tristan Phillips. Officer Truax and I… He's my --" He broke off. Did Michael's cop coworkers know he was gay? He bit his lip. "We're friends."

"I'm sorry," said the woman. "I can only give patient information to immediate family.

"I…is Emma here?" he asked, growing alarmed. "Emma Truax? Michael's mother? Is she here?"

"No, she's been notified, but she is not here." The woman seemed to have nothing further to say.

"But," said Tristan, his throat doing a stinging, burning kind of thing that left his voice scratchy and fading. "He's my best friend. He needs to know I'm here. I promised I'd be there for him if anything happened." He raised his voice. "I *promised* him."

"I'm sorry, son," she said again kindly, but now a little stonier. "It's hospital policy *and* against the law for me to divulge information about a patient."

"Can't you…can't you tell him I'm here?" he asked. "Tristan."

"Son, I'm sorry, I'm going to have to ask you to go sit down. You can wait if you like till a family member gets here." She had other things to do, he could tell.

"But…no!" he cried, starting to get a little desperate, raising his voice, breathing hard. Tears stung his eyes. "I can't. I promised. Can't you just tell him something for me? Can't you just tell him…"

"Something I can do for you?" asked a man, coming up behind Tristan. He didn't need to turn to know it was one of the police officers he'd seen in the waiting room.

"Officer," said Tristan turning to find a man about thirty-five wearing the familiar FPD uniform. "I'm a friend of Michael's, but they won't…" He looked into hard and wary eyes. Implacable eyes.

"Son, this is a hospital. There's no need to raise your voice," he said. "Officer Truax's condition is unknown at this time."

"But I…" said Tristan.

"His mother is on her way from Las Vegas," said the man, whose badge read "Villardo." "We're all worried. Come and have a seat." He eyed Tristan carefully as though he were going to erupt, but led him to an area where Tristan could sit down amidst a group of bored-looking strangers, who all looked like one family, also tiredly waiting.

"Can you tell me what happened?"

"No, I'm sorry," said Officer Villardo.

"The report on the news said he was stabbed," said Tristan, a little quieter, but no less angry. "I should think if they can report it to the press, they can tell his best damn friend."

Officer Villardo appeared to think for a moment. It was clear he didn't care what Tristan said. He wasn't family, and he wasn't in uniform, so he just didn't count. "Stabbed? That's accurate," he said grimly.

Tristan sagged in his seat. "Do you know how bad it was?" he asked in a whisper.

Officer Villardo sat opposite Tristan, his elbows on his knees, his fingers steepled in front of his mouth. It took him a long time to answer. He seemed to give the question a great deal of conscious thought. He sighed. "Bad," was all he said.

Tristan nodded, getting up. He left all his personal belongings on the chair to mark his place and then found the men's room and threw up until he had nothing left in his body to purge.

Chapter Twenty-Five

After the first hour of waiting, Tristan stopped hearing the *Jeopardy* theme in his head. It was eleven in the morning by that time, and the hospital was bustling with activity. Different uniformed officers came and went, conferring with each other quietly, the thin blue line stretched thinner with the injury of one of their own. Tristan saw the strain of confronting in real time the danger that they probably didn't allow themselves to contemplate normally on their faces. The danger he hadn't allowed himself to consider at all.

Tristan's head had been throbbing since he'd puked. He'd felt his vertebrae snap with the intensity of his retching, so it didn't surprise him that his head ached. He wondered briefly if he was like his dad, and he had a flaw somewhere that would just give way someday, like maybe when he puked, only to burst like a dam to drown his brain and end his life. His father had been dead before he'd hit the ground. Express lane, no stops, no waiting. For his shocked family, it had been hard, but not like this. Not like sitting in this crowded room waiting for word. Not like for Tristan, who was no one to these people; they passed him by and looked beyond him like he didn't exist. He wondered bitterly if he'd been a pretty nineteen-year-old girl with an engagement ring on her finger, if they would have treated him differently. He *knew* they would have.

The challenge had been to close his eyes briefly and to find solace in a kind of quiet contemplation and prayer, except Tristan couldn't remember how to do that. His eyes were closed against the harsh fluorescent lighting, and he was trying, when he felt a body drop into the seat next to him. The vinyl cushion exhaled a sigh, and he opened his eyes to find his mother by his side.

"This blows," she said, in that way she had of expressing herself in an endearingly inarticulate manner when it counted the most. Tristan couldn't help it; the eyes he thought dry swam with tears, and he sobbed a greeting to his mother, who took him in her arms as if he were still four.

"They won't tell me anything," he said, pulling back. "I'm no one. I've been trying to call Emma."

"Shh, baby," Julia crooned to him. "Shh. Emma called my cell; she's on her way. She's flying back from Vegas, honey, and she can't take calls. She'll be here soon, as soon as she can."

"Mom," he said, but he couldn't go further. Here was a woman who'd lost her life partner in the time it took to choose a drive-through, and he couldn't ask her what he wanted to ask. He couldn't bear to ask her how she survived.

"Has there been any change?" she asked.

"They won't tell me anything," he said bitterly. "I don't count. Hospital policy. He could be dead; no one will even talk to me. He could just be lying there waiting for Emma to come so they can turn off…"

"I saw on the local news he was out of surgery and in serious but stable condition, and they're cautiously optimistic."

Tristan stared at her. "Am I going crazy? They wouldn't tell *me*, but they announce it on the damned news?" He slumped farther and rested his head on his mother's shoulder, something he was really too tall for now. "That's good news anyway," he sighed, feeling the first blush of hope in his heart. "How could I even…"

"You could. You just would," she said. "It's not a multiple choice questionnaire where you get to check the best answer box."

"You ought to know."

"Yep," said his mother, her face like a marble madonna. "I ought to know."

"Mom?"

"Hm?"

"I don't know if I can lose someone again. I don't know if I can stay sane if it happens."

Julia looked at Tristan and interlaced her freckled hand with his. "You shouldn't have to, but you'll cope. I believe you'll cope," she said.

"I don't know if I can put myself through this," he said, for the first time admitting what was creeping into his heart. "Maybe I can't be with someone who's on the job."

"It's something to consider," said Julia carefully.

"I feel like crap even thinking it."

"Why?"

"What kind of shit would I be to give up on love like that?"

"You wouldn't stop loving him, Tris. But it *is* fair to ask if you can live like this. It's fair to say you've been through enough loss and pain and can't lose someone again. You wouldn't even be asking if he were a drug addict or an alcoholic."

"Mom, he's a damned hero; it doesn't compare!"

She gestured around her at the sterile hospital waiting room. "Doesn't it? From where I sit, his choices place his life at risk. Sure, he's a hero. No one is saying anything to the contrary. I happen to think he's a really, really good man. But only you know whether you can live with the pain of knowing every day that this is one possible scenario."

"Oh, Mom." Tristan began to cry again.

"I'm not strong enough to love anyone except you kids. That's my choice. I feel like I can live with that."

"Shit."

"On the other hand, baby, everybody dies," Julia murmured, putting her arms back around him. "Everything ends. It's not good enough to find yourself a nice, safe architect."

"I know. *I know.*"

"So you either love or you don't; the end is out of your hands." She gave him a hard squeeze. "But how you live and what you can stand, that's on you, Tristan, and I urge you to make your decision with your eyes wide open and cherish what you get."

Tristan closed his eyes and just leaned on her as he always had. Always would. "Love you."

"Love you back," said Julia.

They stayed like that for a while, until Julia decided Tristan needed to eat and over his protests went to Carl's Jr. to purchase some lunch for him. He was enjoying a shake when a commotion started at the door, the officers in the room getting up and moving all at once. At first his heart stopped because he thought something might have happened to Michael -- that he might have taken a turn for the worse -- and he closed his eyes against the pain of that. Then he felt a strong, sure hand tug at his, and he realized Emma had returned at last.

"Come on, baby," she said. "I got your messages. Let's go kick some ass."

"Huh?" Tristan said as she pulled him to the information desk.

"My name is Emma Truax; I'm Officer Truax's mother. And this?" she said. "Is Tristan, who for the purposes of this discussion is also my son."

Tristan noticed the doctor seemed tired when he'd looked briefly at his eyes, but after that, he found he could focus only on the man's clogs, which were screaming red polyvinyl and looked like nothing so much as red licorice made into footwear. While focused on the whimsical shoes, critical information that included the words perforated, collapsed, nicked, hemorrhage, the number of units of transfused blood, the nature of each and every lurking danger, and Michael's prognosis for recovery bounced off of him and around the sterile hallway like little steel ball bearings.

"Anyway," the doctor said at last, replacing the pen he was making notes with into the pocket of his lab coat. "It's a very serious, life-threatening injury. I don't mean to frighten you, but the only reason he made it this far is that he had an EMT on scene at the time of the stabbing, and he was less than ten minutes away. He's a lucky man, and I'm counting on his luck to hold a little longer." He looked at them seriously, wanting them to understand the truth of his words. "It needs to."

Tristan blinked at him. The doctor seemed to be done. He wanted to ask the only question he cared about at that moment, but fear clogged his throat.

"Can we see him?" Emma asked for him.

"One at a time and for no more than a few minutes." He looked at Tristan closely. "Are you Tristan?" he asked.

Tristan couldn't imagine how he knew. "Yes," he answered. "Was he conscious? Did he ask for me?"

"No," said the doctor. "The ink." He pointed to his own ankle. "The rules are immediate family only," he began, and Emma drew herself up into what Tristan could only think of as a fighting stance and pulled him to her, standing as tall as she could at his back, which was not very, really.

"But you're not going to be a jerk about it." She smiled. "Isn't that what you were going to say?"

"No," said the doctor. "I was going to say if you need anything and anyone gives you any trouble, page me immediately." He gave a card to each Tristan and Emma. "I'll handle it." He stared at Tristan. "Love makes people get well faster. But not too much love." He shook his head at Tristan before he left.

"What the…" said Tristan. He turned to Emma. "You go." He gave her a little push.

"No, honey, I can wait," she said. "You go on. I think I've had longer to get used to the idea of this."

Tristan swallowed hard. "I'm…" he began, in a whisper. "I'm scared. You go first. Tell me what to expect, okay?"

Emma stroked his arm. "All right, baby. I'll go in. You lean against the wall; you look like you're going to fall right over." She slipped quietly through the door.

Tristan stood with his back against the wall. The *Jeopardy* theme was back. He looked at the fluorescent lights in the ceiling, going over in his mind all the things he knew about light as if remembering what he knew about science could somehow tilt the scales of fortune in his favor in this place.

It seemed like an interminable wait before Emma came out. Her eyes were red. "I think I was kidding myself," she murmured. "I could never get used to the idea of that."

Tristan put a hand out to steady her. "Mom's out there." He indicated the waiting room.

"Thank you."

Tristan watched her walk away. It only remained now for him to open the door to the small room where Michael lay injured, yet he found he had little courage to do so.

Heart pounding, mouth dry, Tristan entered the room, immediately aware of the beeping of the monitors and the stillness of the form on the hospital bed. Michael was connected to tubes everywhere. Bags hung from poles to hydrate and deliver medication, a nasal cannula brought oxygen, and tubes entered his hand from the I.V. and exited from under his sheet carrying urine. Everything was monitored, his heart rate, breathing, and blood pressure glowing green and red on machines. A small sound from the bed captured his attention immediately.

"Michael?" he asked, taking Michael's still hand in his. There was no response. The doctor said Michael was medicated and would remain unconscious for a while. That much he remembered anyway. He held Michael's hand in his, the tanned skin against his own very white and freckly hand reassuring.

"Did I fail to mention how very impossible it would be for me to live without you?" he whispered. He continued stroking Michael's hand, murmuring to him, and found the courage to sweep the short hair back from his brow, placing a kiss on his lips.

"You're my guy, remember?" he asked. "I need you, Michael." Tristan continued his soft-spoken and one-sided conversation until he realized his time was up. He kissed Michael one more time, whispering, "Don't go anywhere, I'll be right here," and then he was at the door, prepared for the interminable wait until he could see Michael again.

"Back soon, baby," he said and then left the room. Maybe he felt better than he had since he'd heard of Michael's injury, but that wasn't saying a whole lot.

In the waiting room, Tristan was restless, his legs dancing as he tapped his feet on the hard commercial flooring. It would be hours before they'd let him see Michael again, and he felt he ought to be doing something constructive, not just sitting. His mom had gone back to her work, and Emma was dozing, snoring softly by his side. They'd begun a camp of sorts, with coffee and a box of pastries someone brought, along with books and magazines strewn about.

At one point Tristan made a half-hearted attempt at some homework, but found he couldn't concentrate, reading the same paragraph in his philosophy text over and over until he realized it and just shoved the damn thing away.

"Emma," he said, forgetting and waking her up.

"Huh?" She jumped, her eyes wide. Tristan felt instantly contrite.

"Oh, shit, I'm sorry, I didn't mean to scare you." He swiped tired hands over his eyes. "I've got to take off, get some air. I'll have my cell. You'll call me if…"

"I'll call you when they say we can see him again," she said. "Stay close by."

"No more than ten minutes away," he agreed.

"It's okay, baby. Go get some air."

The car still sat where Tristan had parked it that morning, beeping cordially when he opened the door with the remote. He knew he should have stayed. He'd said he would stay, wouldn't leave Michael, but the war was lost. He *had* to move. He'd left his heart and his soul and probably the part of his brain he thought with in the hospital room in that bed with Michael. The part that remained just needed to *do something*. He parked along Harbor Boulevard, thinking about the last time he'd been here, and purchased coffee that he didn't want or need at the bakery around the corner from I.N.KD. He stepped into the small boutique and saw Jim looking at him through concerned eyes.

"Tristan," he said, leaning a hip against the counter. He had light brown hair, what was left of it close-cropped, and glasses. He had a mustache and a tiny V-shaped beard and was pierced in the crease between his mouth and chin. "How is he?"

"Bad," said Tristan numbly. "Not dead, which is good, right?"

Jim just stared at him, his sad eyes willing him to confide, to trust. "Yeah."

"Anyway, I wondered if Meghan was here." Tristan looked around again and back at the curtain separating the boutique area from where the office must be.

"No, Meghan's home today," he said. At Tristan's crestfallen expression he added, "I could call her. She'll want to talk to you."

"You could?" said Tristan. "I don't want to bother her on her day off…"

"Let's see what she says," said Jim.

Tristan was holding himself together by sheer force of will. He knew he must seem whacked at best; too much caffeine and too little calm. Crazy.

"Meghan?" Jim said into the phone. "Michael's friend is here to see you. Do you have time to stop by?" Tristan noticed Jim was treating him like an unexploded bomb, and he didn't care. Jim seemed to listen and then nodded. "Fine, I'll tell him."

Tristan looked at him as he hung up the phone.

"She'll be here in about ten minutes."

"Why?"

"She went to school with Michael. We both did. He's one of our best friends, Tristan. She's sick with worry."

"Oh," said Tristan. It had never occurred to him that someone else would feel that way, although he didn't know why not. Michael was well liked locally as a police officer and by everyone who knew him. Anyone on the force was bound to be anxious and angry that he'd been attacked, but Tristan hadn't even considered his friends, hadn't thought beyond himself and Emma, and maybe Edward. "*Oh.*"

"Don't worry, he's tough. He'll make it." He cleared his throat and turned to look at the street through the window.

"Thanks." Tristan sipped his coffee in order to have some reason to be holding it. They stood in silence, not really aware of the passage of time until a gust of air blowing the back curtain told them Meghan had come. She went straight to Tristan, her eyes red from crying and allowed him to fold her into his arms.

"Shit," she said. Apparently she had the same etiquette book his mother had, or at least had gone to the same finishing school. Condolence 101. "This is such shit. In high school he was my rock.

When the other kids gave me crap, he was always there for me." She sniffed loudly, bringing a tissue to her nose and eyes.

"He's going to be okay," said Tristan, his mouth working the words, but his head and his heart were someplace else, so they were hollow in his ears.

"You can probably tell how easily I fit in at school," she said wetly, tears streaming down her inked face.

Tristan laughed.

"He's going to die inside when he hears about Mary," she added, squeezing her eyes shut. "Even though she stabbed him, he's going to think it's his fault Mary died."

Tristan stared at her. "I don't know what you're talking about." He looked from one to the other. "Mary died?"

Jim and Meghan looked back at him with wide eyes. "How much did you see on the news?"

"None of it. I was in school, and my mom called me. I listened to the radio on the way to the hospital, and they only said --" He looked out the front window where the sun was beginning to set between the office buildings across the street. "Was that just this morning?"

Jim quietly told him how Michael came to be stabbed. "I have a friend who works for the FPD in dispatch; she went to school with my brother, Ian. She filled me in."

"Oh, shit," said Tristan, who knew very well Michael would carry Mary with him until he died. If he…

"Sparky," said Meghan, almost as though she hadn't meant to say it aloud. "He calls you Sparky."

"Yeah." Tristan took her hand in his. He had come up with an idea sitting in the hospital, and the more he thought about it, the more inevitable it became. "Can you mark me?"

"What?"

"Can you mark me with the same band that's on his ankle, the exact same thing? On the small of my back, here?" He turned and pointed to the base of his spine, an inch or two above the crack in his ass. "Exactly like his?"

"Yeah," she said. "I can do that."

"Okay. Now?"

"Yeah. You want his name?"

"No…yes." He thought about the police officers with their implacable eyes, the clerks and the rules and the hospital policies. "Put his name, with the lock in the 'a' like it is on Michael's ankle, but put his badge number," he said. "Put FPD and his badge number, do you know it?"

She shook her head.

"I do," said Tristan. "I'll write it down."

Tristan lay face down on a clean white towel, listening to the crunch of the paper that covered the vinyl-padded surface of the table. He could hear the grinding buzz of the needle as Meghan applied it to his skin. He needed the sting and the burn and the almost-pain that she was inflicting on him. It was like a hard hand holding him down, anchoring him to the earth when his biggest fear was that he would fly apart and drift away with no one the wiser. The pain held him in place like a drug he needed.

"This hurts too much in one place, you say so. I can move away and then come back to that spot later."

"No," said Tristan, gritting his teeth, liking the tears that burned his eyes and the ache in his throat. "It's fine."

Meghan put her head down and kept going, stopping every so often to look at her work and dab specks of blood away with a piece of rolled-up gauze. She sniffled every so often, but other than that made hardly a sound unless she spoke, periodically, to see how he was taking the procedure.

The white towel beneath Tristan was damp with sweat and drool and the thousand tears he shed as he lay there. When Meghan was finished and had covered his new ink with a dressing, she helped him rise from the table, giving him the same talk about aftercare she'd given Michael only a couple of weeks before. He nodded every so often, his mind wandering.

"And that means the ink will still be there when the skin finishes peeling, so don't be thinking your tattoo is peeling off and panic, okay?" she said finally, squeezing his hand in hers. He hadn't paid much attention until that moment, and she probably knew it.

"I've got to get back," he said. The sky outside was full dark, and he had no idea what time it was or when Jim had left, although he clearly had.

"Hey," she said quietly. "Can you leave your phone number so we can call and check up? We don't have Emma's; I tried earlier. She must have changed cell numbers."

"Sure, but I can't have it turned on in the hospital. I'll check it periodically." Tristan wrote his number down on the appointment book for her. "Thank you for seeing me today," he said.

"You're welcome. I hope you never regret having Michael's ink on your ass." She looked at him, her sad eyes going sadder. "Seems like every day I'm changing Sarah to Sherry or scratching it out and putting Nancy next to it." She blinked back tears. "I did a Larry to Harry on a guy just the other week with a little Harry Potter face next to it."

"Oh, man," said Tristan, picturing picking up a guy and finding out he had Harry Potter's face on his ass. "Look, whatever happens…I'll never belong to anyone else the way I belong to Michael right now. I know that. I just hope…" He trailed off. Tristan was thinking he hoped he had the balls to stay with Michael. He was thinking that if he lost Michael, he'd never smile again. He was thinking of the very real possibility that Michael might not make it and what that would mean to him, when his cell phone rang. He looked at the number and saw it was Emma's.

"Emma." He told Meghan, just looking at it. She gripped his hand hard. "Hello," he said, swallowing.

"It's time," said Emma. "They say we can see him for a few minutes each." She seemed to wait for him to say something.

"Any change?"

"No, baby, he's still unconscious. But he hasn't taken a turn for the worse."

"Okay," he said. "Ten minutes, fifteen if parking is a problem."

"Fine." She hung up. He smiled at Meghan mechanically.

"I'm going to see him; there's been no change, better or worse."

"Go," said Meghan simply. "I'll call you."

He began to remove his wallet, tensing when he felt the rasp of his trousers against his new tattoo. "What do I owe you?"

"For heaven's sake, go!" she said. "I know where Michael lives. We'll worry about that later." She tugged his hand one more time and then let go, and he left.

Chapter Twenty-Six

A warm spring breeze scented with onions and peppers cooking rushed past Michael as he rode his Harley out old Route 66, past the business district and the little gas stations and restaurants and souvenir stands that went mostly belly-up when the powers that be decided that Interstate 20 would be a good idea, and relished the feel of his Sparky holding his waist as they sped up. How he loved the feel of the road beneath him, his boy behind him, and the sun on his shoulders. It just didn't get any better than this. They passed a small historical car museum and dumpy hotel, and he could hear, although he really didn't know how, Tristan keeping up a steady stream of chatter in his head about all the interesting places along the side of the road.

Fantastic places whistled past, the Grand Canyon, Mount Rushmore, the bright green grass-seed farms of the Willamette Valley, and the battlefield at Antietam. All the while, his boy talked and held on as they sped over the road together. At last, the motorcycle slowed to a stop to wait for a procession of pedestrians in a crosswalk. They all walked behind a casket crossing the road in a carriage, New Orleans-style, with a jazz band and men and women carrying umbrellas dancing along behind it. Walking slowly behind the casket was a solemn, copper-haired boy, who looked at him as he passed, tears and accusations glowing in his eyes.

Michael looked down to see the hands that clasped around his waist and found, not the soft, freckled hands of his boy, but the gnarled and filthy hands of someone entirely alien to him, and he turned in the seat of his motorcycle to see Mary behind him, her eyes cold and dead, still holding him around the waist in rigor mortis.

Emma's voice came to Michael from far away, murmuring over the pings of something droning and mechanical that he could hear distantly as he fought to understand what had happened to him. After a while, the voice that had spoken softly beside him drifted away, the sound of a door closing firmly behind it.

It hurt him somehow to be without a human voice in this impersonal place where he was cold and fuzzy-headed, and pain exploded in the cave behind his eyes as he tried to make them open. Failing that, failing everything it seemed at that point, Michael wept tears of bitter frustration, which leaked down the sides of his face and fell into the hair by his temples. He heard the door open again and tentative footsteps approach him. He felt a warm hand flutter briefly along the side of his face, encountering the wetness there.

"Michael?" he heard Tristan's voice and tried to make his gritty eyes open again. "Michael, can you hear me?" He felt a warm hand on his own and weakly squeezed it.

"Hey!" Excitement pulsed through Tristan. "Hey, I've got to get Emma. Wait." He skittered to the door of the private hospital room. "Don't go anywhere. I'm coming right back."

Tristan careened out the door into the doctor, whom he told first thing that Michael had squeezed his hand, and then ran to the waiting room to get Emma, tugging her back to where he'd left Michael, heedless of hospital policy. When he returned, Michael's blue eyes were open and rested on him, dazed, while the doctor spoke quietly with him.

"Tristan," Michael said hoarsely. "Mama." He lifted a hand, which Tristan caught and held in his. Emma clasped the other.

"Hey, Sparky." Michael smiled weakly.

"Hey, Michael," said Tristan, his tears spilling onto the hand he was holding as he reached down to kiss it.

"Mama, this shit sucks. Sorry," Michael said to Emma. She wiped her eyes.

The doctor looked at Michael seriously. "You've used up all the luck you're probably ever going to get. You know that, right?"

"Yeah," said Michael grimly.

"Do you remember what happened?"

"Not really, no," said Michael. "I dreamed we were riding," he said to his mother and Tristan. "Out on old Route 66."

Emma shook her head. "There are some cops who'll be anxious to see you too. They're crowding the waiting room. It's déjà vu all over again. I kept thinking maybe I ought to just start singing 'We Shall Not Be Moved.'"

"They're here for me, not you." Michael tried to smile. "This time." Seconds later the same eyes drooped tiredly, and Michael's hand fell back on the bed, out of Tristan's. "So tired," he sighed. "Can I see Tristan alone?"

Emma looked at the doctor. "Sure," he said. "Five minutes, don't tire him out."

"Okay," said Tristan, still looking only at Michael, noticing every movement, every nuance that crossed his exhausted face.

Emma and the doctor left them alone, silent, against the backdrop of mechanized beeps and the hiss of oxygen as it flowed into Michael's nose through the cannula.

"I'm so sorry, Sparky," said Michael, gripping his hand tightly.

"Oh, shut up," said Tristan, caught so suddenly and wrenchingly by tears that he half snorted and half gagged. "Shut the hell up and kiss me," he said, his lips descending on Michael's, his tongue running along the chapped skin. "I'm so getting you ChapStick as soon as they kick my ass out of here." He laughed and cried.

"Tristan," said Michael. "Love."

"Yes," hissed Tristan fiercely. "Yes. Love." He pressed his cheek against Michael's.

"This is the worst. So tired. I'm all out of…stuff." His eyes tried to close again.

Tristan laughed with his lips against Michael's abrasive chin. "Yeah, you used up all your stuff, so rest. I'll be right here. Not going anywhere without you."

"Keeping you, Sparky."

"Love you," said Tristan before he practically tiptoed out of Michael's room. Michael had already drifted off.

* * *

Tristan was sleeping on the vinyl waiting room chair the following day when his mother sat in the seat beside him.

"Hey," he said, swiping at his eyes with the heels of his hands. "What time is it? I've lost track."

She grinned at him. "One in the afternoon. Have you eaten anything besides doughnuts?" she asked, looking at the pink boxes scattered in what was now plainly considered the "fans of Michael Truax" area of the waiting room.

"I honestly can't remember." He sighed, sat up, and immediately remembered getting a large tattoo on his ass. "Shit."

"What?"

"Nothing. Maybe I should go to Michael's and take a shower, get some clothes."

"I wanted to talk to you about that."

He winced a little. "Stiff," he murmured.

"Listen," she began. "I don't know when Michael's going to be discharged, but he's going to need a lot of help at the house at first. His mom is next door, of course, but he isn't likely to want her around all the time fussing. And she's just worried sick. I was going to suggest that you stay with him while he convalesces." She put her hand on his.

"Well, sure," he said. "I know it's been crazy since Michael got hurt, but I can come get the boys and get them to school in plenty of time to get to class and take them to band and the orthodontist. I can stop by the house a couple of times a week to cook and do laundry, too. Anyway, it's finals week, starting…shit, tomorrow. After that we'll be on Christmas break, and they won't need a chauffeur until after New Year's, and by then…" He absently rubbed his chin, acknowledging that even he probably needed a shave as rare as that was.

"About that, baby," she said. "I thought if I got Lily a car she would be able to drive the boys where they need to go. The boys are old enough to start taking on some of the responsibility you've been shouldering, and really, it would do them good."

"What are you saying?" he asked, his heart pounding. On the one hand, he would love to be there for Michael, on the other, his mother needed him, *didn't she?*

"I love you, Tris. You're such an amazing kid." She shook her head and started to cry. "You've helped me so much. You never needed asking."

"Mom." Her tears were like acid rain, dissolving all of his hard-won cool.

"Tris, it's okay if you go with Michael when he gets out. He'll need you… You're so lucky to get a second chance…"

"I've just got to get through finals." He was grimly determined not to have to do the classes over again. "Maybe you guys could help me keep it together until then."

"Of course, we'll talk about it more," she said, getting up. "But first, you've got to eat something that doesn't come out of a pink box. Come with me." She grabbed his hand and dragged him toward the exit.

"Wait." Tristan ran back and picked up his messenger bag and any trash lying around, leaving the doughnuts for anyone who stopped by to check on Michael in what was arguably his waiting spot.

"Ready," he said, going out into the sunlight with his mother. "We have to be back at three. That's the next time we can visit."

* * *

Michael woke to something smooth and fruity being massaged into his lips. "Hm?" he said, smiling as the sensation changed to a light brush of lips on his.

"Hey there." Tristan finished coating Michael's lips with lip balm and gave him another sweet kiss.

"Thank you," said Michael, for both the kiss and the lip balm. He'd been feeling his chapped lips since he'd regained consciousness, and it was just one more thing that was bugging him.

"You are so welcome. Do you know what?" Tristan asked, pulling up a chair and sitting in it with one leg under him. "I've got finals this week. You could have thought of that."

"Man, I knew it wasn't a good week to get stabbed," said Michael, trying not to laugh and finding out that everything, *everything* hurt.

"Well, milk spilt," said Tristan, looking over the skin on Michael's arms. "It's amazing how badly they bruised you just getting an I.V. in. You look like someone beat you with a wrench. The EMT told me he was terrified he'd lose you. You scared the hell out of a lot of people, Officer Truax."

"I know," said Michael, taking Tristan's offered hand in his. "I'm so sorry."

"I cannot lose you, love," said Tristan, quietly. "I. Can. Not."

"I understand." Michael was silent for a while and then spoke again. "I dreamed we were riding together, all across the country, just the two of us."

"Really, the Harley?" Tristan's spirits rose just thinking about that bike.

"Yeah, just you and me. All over." He didn't mention the cold, dead hands gripping his waist. That part he didn't have to share.

"From what I understand," Tristan began carefully, "You'll be phased back into work from a desk first and expected to see someone about your attack."

"I know," said Michael. "They'll evaluate me. See if I'm fit for duty."

"Yeah, nothing worse than an uptight cop," said Tristan, whose opinion of the police had been formed in his days as an intrepid skate park hooligan.

"Sparky," warned Michael.

"Sorry," said Tristan. "Probably."

Michael smiled, and for the first time it didn't hurt. "How's Mama doing?"

"She's holding up," said Tristan. "I think so, anyway. She's working now, and she'll be here later. Starting tomorrow, I won't be here as much because of finals, but I'll be here at night and whenever I can. When they kick me out, I'm going to your house to take a shower and change and maybe review my chemistry notes."

"Our house," Michael corrected him.

"What?" asked Tristan, his surprised blue eyes meeting Michael's.

Michael gripped his hand. "I want it to be our house, Tristan. I don't want to go slow. I want to race into the future, and I want it to be *our* future together. Stay with me. Live with me. Be mine. Everything I have, everything I am is already yours."

"Oh, jeez," said Tristan, running a nervous tongue over his lips. "*Jeez.*"

"That's it?" asked Michael arching a brow.

"Baby, it's not like I spent my childhood practicing for the day when some guy would say that to me," said Tristan, his cheeks flaming up.

"But, jeez?" said Michael. "Jeez is something you say when the waiter brings that big pepper mill for your salad and you forget to say 'when.'"

"Don't get worked up," said Tristan. "You're going to rupture something, and the doctor is going to blame me."

"You little shit." Michael smiled, his eyes on Tristan's lips.

Tristan noticed the look immediately. "Don't look at me like that!"

"How come?" said Michael, although he knew perfectly well and was already tired to the point of exhaustion from the conversation alone. Looking was all he could do for a while.

"You should probably wait till they remove the catheter before you start something, don't you think?"

"Uh, yeah," said Michael. "But you do realize that something starts the moment you walk in here, don't you?"

"Even now?"

"Oh, yeah, my heart's on fire, but my body? Not so much." His eyes started to close again.

"Well, lie there and get well," said Tristan. "My time's up, and I'll see you soon."

"And you'll consider it? Us?" Michael caught his hand.

"You just get better. The future is too far away," said Tristan hoarsely, kissing him.

Chapter Twenty-Seven

On December twenty-third, Emma gave Tristan keys to Michael's truck, and he used it to bring his belongings to the house to move in. He felt a little breathless when he thought of it. He had so very little of his own that the truck had hardly been needed, but his bicycle wouldn't fit in the Beemer, and his mother insisted he take his father's favorite art books. He hoped he and Michael could make space for them, because they were all photographic studies of architecture, and he loved them very much. He thought they would interest Michael as well, but the house wasn't that big, and he didn't want to presume.

Tristan made short work out of stacking most of the boxes either in the bedroom or the office and was placing his bicycle in the garage when a low, gravelly voice spoke behind him, and he turned to see Ron standing in Emma's yard.

"Moving in?" asked Ron.

"Yes," said Tristan neutrally.

"Look, I know you don't have a lot to say to me," began Ron. "But we both love Michael."

"Yes, we do," agreed Tristan. He closed the garage and turned back.

"I just wanted to talk to you," said Ron.

"Okay," said Tristan. He walked to the back door, holding it open. "I have coffee going."

"Thanks." Ron looked over the small kitchen. "He sure did a beautiful job on this one."

"Yes," agreed Tristan. "It was a labor of love. He really likes this place, and it shows in the attention to detail."

"It does. Look, I don't know what Michael told you about me…"

"He told me you used to be lovers," said Tristan. "And that maybe the two of you had different expectations of what that meant."

"That's diplomatic," grunted Ron. "I like to play games. I never made a secret of it. It still makes me sick that he didn't feel like he could tell me he wanted something different."

"I don't think he knew how."

"Well, he's got you now, and it's good," said Ron. "Although you're a mouthy little thing."

"That what you wanted to talk to me about?" asked Tristan with his chin up. He wasn't going to let Ron push him around. Ron had no idea how far he'd go to protect Michael.

"Look at you." Ron whistled. "You aren't afraid of anything are you?"

"Yes," said Tristan honestly. "I'm afraid of losing Michael."

"Me too, and that's what I wanted to talk to you about." He seemed suddenly at a loss for words.

"Cream and sugar?" Tristan asked, handing him a large mug of coffee.

"No, thank you," said Ron. "Have you given any thought to what your presence in this home might mean to Michael?"

"Well, he *asked* me to move in. I can't say I've thought beyond that," said Tristan carefully.

"Well, he's a little naive, isn't he? He's a cop, Sparky. Surely you know that's not the most gay-friendly occupation."

"Yes, but…"

"In the hospital, the other cops were probably thinking, *Look at that boy.* Michael's got himself a fan club. They look at you, and they know that you love him, and you're not exactly hiding it, are you?"

Tristan blushed to the roots of his hair. "I know. I didn't say anything, but I know they could tell."

"Still, anyone can have a fan, right?" said Ron. "And it happens. A guy makes a friend, someone younger who looks up to him. Nobody holds it against him if the kid gets a crush. But the minute you move in here, Michael is *out.* And maybe that's not so good. Maybe it's not even safe, you know?"

"Safe?" asked Tristan numbly.

"Yeah, *safe,*" repeated Ron. "Michael has a dangerous job, and he needs to know that his brother officers are going to have his back. I'm not saying anything would be deliberate, although it's certainly happened in the past. I'm saying what if someone hesitates? What if someone thinks, if it's him or me, maybe it should be him?"

"You're saying if I move in here, Michael could suffer."

"I'm asking you to think about it very carefully, for Michael's sake. It's not jealousy talking. He's like family. We tried something, and it didn't work. Someday we'll all get past it and be family again. I'm happy when he's happy, and he's happy *with you.* But he's not a doctor or a lawyer or an Indian chief." Tristan could tell this was probably the most Ron had said for a week. "He's a cop, and maybe he needs to hide that he's gay so he can stay a safe cop."

Tristan put his head into his hands.

"I'm sorry, Sparky. I'm not sure I'm right; I'm just asking you to think." Ron put his hand out and stroked Tristan's hair, and Tristan had the impression that Ron had been more of a father to

Michael than a lover. That it had been a bad thing for both of them to try something different.

"He is *not* going to understand," Tristan said quietly.

"No, probably not," said Ron. "It doesn't mean you can't still be together, though. Hiding homosexuality is a time-honored and little-respected art these days. I ought to know. I kind of liked the drawn-out tension of seeing a big guy in leathers and not knowing. When it was all about dropping hints. What a rush, wondering if you were getting pulled into an alley to be blown or beaten senseless. Now, it seems everyone has to wear signs." He rolled his eyes.

Tristan laughed, although he was also crying, so it made a snot bubble come out of his nose. "Shit," he said, grabbing a napkin.

"Hey, *green wood*," said Ron. "I'm wondering if you might actually like me someday."

"Yep," said Tristan. "I'm wondering if I like you already, you shit." He blew his nose, and Ron laughed.

"Maybe I deserve that."

"Ron?" Tristan said quietly. "I don't know if I can do this."

"What, leave? It's not forever. There are other cities. Michael could work someplace they don't know him."

"No," sighed Tristan. "I'm not sure I'm cut out to marry the job."

"Shit," said Ron, as he began to comprehend what Tristan was saying. He took a sip of his coffee. "Michael know you feel that way?"

"Oh, hell, no, what was I going to do? Tell him when he was in the hospital? Say, 'Sorry -- the job that almost got you killed? I hate it.'"

To his credit, Ron remained silent.

"I lost my dad two years ago. Never mind how *I* felt about that, I watched my mom die with him. I feel like I'm up to here with grief, and I finally, *finally* find someone..."

"Sparky," began Ron, but Tristan wasn't finished.

"I love him. Every cell in my body is screaming his name. But then it hits me, like I'm gagging on an ice cube, and I feel nothing but cold, blind terror."

"*Oh, Sparky,*" breathed Ron. "This will kill him."

"Shut up!" Tristan raked a hand through his hair. "You've got no right to judge me."

"I'm not judging you -- I swear I'm not." Ron put a warm hand over Tristan's. "I get what you're saying. I know it's hard."

"Help me move the boxes back out," Tristan said. "I'm not saying I'm not moving in, I'm just...I'm going to wait until I can think of something besides how close Michael came to being...not alive."

"*Pussy.* Can't even say it, can you?"

"Can't even think it," said Tristan, getting up.

"That makes two of us," Ron murmured as he followed Tristan to the office and started helping him load boxes.

By the time they had all the boxes in the truck, Tristan realized all he had to say to Michael was that he didn't feel he could leave his mom right then and get his mom to understand and back him up. Ron left him with a coffee in a Styrofoam cup and a sad smile.

Tristan sat quietly in the suddenly too-silent house. He had decorated every inch of it for Christmas, inside and out, making a special effort to keep in mind Michael's love of the house and using mostly natural elements, clove-studded citrus fruits and fresh greenery. He'd kept the colors muted, earthy, and real. He'd done the tree with Emma and his family, putting up Michael's own German bubble lights and Christmas ornaments, purchasing a few of his own, and hanging elegant black velvet Christmas stockings on the mantle. *Our first Christmas together.* Emma had reassured him that Michael would be thrilled that he'd taken the time, even if he wasn't home by Christmas.

In the week after finals, Tristan had alternated his time between the hospital, decorating the house for the holidays, and baking enough tea loaves and cookies to fill not only Michael's freezer, but Emma's and his own family's as well. As the boredom became crushing, the only thought that saved him was that he was going to share his first holiday with Michael.

Now, sitting in the kitchen in the wake of Ron's visit, he let himself go and cried.

Hours later, Tristan drove the truck back to his mom's house and emptied his things back into his old room. He called his mom and told her he wasn't going to be moving for a while, and that he'd explain some other time, but that she shouldn't worry, everything was fine.

Emma was waiting when he arrived at the hospital that afternoon, smiling so fiercely with her eyes shining that he knew something must be up.

"They're going to let us take him home tomorrow," she said in a rush as he got off the elevator. "We can spring him for Christmas Eve; isn't that just the best news?" She hugged him tightly around the waist, and they walked together to Michael's room. "They say he'll just need to take it easy for a while and that he needs someone to stay with him. He can't drive for four more weeks, can you imagine? He'll be beside himself."

"That he will," said Tristan, heartened by the news. "Is it really all right?"

"Yes," she said. "They've been gradually giving him water and food, to make sure everything goes where it's supposed to, and the doctor says his body is beginning to function normally. He's passing things properly, and they expect him to continue recovering as long as he rests at home."

"Look, Emma, I didn't get a chance to tell you. I didn't move into Michael's today." He looked at her apprehensively.

"What?" She seemed shocked. "Why not?"

"I guess I…didn't think it completely through. It's a huge step, and everything's so crazy right now. I need a chance to think, some time when I'm not scared to death."

"I see," she said thoughtfully. "It's been a shock."

"Emma, I love him," he said sincerely. "It's just that this is huge, and I'm not ready."

"It's okay to feel that way," said Emma, squeezing his hand. "If you need to wait till you're ready, I understand and so will Michael." Privately, Tristan thought Michael would never understand until he understood it himself.

Emma opened the door to Michael's room. "Which lazy policeman do we get to take home and spoil rotten for Christmas?" she asked, grinning like a lunatic.

"Did you hear that, Michael?" asked Tristan, seeing him smile. "You get to go home!"

"And rest!" emphasized Emma. "We will look the word up when we get home to refresh your memory, but I'm already certain there are no power tools involved."

"I plan on staying in bed for a month," said Michael, looking at Tristan, who pinked right up.

"And *rest*!" Emma reiterated.

"I can assure you, I'm not good for much else."

"Don't be a baby. You can knit scarves for orphans or something," said Tristan.

"See?" said Emma. "He'll keep you plenty busy."

Michael fairly leered, but Emma was busy digging a phone list and a cell phone out of her pocket.

"I have to phone all these people. There have been so many people who have called and e-mailed. I'm going to let them know the good news, and maybe they'll bring casseroles so we don't have to cook too much the first few days," she said. "I don't know. Do people still do that?"

"Yes," said Tristan. "My mom does. Tell them we're good to go for desserts."

"Will do," said Emma, waving on her way out the door.

When the door closed behind her, Tristan took Michael's hand in his. "I'm going to bring the Beemer to pick you up tomorrow. I'm thinking it will be hard for you to get up into the truck. Still the Beemer's kind of small. I feel like Goldilocks. This one's too big…"

"Yeah," said Michael. "But it's just a short drive. Small is okay. Did you get your things moved in yet?"

"No, I didn't. I've been Christmas shopping, helping Mom out, taking the kids to get stuff, and on top of that, I have this gorgeous man I have to daydream about all day. Who has time?"

Michael worried his lower lip a little. "Didn't your mom get Lily a car yet?"

"No, not yet. We're going car shopping between Christmas and New Year's when my mom has the time off."

"Oh," said Michael, looking a little sad. "I guess I was thinking that when I got home it would be *our* home, you know?"

"It *is* our home," said Tristan. "Even if I don't live there. You're my home, Michael. I live here." He placed his hand carefully over Michael's heart. "The rest is just stuff."

Michael smiled. "Yeah," he said. "I guess." Tristan leaned in to kiss him gently on the lips, their tongues touching briefly.

"I love you so much," said Tristan. He heard the door open and jumped away, startled. Michael looked surprised, but turned to the newcomer.

"Hey, Doc," said Michael. "I guess time's up, and you can't hold me any longer without charging me with a crime."

"That's right," said the doctor, shaking his hand. "We seem to have fixed you, and tomorrow is Christmas Eve, after all." He winked at Tristan.

"I still have all the lights to put up and the tree to buy and decorate," Michael joked. "Can't I go today? There's all that last minute shopping to do. And there's the baking. Where does the time go?"

"Are you trying to get me to rescind the order letting you leave?"

"No!" said both Tristan and Michael at the same time.

"Good, then you behave, or I'll come to your house and bring you back here myself. I have spies everywhere. Try not to forget that." The doctor left the room.

"I did want to do one thing," said Michael. "But now it's out of the question for a while."

"What, baby?"

"I wanted to go ring shopping before Christmas." He took Tristan's hand in his. "I was hoping…"

"Let's just get you home," said Tristan gently. "I think you just need to get well."

"Yeah," said Michael. He looked tired again. "That's right. I'm sure to have more energy soon. They still wake me up at all hours, and it's cold in here sometimes."

"Well, when you get home, I'll wait on you hand and foot. I'll keep you warm, I'll compose epic poetry to the dimples in your buttocks, and I'll take care of your every need," said Tristan. "You just wait."

"Don't want to wait, Sparky," said Michael, drifting off to sleep. "Can't sleep well unless you're with me. I'm sure that's why I always feel so tired."

"I'm sure," said Tristan, stroking his hair. "Love you," he murmured, blinking back tears.

"Love you. Gonna get matching rings and tell the whole world. Won't be lonely anymore…" Michael drifted off.

Chapter Twenty-Eight

Tristan pulled his BMW around to the patient loading zone and saw that Michael was not the only person in a wheelchair waiting to be picked up. He was chatting amiably with a woman who was holding a brand-new infant in her arms, waiting to be picked up, presumably by the baby's father. The nurses who held their wheelchairs were also smiling and talking. The air was cold and crisp, the sun shining. It was a beautiful, clear Southern California kind of Christmas Eve, the kind where Santa shows up in khaki shorts and a Hawaiian shirt and shades, flashing a peace sign with one hand and sipping a Corona with the other.

Tristan's heart was pounding hard in his chest as he and the nurse, whose name was Tammy, helped Michael into the front seat of the Beemer. It was obvious that Michael still had plenty of healing to do. The pain when he moved was etched on his face. Several of the other nurses had drifted down from his floor to say good-bye. It wasn't hard for Tristan to imagine that they were all half in love with him. Everyone was. Tristan most of all, and he was sure he would explode with it the minute they were finally alone, causing chunks of himself to fly all over like so much lovesick shrapnel to ruin all his hard work decorating the house.

Once Tristan was behind the wheel, the nurses said their final good-byes and closed the car door, leaving them alone for the first time in weeks.

"I can't wait to go home, Sparky," murmured Michael, who was maneuvering the seat around trying to get comfortable. "I want to be alone with you in our house."

Tristan smiled. "I'll bet it will have to wait. I think everyone and their little green dog will be coming this afternoon to welcome you back. Are you up to lying on the couch?"

"Sure. It's comfortable, and I need to be lying down." Michael got quiet for a long moment. "Sparky, I know you didn't sign on to be my nurse. You don't have to take care of me, you know. My mom…"

"Michael, just so you know, I'm going to be on you like white on rice until you're well, so don't even bother." Tristan made the left onto Chapman. "I almost lost you. I can't tell you what that did to me."

"I'm sorry," said Michael quietly.

"Not something you did on purpose, is it?" asked Tristan, but he was gritting his teeth. Tristan's heart could beat at a steady pace now, while he was driving the tree-lined streets of Michael's neighborhood, but it began a skittering, frantic tattoo when he thought about Michael getting well. Michael back on the job, and Michael leaving in the morning and maybe not making it back home at night. Tristan tried to put it away, to think about it later when he had more time.

"I drove these streets alone for days after your…when you were hurt, not really knowing whether we'd be here together again." He stopped the car for a minute to let his roiling emotions settle. "I will thank God every minute of every day that you're here with me. If you don't let me take care of you now…" The thought made his stomach churn.

"I'm sorry, Tristan." Michael reached out a hand. "I'm so sorry."

"Will you stop saying that?" Tristan wiped the tears from his eyes. He started up the car again, weaving through the familiar streets until he pulled into the driveway behind Michael's truck.

"Home," Michael said aloud.

Tristan gazed at it.

"Let's go in. Will you make a fire?" said Michael, grinning.

"Yes," said Tristan happily. "I'd love to." He helped Michael to the front door, unlocking it and turning off the alarm. As soon as he got Michael settled on the couch, he started a nice, crackling blaze in the fireplace. Michael looked around curiously at the Christmas decorations everywhere.

"Somebody's been busy," he said, as Tristan brought him pillows and a warm quilt to make him comfortable. Tristan turned on the tree lights and began to light the candles, which glowed in the dimly lit room and warmed it almost as much as the fire did.

"I was running on a lot of adrenaline for a while." He looked around and thought that maybe, yeah, he'd been a little over the top. "I had some help from my family and Emma."

"I'll bet," said Michael. "Come here." He patted the couch. Tristan kneeled on the floor in front of him, still too afraid of causing harm to get close.

Michael took his face between both his hands and kissed him tenderly on the mouth. "You are so special."

Tristan rolled his eyes. "Special good, or special ed?"

"I love you, Tristan," said Michael. "Always. I'm so glad to be able to say that to you today."

"Love you too," said Tristan, unwanted tears staining his cheeks. "Me too." He wiped at them jerkily, clearing his throat. "Okay, enough of this. Are you hungry? Thirsty?"

Michael merely smiled tiredly and let Tristan fuss, allowing him to remove his clothes, make him comfortable, and push up a small table with water and fruit on it. He turned on music and then babbled on about what type was most conducive to healing. It was exhausting to watch, but Michael let him do it. About an hour later, the doorbell rang, and the first of the visitors arrived with food.

Tristan and Emma, who was among the first to arrive, ushered friends and family in and out of the living room. They kept the fire going and the conversation light, and quietly saw to it that Michael never had to ask for anything.

A short hour later, Michael was drifting off, and people came and went without his knowledge, filling the space under the tree with gifts and the refrigerator with casseroles. He had vague impressions of people, like Meghan and Jim from I.N.KD and Ron, who seemed to be talking with Tristan as though they were longtime friends.

Some of his fellow officers from work came, and at those times he noticed that Tristan seemed strained, coming and going from the living room and acting subdued, which he didn't understand. Sometimes his boy allowed Emma to visit and play host, while he simply came and went silently with refreshments, like good domestic help.

After another hour still, Michael could no longer keep his eyes open at all, and by some silent communication, Tristan and Emma evicted the last of the guests. Emma went home, first putting a sign on Michael's porch support that he was sleeping and any visitor should knock on her door instead.

Tristan turned out the porch light, but left the Christmas lights on, remarking out loud to no one in particular that he liked the way they looked through the front window. Tristan pulled the futon from the office and dragged it to the front of the fireplace, adding another large log to catch. He shucked his pants and shirt off and then his underwear, preferring to sleep nude in the warmth of the fire.

For a long time, he sat and watched Michael, taking in everything about him, his slow, even breathing, the way the light scintillated off his golden hair, his hands, so beautiful, curled up on his abdomen as if to protect himself where he'd been stabbed. Once again, Tristan thought that even if he had forever with this man it would not be enough. He leaned over and kissed Michael gently on the lips and folded himself into the futon to sleep.

Sometime in the middle of the night the slightest scuffling noise awoke Tristan, who jerked at the sound, trying to orient himself to it. He turned to see Michael, pulling the blanket back to rise from the couch with obvious difficulty.

"What is it, love?"

"Don't worry," said Michael, rising painfully to a sitting position. "I just have to pee, go back to sleep."

"Not a chance." Tristan rose quickly from the futon. "Here, I have this thing they gave me from the hospital," he said, indicating a bag by the couch, which contained a plastic jug.

"Sparky, you don't seriously expect me to pee in my living room, do you?" asked Michael, aghast.

"I expect you to do whatever the doctor told me you should do, and they told me you shouldn't be walking around too much yet. This is a piece of cake. Think of yourself as a long-range trucker." When Michael remained resolutely disinterested, he added, "Should I make water noises?"

"Sparky," whispered Michael. "I don't think I could do that. You know, with you here."

"You do it all the time when I'm in the bathroom with you," Tristan pointed out.

"Not in a jug." He looked at the plastic bottle in question, horrified.

"It's not like I'm going to drink it; I'm just going to flush it the second you're done. *Michael,*" he said sternly. "You do not want to fight me on every little thing. Save your strength for the big stuff, okay?"

"Okay," said Michael. "Leave the room." Tristan glared at him, but did as he was asked, wrapping a blanket around himself and adding another log before he went to the kitchen. He made himself a cup of herb tea in the microwave and heard Michael call out to him a few minutes later. He returned to the living room, looking innocently at Michael, who gave him the jug, his cheeks like red flags.

"Oh, yuck," teased Tristan. "It's warm and oh…grooooooosss." He took it to the bathroom and flushed it, rinsing the jug with hot water and antibacterial soap. "Ew, penis germs…" he called out, laughing at Michael's discomfort.

"Ah, crap," said Michael, turning away. "Don't make me laugh!"

"Sorry, Michael," said Tristan. Michael was still sitting upright on the couch, his expression unreadable. "I know that was pretty intimate, but it's not like we haven't been more intimate than that. I promise you I'll take care of stuff like that. It doesn't bother me at all."

"It's just that --"

"It doesn't bother me at all." Tristan said again. He relaxed onto his back on the futon, rocking a little from side to side to get comfortable. Michael smiled at him in a way that made Tristan think he'd mostly forgotten about peeing.

"Wish I were down there with you," said Michael.

"Me too… I've slept here almost every night." Tristan smiled up at Michael, who felt his body tighten a little in response.

"Is that so?" he asked, feeling a kind of restless energy around him.

"Mmmhmm," Tristan murmured, working it a little. "You know, I like the way you're looking at me right now."

"Do you?"

Tristan bit his lip. "I do. And it's been so long since you've looked at me that way." He arched his back a little as if he couldn't help it.

"Yep." Michael smiled. "It has."

"And I sort of…kind of…I don't know, thought about this before, when you weren't here." He gave Michael a look that very definitely said, *Let's play.*

"Ah, well." Michael's eyes shone in the firelight. "You see, I probably can't do very much more than watch right now…"

"Oh." Tristan sounded disappointed.

"But I'd like to watch," Michael said. "I want you to tell me what you were doing without me, on this futon, in front of my fireplace while I was gone… In exquisite detail." He snaked his foot over and removed the blanket from Tristan's torso, exposing his very lovely body and rock-hard cock.

Tristan smiled like a debauched angel. "I was thinking about you," he said, warming to the opportunity to put on a little show. "I was thinking about how you touch me," he sighed, his hands skimming down his arms as he hugged himself against the sudden cold. Those same beautiful hands raked through his long red hair. "I'd imagine that you're here with me and that I'm lying on my back, and you're running your hands all over me." He ran his hands down his sides and his hips, over the fronts of his thighs and back up, not touching his cock or his balls yet. "But you're teasing me, touching me everywhere, making me need you more and more."

"Am I?" asked Michael hoarsely. "Would I do that?"

"Mmmhmm. And then, just when it makes me insane, you take your hands away and say, 'Touch yourself, Tristan,' and I have to, you know, because I want to please you."

"You do?"

"Oh, yes," said Tristan. "Because I know if I please you, you'll touch me some more, and that's the only thing I can think of, see. Getting you to touch me. So I'm kind of desperate, you know? And then I start touching myself, here, like this, see?" he said, referring to the way his hands stroked the hollows of his hips on either side of his pubic hair, in round little circles that seemed to make his cock jump as he writhed. "And it feels...oh...good, you know? Like a secret place that makes me...uhn."

"Mmmhmm." Michael's mouth went dry. His own cock was throbbing now, so much that he loosened the drawstring on his pajama pants to release it.

"And then I think, what if you put your big, callused cop foot on my chest," said Tristan, who was clearly getting into this. "You know, to hold me down a little and let me know I belong to you." He gasped as Michael's foot scraped across one sensitive nipple and then the other, exerting a small pressure on him so that he could move his hips and arch his back, but not much else. "Because I do, you know. I belong to you, Michael. And I think no one can make me feel this way but you." Tristan began to stroke his dick with one hand. He reached down and cupped his balls with the other. "Only you," he sighed, as he began to rock against his own hands.

"Me," said Michael, breathing hard now. He didn't touch himself; he was enjoying the show. His Sparky was going to burn the place down.

"And then," said Tristan, lost now in the fantasy. "I could just imagine you touching me, you know, in deeper places. Places that make me burn," he said, removing his hand from his balls and sucking on his fingers, pushing them in and out of his mouth until Michael could almost feel that mouth on his dick, tonguing him and making him ready. Michael removed his foot so Tristan could get the leverage he needed to finger his own hole. "It would be your fingers inside me, and I'd rock between your fingers and your hand, and either way I go…I…oh…yes…*Michael*," he said, lost in it.

"Then what," asked Michael thickly, his voice grating even to his own ears.

"Oh, then…" said Tristan. "I'd imagine you talking to me, telling me I'm your boy and that you need me to love you. You want me to come on your cock, and you want to taste it. Want me so bad…" Tristan gasped now, panting, biting his lip as he brought himself to the brink of orgasm. He moved then, coming to his knees right below Michael, so his face was looking up at Michael's like a slave, his eyes glazed and heavy, the burn slowly creeping up his skin to his fair neck. He rocked between his fingers and his hand, jerking now, his hips snapping, and he said, "I just want to…be…so…good…only for you…so good." He bit his lip, and ribbons of sweet white cum undulated through the air, falling in lines like silly string all over Michael, the couch, and the futon.

Michael stared at him for a second, then exploded completely without warning, without even touching himself, adding his own jets of cum to the air, which landed all over Tristan's face and chest.

Tristan raised his hand and raked it through his hair, smoothing it down and catching bits of cum on his fingers and licking it off.

Michael slumped back onto his pillows, panting for breath. He lay there a long time, trying to wrap his mind around what had just happened. Finally, he began to make a noise low in his throat that sounded as much like sobbing as it did laughter. He held a pillow tightly against his abdominal muscles and groaned.

"*Shit*, Tristan," he said. "Nothing's going to kill me but you."

Chapter Twenty-Nine

Tristan went to sleep slightly subdued after his performance. He had retrieved a warm washcloth from the bathroom and cleaned up as much as he could and tried to keep Michael from laughing, which hurt him. He'd given Michael his pain medication, making careful notations on a chart he'd made on the computer, and settled him back to sleep on the couch with a kiss.

Tristan was a little concerned by how much he liked jerking off for Michael like that. He'd really, *really* enjoyed that. He had discovered a kink in his own personality, and if it didn't correspond to anything in Michael's, he was in big trouble. Because that? That was damned hot, and he was ready to do it again, and again, and again.

The sun was fully up on Christmas morning when they finally opened their eyes, and Tristan got up and put away the futon. He made Michael's breakfast and sat him up with the paper, then went to take a shower. In the steamy bathroom, he looked at himself in the mirror in a totally different way. He explored himself from different angles, pulled his hair up, bent over, and checked out his own ass. No doubt about it, he was an exhibitionist. Tristan studied the tattoo he'd gotten from Meghan when Michael was still in intensive care. He'd kept quiet about it, partly because he thought it would be a fun surprise and partly because it was almost sacred to him. He'd wanted to brand himself Michael's property, and if something had happened and Michael hadn't made it, he'd wanted a permanent reminder of his lover on his skin.

After his shower, Tristan drew on a pair of low-slung jeans and a ribbed-knit shirt that didn't quite meet them, smiling to himself when he saw that his tattoo could be seen quite clearly between the two. He came out to the living room just in time to see Emma coming up the porch steps with Ron.

"Merry Christmas," said Tristan, opening the door. "Michael's just finishing his breakfast."

"Hey, baby," said Emma, kissing Michael on the temple. "Did you sleep well?"

Michael looked at Tristan, who was trying to look innocent. "I was up a little in the middle of the night, but Tristan got me my meds, and I slept after that." He glanced Tristan's way and found him turning a dull shade of red.

There was another knock at the door, and Emma opened it to find a couple of off-duty cops on the porch, along with their wives. Michael, who was watching Tristan idly, saw him exchange an odd, fearful look with Ron and leave through the dining room, effectively disappearing before their guests could come in. Throughout the morning, Tristan's odd behavior continued. He came out and visited with Emma, Ron, and his own family when they arrived and yet made himself scarce when friends from the department came by. By the late afternoon on Christmas Day, Michael saw the pattern clearly.

"I'm tired," he announced, and it was true. Even though he'd done nothing all day, he was exhausted. "Maybe you guys should put up the sign, and Tristan and I can get a much-needed nap."

Emma got to her feet, pulling Ron with her. To Tristan's family, she said, "Okay, guys, party's moving to my place, and we'll eat there. Then we'll see if Michael and Tristan feel up to opening some presents later."

"Tristan," said Julia. "Call next door if you need anything, okay?"

"Sure, Mom. Michael's right. I know I'm tired, so he must be totally beat." He smiled down at Michael, who was beginning to doze on the couch.

"Sure am," he sighed.

When the family left, Tristan dragged out the futon again and pulled the screen away from fireplace to shovel the ashes into a can Michael kept for that purpose. He matter-of-factly handed the plastic bottle to Michael, who filled it without histrionics, and started up a nice fire, leaning over and blowing on the kindling instead of using the gas to get it started.

"Sparky?" said Michael.

"Hm, what?" said Tristan, turning around for a minute before returning to working on the fire.

"What's wrong?" asked Michael. Tristan could see he was drowsy, could tell by the way he tried to keep his eyes open that he worried.

"What do you mean?"

"Something's different. You're different." Michael held his hand out, and Tristan took it.

"Things are different, Michael," said Tristan.

"Yeah, but" -- he squeezed Tristan's hand in his -- "I'm going to be fine. The doctors said I was lucky and am going to make a full recovery."

"Mmmhmm," said Tristan.

"Things are good, baby. I'll be back to normal in no time, and then we can make this place just the way we want it."

Tristan held onto his hand and listened.

"I'll have to do all the psych crap. I'll have to think about Mary." His face folded inward like a burning ball of paper. "Oh, crap. *Mary.*" Michael turned his face and hid his tears.

Tristan said nothing, but came to him and held him gently.

"I had a dream about Mary," said Michael. "When I was in the hospital. I was riding my Harley, and I thought you were riding behind me. I was so happy… Then I looked down and saw dead hands around my waist…skeleton hands…Mary's hands."

"*Oh, Michael,*" said Tristan, whose own tears fell into Michael's hair.

"It's going to be okay, Tristan, you'll see…"

Michael looked at the fire, where a sudden shower of sparks caused by a shift in the wood puffed into the air like fireworks. A large chunk of ember fell from the grate onto the brick hearth.

"I'd better get that, Michael," said Tristan, letting him go to lean over and grab a shovel. "At my house this sets off the smoke detectors." He reached over and scooped up the smoking wood, tossing it back into the fire.

"Hey," said Michael, suddenly. "Come here, baby." He waved him over. When Tristan got there, Michael took his hips and turned him around, running his hand over Tristan's tattoo.

"What the hell? That's exactly like mine," he said. "When did you get this?"

"When you were in intensive care that first day. Meghan did it." He let Michael run his fingers over the swirls. The hand holding his hip tightened. "Sparky! That's my…"

"Badge number, I know," said Tristan. He felt Michael's lips on the small of his back.

"Thank you," said Michael. "How did I miss this last night?"

"I think you had your eyes on…other things. It's not much of a Christmas present," Tristan sighed, as Michael rubbed little circles into his tattooed skin.

"It's the best. It means you belong to me, doesn't it?"

"Yes." Tristan still wasn't sure what he meant by that.

"It's the best," Michael repeated. He settled himself on the couch, lying down, and sighed. "I wish I could sleep on the futon with you, Sparky. I miss your skin."

"Miss you too." Tristan slipped down to lie before the fire. "Soon, love."

"Soon," echoed Michael, his heavy eyelids falling. He fell asleep with his hand grazing Tristan's red hair.

* * *

By the morning of New Year's Eve, Michael was so over being taken care of that he'd begun snarling like an angry badger, and nothing, *nothing* made him angrier than seeing his Sparky slink off to the kitchen or the office while his brethren in blue visited, like some hired help whose only job it was to bring out the drinks and retire till the master rang again. He thanked God every day for his ego, which did not allow him for one second to contemplate the tiniest possibility that his Sparky was ashamed of *him*. The way his boy kept making guilty eye contact with Ron made him think there was something altogether different going on.

So he bided his time and waited, wondering if Sparky would ever talk about what was bothering him. Yet at the same time, he was in pain, exhausted, and in no shape for an emotional scene. Right then there were no less than twenty men and women from the FPD in his living room. He'd seen his boy looking like a monkey with a shock collar someone was setting off at intervals, just for fun, and it had to end, now.

"Ron," he caught his old friend's attention, motioning him over. "Pull up a chair and talk to me for a while."

Ron looked concerned, maybe even a little afraid.

"Come on, no hard feelings, you know that, right?" Michael gave his arm a weak squeeze.

"I always made you scared, after. I hated that most of all." Ron looked down into the beer bottle he'd been holding, swirling the last of the amber liquid around.

"Scared you didn't like me anymore. Scared I'd lost more than I wanted to lose," said Michael quietly.

"Oh, hell, you could never lose me. Let's imagine that we never…"

"Done," said Michael. "It didn't fit, it's over."

"Done," said Ron, thickly. "Still love you, buddy, like always. Real proud." Ron turned away to hide what Michael thought might be tears.

"You like Sparky?"

"Yeah, the little turd." Ron grinned. "What's not to like? He hasn't got a lick of fear, and he's good, you know? Deep down."

"Then can you tell me what's up with him? Come on, I know you know what's going on. I'm a cop. I notice things." Michael folded his arms and waited patiently.

"Look, I don't think now's the time. You've got half the force here, man. We'll talk later." Ron got up to leave, but Michael caught him, grimacing in pain as the movement yanked the healing muscles in his abdomen a little.

"Oh, baby," said Ron, sitting back down guiltily. "You hurt? Do you need your meds?"

"No, I just want an answer, Ron," said Michael tiredly.

"Sparky and I had a talk, Michael. He was moving in here, and I asked him if he thought about what being out would do to your career, to your safety." Michael opened his mouth to say something, but Ron went on. "Don't look at me like that! I've known cops who died because people didn't much like their lifestyle. Tougher guys than you got fragged when I was in the military, Michael, for no more than the hint that they were gay." Michael could read the worry and the love on Ron's face and didn't hold it against him.

"Times change."

"People don't," said Ron peevishly. "And people with guns change less than most."

"Come on, Ron. Tell me that my boy is not hiding in the kitchen because he's afraid he'll get me killed."

Ron said nothing.

"Aw, *shit*." Michael caught his mother's eye. Emma came to him, sensing the change in his mood.

"What, baby?" she asked, concerned.

"Can you make all these people go away?" he asked, feeling surlier by the moment. "I just need some damn space, Mama. Give me some time, okay?"

"Oh," she said. "*Oh*. Sure. We've been thoughtless. I'll hustle everyone to my place, okay?"

"Okay. It's not thoughtless… I'm just tired, I guess."

"Sure you are, baby." She smiled at him. "I'll take care of it."

"Thank you."

Michael watched as his mother effortlessly gathered his guests and moved them, snacks in hand, out the door. When Tristan returned to the room carrying a meat and cheese tray, everyone was gone, and the silence hung thick in the air.

Michael rubbed his eyes tiredly. "When were you going to tell me?"

Tristan advanced into the room and placed the food on the table next to Michael. "Tell you what?"

"Tell me what's going on in that hyperactive brain of yours. That you're scared." Michael said it like an accusation, and Tristan reacted defensively.

"Is that such a surprise? You were very nearly stabbed to death. If I weren't scared I'd be a pretty shitty boyfriend all around, wouldn't you think?"

"Tristan, listen…"

"No, you listen to me. It's not rocket science. I'd probably understand it better if it were. You almost *died*, Michael."

"I know that… I know. It's part of the job. What did you think? That I'm Barney Fife and the most dangerous thing I do all day is put my gun in my holster?"

Tristan slumped into the futon, going down hard onto his ass. "We cannot have this conversation now, baby. Now you need to heal and rest. Now is when you need to just…"

"We sure as shit will have this conversation now." Michael put a pillow over his abs and held it there, hoping it would keep him from feeling the stabbing pain in his gut when he took a deep breath. "I'm a cop, Tristan. I know you don't have much respect for the badge, but --"

Tristan cut him off. "You know damn well that's not true."

"Sparky, listen to me… I was stabbed, I almost died, I got lucky, and now I want us to be a forever couple, hell, even a family, if that's what you want. I could do kids… I could do anything…"

"Can you fucking *hear yourself*?" spat Tristan. Michael jumped at the sound and looked up. "I want, I'm fine, I got lucky, I could do kids." Tristan was clenching his hands together, the muscles in his arms bunching as if he wanted to hit something.

Michael froze. How could he have failed to notice how tired Tristan looked? He'd never heard Tristan curse like that, ever. There were dark circles under his eyes, and his lips were white and pinched.

Tristan stood and started to pace. "I want, I want, I want. Shit!" Tristan raked his hands through his long hair. "Let me tell you what I wanted. I wanted to get laid. I wanted to find out what it feels like to be fucked by a man. I wanted to start on a long journey of self-exploration. I did not want to fall in love. I did not want to live in a world where the sun rose and set on one man. I did not want to give my heart away to a guy who took it and went out and got himself almost killed because that was his *job*. Can you understand that?"

"Sparky!"

"No, let me say it." He began to cry. "I have to say it. I'm nineteen fucking years old. I took off the training wheels, and now I'm racing down the damned autobahn. I've had you for what, a month?"

Michael held his arms out, but Tristan stayed where he was.

"I live for you. I breathe for you. Every cell in my body wants you *right now*. And I'm not fucking ready!"

"Tristan, the doctor said it's going to be fine… I'm going to be okay… It's not over."

"No, it's not," said Tristan suddenly too quiet. "Because you're going to turn right back around and go back out there and do it again."

A thick, smoky silence fell over them, and each waited.

"It's the job, then," Michael said in a sepulchral voice.

"Yes." Tristan shook his head. "No. Not entirely. I…I just wanted to get laid. I'm not ready for any of this."

"You said you love me. Didn't you love me?"

Tristan closed his eyes. "Oh, wouldn't that be easy." He knelt in front of Michael, holding both of his hands. "I know what it's like to lose someone who means the world to me, Michael. To know I'll never, ever see him again in this lifetime. I can't go there again. Not and stay sane."

"So what do you want? If you leave, you won't see me again in this lifetime, either," Michael snapped. He hadn't meant to; he was tired, in pain, and dissolving in disappointment.

"So if I say I'm not ready, it's a deal breaker?"

"I didn't say that. It's just that… I looked it in the face, Sparky. It changed me. I want new things."

"I want to think, Michael. One thought where I'm not drowning in the enormity of my feelings for you!"

"Jeez." Michael looked away.

"I'm sorry." Tristan swallowed hard. "I told you I didn't want to have this conversation."

Michael's laugh was mirthless. "Maybe if you'd told me why…"

"Shit," said Tristan. "Don't joke. Not about this."

"What do you want?" Michael asked again.

"I don't know." Tristan's blue eyes were troubled. "I cannot lose you."

"But you'd push me away."

"I. Can. Not. Lose. You."

"That's not rational, Tristan. If we're over, then you lose me," said Michael gently. "Have you realized it yet? One of us is going to repeat the past. You live with loss…or I live with abandonment."

"Oh, *fuck*, Michael." Tristan melted onto him.

Michael held him gently and kissed him tenderly on the lips. “Better go. Be like ripping off a Band-Aid. Get her done, you know?”

“I know.” Tristan left by the front door.

Michael stayed on the couch in the living room of the house he’d begun to really consider a home. “Happy. Fucking. New Year.”

Chapter Thirty

Tristan took the mountain roads carefully, not quickly, because he was certainly not the only person with the idea of snowboarding on New Year's Day. When he'd decided a little rush would be a good thing, he'd called his friends, most of whom already had plans, but P.K. -- *Pankage* -- had been home watching the Rose Parade and packed a bag with little persuasion, ready to go when Tristan arrived at the student housing complex to pick him up.

"I can safely say that snowboarding isn't something I would choose to do on purpose," he admitted when he threw his duffel into the back of his car. "But getting out of town sounds like fun."

"I need clean air," said Tristan simply, as he took off up the 55 Freeway.

Whether P.K. noticed his unusual mood or not, they drove companionably, winding from one freeway to the next until they had to get out and struggle with tire chains.

P.K. broke the silence between them as he watched Tristan work on the cold ground. "So do you think it will be possible to rent snowboarding equipment? I brought my warmest clothing, such as it is, but frankly, I don't see myself as a mountain man."

"You can rent equipment; if you don't want to snowboard, you can ski, if you like. I can do both, so I can help you if you want to learn. I only brought my board, though."

"Is it difficult?"

Tristan turned to him. "For a rocket scientist like you?"

"I was not exactly the first chosen for team sports, Tristan."

"You'll be fine," said Tristan. "We're lucky my mom found a place for us to stay. Apparently someone had a cancellation, or we'd be S.O.L." He was straining and jerking, linking the chains in place. "I had to get away for a while. I need air."

"I'm sorry Jonathon and Daniel couldn't make it. That would have been fun. I imagine we'd all be wading through your cast-offs. Ah, well, more for me."

"What?" asked Tristan, completely in the dark. He moved onto another tire.

"Well, it did occur to me that I would have the opportunity to watch you in action, as it were, with the ladies." Pankage grinned, his white teeth dazzling in the golden brown of his face.

"Oh," said Tristan. "I planned on just boarding till I couldn't stand upright anymore, man. I'm not feeling very social at the moment."

"I see," said P.K.

"Not that I don't want to have fun or anything," Tristan added quickly, thinking P.K. might regret coming with him. "I just…I'm not here for that."

"Trouble in paradise?"

"You could say that."

"Fresh air is good," replied P.K. as they worked, mostly silent again. Once the chains were safely on, they continued up the winding mountain road.

Tristan pulled into the parking lot of a resort that had a series of cabins in a horseshoe around a lodge. "This is it." He got out and stretched his legs.

"Ponderosa Pines," said P.K. in his clipped Pakistani/British accent. "How utterly *Bonanza*."

Tristan looked at him. "Dude, you watch *Bonanza*?" He didn't seem like a *Bonanza* kind of guy.

"Every chance I get. But if you tell anyone, I'll have to kill you." P.K. made to get his duffel out, but Tristan stopped him.

"Leave your stuff; we'll drive around to the cabin as soon as we check in." He walked ahead of P.K., who was looking around with shameless delight at the Western décor.

Tristan went through the motions of checking in, then drove the car around to their cabin. He dragged his gear into the small building and suited up, itching to get out and move. "I'm going to grab my board and go. If you want, you can come with me."

"I think I'll stay here and watch the rest of the football games. I'll come tomorrow."

"Do you want to ski or snowboard?"

"Either one. I'll probably seriously suck at it, whatever."

"Don't be like that." Tristan smiled. "It's really not that bad. Have you ever tried a skateboard?"

"No."

"No time like the present. I'm sure you've got the moves. I hate to just leave you here, P.K. I just need to…"

"I know. Go ahead. Maybe I'll make the acquaintance of injured snow bunnies or something."

"I hope so." Tristan left the small cabin and P.K. behind.

Tristan parked his car and shuttled to the mountain, glad he'd purchased his lift ticket online. The temperature was probably in the low thirties, crisp and biting, and his breath fanned out before him. Already he felt better, freer than he had in weeks, and he consciously tightened and relaxed his shoulder muscles, letting the fear and anxiety roll off him in thick waves. He slipped on his sunglasses and waited, intent only on the feel of the air as it rushed past his face. He moved forward in the long line, clamping his front foot on the board and taking the lift as it came, natural as breathing.

Once Tristan slipped off the lift chair, he found a level spot and clamped his other boot onto his board. All that was left was carving the snow, several fresh inches of it spewing out behind him like white sparks off a welding torch. He repeated the whole process over and over again, until all that existed was the cold and the rush and the exhaustion of his body as it gave itself to the mountain. Line… Lift… Freedom. Over and over again until the lifts stopped, the light faded, and the last shuttle came to deposit Tristan by his car.

Tristan entered the tiny, rustic cabin to find P.K. dozing in an avalanche of junk food, so he stripped down to his boxers and made his way to the tiny shower. Once inside, he let himself go and sat on the floor, crying, until the water turned cold.

P.K. was up and tidying things when he returned from the shower with a towel wrapped around his hips. Tristan knew his eyes were red and puffy, but P.K. said nothing, preferring a tacitly agreed upon silence to probing questions that might upset the delicate balance of domestic harmony.

"I'm hungry," said Tristan. He didn't feel hungry, but thought it might appear more normal if he suggested they go somewhere to eat.

"The man in the office told me there's a German restaurant that lots of people seem to like."

"Oh. Yeah, I know the one. My dad used to like that place. Sure. Let's go." Tristan dressed in jeans with a couple layers of T-shirts and sweatshirts, and grabbed a hat. P.K. seemed to watch him and follow his lead.

"I don't think I'm used to the mountains," he said, putting on his own hat.

"It's a good idea to remember to stay hydrated," said Tristan. "Hydration and Tylenol help with altitude problems if you're prone to them."

"I might be," said P.K. ruefully.

"Let's get you some carbs too. I read somewhere that helps. *Kartoffeln.*"

"What?"

"Potatoes." Tristan opened the car door and let P.K. slide into the passenger seat, crunching through the snow to the driver's side. Tristan raised his head and tasted the air. "It feels like we're going to get fresh snow." He would *not* think of how much he wished Michael were here to see it. "That'll be good."

"The man from the desk came by with wood for the fireplace," said P.K. idly. "I think he wondered what I was doing just lying around when I could have been skiing. I guess I really will have to try it out."

"You should. Even if you don't like it. We'll rent some gear for you and get you a lift ticket. You've got to try it once."

"I warn you, I'm not an action figure."

"I know, but wouldn't it be better to be able to say you did it?" Tristan grinned.

"I guess." P.K. didn't sound convinced.

They ordered Weiner schnitzel and fried potatoes, which came on a huge plate with scoops of red cabbage. They drank a lot of water at Tristan's urging, and P.K. did seem to be feeling better once they'd eaten. They split an apple pie-like tart with almond paste that Tristan really liked, but left P.K. cold.

"I don't like sweets too much. I'm all about salty things. Jonathon got me eating fried, spicy pork rinds, and now I can't stop."

Tristan nearly gagged. "I guess it's not just water that finds the lowest place to run."

"Hey!" P.K. threw a napkin at him. After they paid the bill, they walked into the cold mountain air.

Tristan shivered. "I like the cold, but whenever I go anywhere that's cold like this I roast going inside so much that I freeze going back outside. I think they must be hatching eggs in that restaurant."

"It was rather warm by comparison. Hey." P.K. looked around. "Is that snow?"

Tristan looked around as well, noticing that a few flakes were falling. "Yeah," he said. "It's just beginning. I hope it doesn't get too bad. I hate digging my car out."

"It's beautiful," said P.K., just stopping in the middle of the parking lot to stare. "I've never seen snow fall."

Tristan felt P.K.'s gaze on him and tried to hide the tears that had begun to fall.

"Well, shit," said P.K.

Tristan looked away, using his remote to open his car door. When they got in, he murmured an apology. "I'm sorry, P.K. I'll bet you wish you'd stayed home." He tried for a laugh, but it came out wet.

"Nah, I've never seen snow fall before. I'm thoroughly engaged." P.K. looked at him thoughtfully. "Though perhaps you'd like to talk about it?"

"Not really."

"Because it's a man's name that's tattooed on your ass?" P.K. asked gently. "I couldn't help but notice when you returned from the shower."

Tristan raised his eyebrows.

"It's a large tattoo." P.K. averted his eyes. "And I have excellent eyesight."

"I know." Tristan started the car, pulling carefully out onto the street now that the snow had begun to fall.

"You seemed so happy this last quarter," P.K. prompted.

"I was. I fell in love."

"And?"

"It didn't work out -- isn't working out." Tristan shook his head. "I'm not ready."

"Ah," said P.K. They drove the rest of the way in silence. Tristan thought then that he was lucky; Jonathon and Daniel didn't know how to value a silence, but P.K. made it comfortable. He was glad he was here with P.K. and not alone in the unbearable silence of snow.

When they got back into the cabin, Tristan handed P.K. a water bottle and told him he needed to drink it and took one himself. They made a fire and watched the game recaps on the news, Tristan finding his body unable to stay awake for more than fifteen minutes or so before he was fading out, fully clothed. He crawled between the sheets on his bed and knew nothing more until morning.

Tristan opened his eyes when P.K. slapped his foot. "Huh?" he asked, rising to his elbows on the scratchy sheets. "What time is it?" he asked.

"Seven. Time to get up. Snow awaits."

Tristan was blinking his eyes and trying to make his dry tongue move. "Wait..." he murmured, rolling to his side to get up and finding every bone in his body hurt and everything, literally *everything*, was stiff. "I...oh."

"Come on, get up. It's not like I haven't seen morning wood before. I live in a dormitory." P.K. turned his back to give Tristan a break then and headed for the door. "I'm going to come back with coffee and a newspaper. I've been psyching myself up, and I believe that if I don't try to snowboard today, I will lose my nerve completely."

Tristan smiled. "Thank you."

"Not at all. I just don't want you to waste my vacation moping."

Tristan headed toward the bathroom, and when he came out he was showered and dressed, and P.K. had coffee for him in a small Styrofoam cup. "This was the largest cup they had, but I imagine that we can get more where we're going, yes?"

"Yes," said Tristan.

"And I imagine the whole plan for this trip was to exhaust yourself so that you cannot spend too much time thinking about things?"

"Yes," said Tristan.

"Good, then in that case, I've taken the liberty of going online and getting myself an itinerary and a map so that we can find interesting things to do in the evening when the lifts are closed. I think I can guarantee that you will not have more than two or three conscious hours during the entire trip in which to pine."

"You're a good friend."

"I am, am I not?" said P.K., smiling his white smile. "Come on. You have a novice to teach on the slopes, and I'm a slow learner."

"As if." Tristan followed him to the door, carrying his coffee with him.

"Really, I still cannot dribble a soccer ball even if someone holds a gun to my head."

"Really?"

"Yes, in secondary school, I had a very angry coach, and he tried it." Tristan didn't know whether he was kidding. P.K. didn't enlighten him.

"But snowboarding is fun," Tristan said doubtfully.

"They said that about soccer too," sighed P.K.

Tristan looked on as P.K. tried his best, but after two times coming down the smallest hill, he gave Tristan the kind of look his mother always had when the toilet backed up. P.K. manfully put up with a third, and then excused himself.

"My quads are going to burn for a week," he said, huffing as he picked up his snowboard. "I will be much happier watching you from somewhere warm."

"If you're sure," said Tristan, looking back at the bunny run they'd been taking. "I'll go up and get a couple of good runs in."

"And I will be better off with coffee and snacks and television sports," said P.K. "I am prepared to wait until you are finished for the day, however long that will take." He smiled and lurched toward the clubhouse. Tristan finally returned at dusk, after the lifts closed, sore, wet, and exhausted. He found P.K. surrounded by a group of people, laughing and talking as though he'd known them forever.

"Did you have a good time?" asked P.K. politely. His eyes narrowed as he took in Tristan's appearance. "You should have worn sun-block, Tristan, you look masked."

"I did. I just didn't reapply. It happens every year. It's okay." He looked around at P.K.'s new friends, who introduced themselves and asked if he'd like to come with them for dinner.

"I'm sorry, I'm so exhausted," he said. "P.K., do you need the car?"

"He can come with us," said a dark-haired girl with fine features, who looked interested in P.K. and wasn't trying to hide it.

"P.K.?" asked Tristan.

"Will you be all right?" P.K. asked thoughtfully, and Tristan waved his concern away.

"Go on, I'm not even going to eat before I pass out, I'm so tired." He got up and stretched. "You have your key, right?"

"Yes, and I know the address of the place where we're staying."

"Okay. If you need me to pick you up anywhere, let me know." He started to leave. "You have my cell number programmed, right?"

"Yep," said P.K. grinning.

"All righty then," said Tristan, happy that P.K. had found some nice people to hang with. "Have a good time."

As he left, he thought he heard some of P.K.'s new friends say it was too bad his friend couldn't come too. He knew he hadn't mistaken the frank female appreciation from one of the dark-haired girl's friends. He was tired and glad to go home alone. The sooner he left, the sooner he'd sleep. He took the shuttle to the parking lot and picked up his car. When he got back to the tiny cabin he tossed off his wet clothes and showered to get warm, then got into bed, more than half asleep before his head even touched down. In the seconds it took to get comfortable and drift off, he wondered if his whole life was going to be like this, like monochrome when it used to be in color.

Chapter Thirty-One

It took a scant seven hours and forty-two minutes for Michael to alienate everyone who loved him and tried to help him. Ron and Emma took turns standing on the porch breathing in deep breaths before one or the other would confront the wounded man in his lair to make him eat, shower, and dress, eventually just confining their concern to eating, as showering and dressing seemed inexplicably to anger the already irritated Michael beyond bearing.

Ron was checking and rechecking meds, and Emma had had just about enough.

"Hey, baby," she said, squaring her jaw and entering the dimly lit living room where Michael lay on the couch reading the newspaper in front of the fire.

"Hey, Mama," he said automatically, flipping to the next page. He seemed to be reading each page completely and going to the next one regardless of how the articles played out.

"You're a mess, son," said Emma. She was tired, and it showed on her face. "Ron is coming by to put the Christmas things away."

"Tell him not to bother; I'll get them when I feel better."

"I will not," declared Emma. "That's a fresh tree, or was, and now it's little more than a fire hazard. You of all people…"

"Yes, yes. I know. It isn't safe. All right, have Ron take it down." Michael flipped another newspaper page. "It says here that there's something about drinking diet soda that makes people fatter. Figures."

"Michael, what are you going to do about this? You can't just lie here moping."

"I'm not moping. I'm healing. I have to heal so I can go back to work," he said in a patronizing, patient voice that was like touching a match to an open can of gasoline.

"Oh, for heaven's sake, *yes*! Let's make sure you get right back on the damn job."

"You too? I thought I just had the one detractor."

"Detractor? How can you call either of the two people who love you most in this world detractors?" She picked up the plates from his lunch and breakfast and started to the kitchen.

"People who love you," he said, "love you for who you are. They don't say, I'll love you if you only just quit your job, Mama."

"Who said that?" she demanded angrily.

"Tristan."

"Did he? Did he really? Or did you just hear that?" She rounded on him, plates in hand. "I may be a damned old hippie, but I know a thing or two about people. I know, for example, that loving someone isn't enough when you want two totally different things. I know that a man could love me and still walk away because he wasn't ready to marry and have children."

"He was a total shit, Mama. He didn't love you, and he didn't want me, and he blew off his responsibility because he wasn't worth a damn."

"You have no idea what you're talking about, Michael. Love isn't a panacea. Sometimes things don't work out. Your father was a med student. He would have had to give up his family's support, his family's plans for him, and his own dreams, to marry and have a child right then. He wasn't ready, and I wasn't willing to let him do it. I can't be sorry for that. It was a tough thing. A hard thing.

But I've never been sorry to have you, and I've never been sorry to have known him."

"He should have made it work," muttered Michael sullenly.

"Maybe. But he wouldn't have been happy. He'd have grown to hate me, and hate you, and hate the prison that his life became. It is possible that to love someone you have to let them go, Michael. It's hard. It sounds like a black-light poster from my childhood, but it happens."

Michael stared at her, and she knew she'd overstayed her welcome. She took the plates to the kitchen and made him a sandwich, resisting the temptation to put something he absolutely hated in it, like store-bought yellow curry powder, and left it next to his sofa. She said nothing further and just let herself out the way she came in.

Michael slept in front of the fire on the couch at night, sometimes so deeply that he feared he might be succumbing to carbon monoxide poisoning, and he'd claw his way back out to open a window. There were patchy bits of rain outside, and the cool air rushed in to replace the warm fairly quickly, dispelling the fuzzy-headed gloom until he felt he must have just imagined it. His phone wasn't silent, but he screened his calls. He really didn't want to answer any more questions about his health or his "incident."

The homeless-person-as-a-wild-card angle the press took enraged him, making him feel responsible for more than just Mary's death, but also for the misperception of homeless people as violent offenders in waiting. He pieced together what he remembered of Mary's behavior and realized that she'd acted wounded, and her behavior had been completely reasonable under the circumstances. She had been attacked, the autopsy showed, and probably robbed and wasn't in her right mind.

He looked into the crackling fire and fed the newspaper clippings about his ordeal into it. They caught and curled, dancing for a short minute until there was nothing left of them. He remembered his Sparky's face as it had been the night he'd stripped and fantasized, fondling himself on the futon before the flames. Michael could almost see the color of his hair and the way his eyes looked if he gazed into the flames themselves, the gold, red, and blue licking at the logs as Tristan's tongue had once so eagerly lapped at him. He leaned over to get the poker, and his abdominal muscles shrieked in protest. Once again, he pulled a pillow to his chest and held on hard, the pain subsiding for a minute.

It was going to take months to come back from this. His body, which had always been something he could count on, betrayed him when he made the slightest move. The fluid grace of his years playing competitive sports in high school and college, of jogging and training with weights in the police academy was completely out of his reach. He'd have to start at the very beginning, taking it slow, working his way up to proficiency even as his body fought him every inch of the way. Just the thought of it was exhausting. The idea of waking up every morning and putting one foot in front of the other, of going to work and coming home and feeding and bathing himself seemed…pointless. His reason for doing all those things was changed and might be gone forever, and he was having a hard time coming up with a new one as fast as everyone around him wanted him to. That's why he figured they could all just go to hell and wait.

In his quiet moments, Michael felt compassion, even gratitude for his mother and Ron, who came and went quietly, checking on him as if he were an unexploded bomb. As if he'd eat his gun. That thought never entered his head. He dragged himself back and forth from the bathroom and ate what they gave him. He read the newspaper. He kept up on current events. Sometimes he'd pull out a book and actually try to read it, but mostly he read the same paragraphs over and over. So he preferred reading the paper because for some reason, he could read the whole thing cover to cover and feel like he'd actually accomplished something. He'd stopped taking the pain meds after New Year's, a little afraid of how good they made him feel. Now, when the burning pain of his repaired muscles got too bad, he found a Tylenol or two, never more than they directed on the bottle. It didn't help him to sleep, but he dozed on and off all day anyway, preferring the quiet darkness of sleep as long as he didn't dream about Mary.

Michael did understand one thing. He understood it wasn't just the job that had Tristan running scared. Tristan wasn't ready for what Michael represented. He wasn't ready for the life that Michael wanted. Whether that meant that Tristan didn't want to be in love, that he didn't want to pick the first guy he'd been with, or that he wasn't ready to be married to a cop, Michael understood. It meant that the ball was in Tristan's court, and all Michael could do was wait. And that jangling fear that knotted in the center of his chest whenever he thought about it? Was becoming an old friend.

* * *

"I still think this is a dumb-ass idea," said Emma.

Michael frowned at her, but Ron spoke up. "Aw, now, Emma, the boy just wants to get away for an afternoon. I promise if he hurts too much I'll call you, and you can pick him up in the car."

"Michael?" asked Emma.

"Yeah, Mama, I'm going to just take it easy and let Ron drive," he said, putting on his helmet.

"Son, I --"

"I'll be fine. We'll get a little air and some lunch. I can't sit inside the house forever." Michael thought then, *Well, I can. I probably will.* But not today.

"Well..."

"Emma, it's going to be fine," said Ron again, pulling on gloves and sweeping a puff of dust off his jeans. Michael gingerly slung his leg over the saddle -- okay, that probably wasn't the best idea. "You okay, boy?" he asked Michael, seeing him grimace.

"No, fine. Muscles pulling. Get on, Pop, don't kick me in the balls." Michael grinned.

"You take all the fun out of everything, boy. You always have." Ron kicked the Harley to life, settling in and sort of checking things out, getting the feel of Michael on the back of his bike again, like when he was a kid.

They roared around the neighborhood, getting the kinks out, and then out onto the canyon road he'd taken with his Sparky. Michael tried not to hear himself think, tried to just feel the wind rush against him, to feel the sun, shining now through thick, puffy layers of rain clouds. He looked around idly for a rainbow, but whether there wasn't one or he just couldn't see it, he found nothing. They rode east for a while, but kept it short and ended up at Esther's Taco House.

"Stiff?" asked Ron, bringing drinks over. "Here." He gave Michael a bottle of water.

"Jeez," said Michael, looking at Ron's beer.

"It's water or nothing for you for a while, boy. Doctor's orders." That wasn't strictly true, but Michael didn't set him straight.

"Okay, it's fine." He started putting his carnitas tacos together, adding salsa, making them just the way he liked. "You haven't called me boy for years."

Ron looked down at his food. "Is it a problem?"

"It feels good." Michael took that first satisfying bite, juicy and meaty, with the crunch of cabbage instead of lettuce snapping like a sharp peppery snap next to the pork.

"Missed you," said Ron.

"Me too."

"Want you happy."

"Thanks."

"It's not happening though, is it?" Ron hefted his embarrassingly large burrito and took a bite.

Michael looked at his food, putting his taco down. "Maybe this wasn't such a good idea."

"Sparky loves you," said Ron. "I see it; hell, everyone sees it. Have some faith."

"He's not ready, Ron. He's too young."

"Déjà vu all over again."

Michael closed his eyes against the pain of that.

"It's not the same," Ron murmured, putting a hand on his. "You were young, sure, but we didn't fit. Sparky…well, he fits, right? He knows that. He'll come around. But maybe you ought to be a little more patient."

"Who are you, and what have you done with Ron?"

"Eat," said Ron. Michael picked his taco up again. "Time you started working out… Sparky is going to notice every ounce of muscle you lose and blame it on the people trying to take care of you."

"If he comes back." Michael took a bite and then a sip of water. He had to admit he was feeling a little better.

"Like you actually believe he's gone for good." Ron's eyes narrowed at him. "If you think like that, it's all just drama. Give him time. He's a rational guy who loves you. Give him a chance to work it out."

"You know how weird it is to hear you give me romantic advice, don't you? Aren't you the guy who doesn't do romance?"

Ron grinned. "Doesn't mean I don't know it when I see it. But you're right; give me a convenient alley and a guy who doesn't fight back any day."

"You're hopeless," said Michael, snatching Ron's beer and finishing it. Okay, he really didn't want to get back on the bike, but he felt better.

"No, Michael, I'm really full of hope where you're concerned, actually," Ron admitted. "And you owe me a damned beer."

Chapter Thirty-Two

Michael didn't know what woke him. The faint scratching sound, the beep of the alarm whistling and then being reset, the thunk on the kitchen floor like a bag being dropped, or the sound of the kitchen cabinet where he kept his liquor squeaking. He made his way cautiously to the kitchen, quietly, in case it wasn't Tristan, although he could think of no one else who had a key and his alarm codes. No one who would sneak in at two in the morning to drink his Bushmills. The sight that met his eyes in the dim light coming in from the porch lantern would have been funny if it weren't so sad.

Tristan stood with a crystal glass in his hand, drinking three fingers of whiskey, neat. His hair was tied up in a ponytail, and his face seemed painfully thin, drawn somehow, as if he'd aged. A plain-as-day mask of white skin stretched from ear to ear across his eyes, and the rest of his face was deeply sunburned, even starting to peel. His lips were so chapped, they'd cracked and bled.

"Sparky, I think you've got the whole mask thing wrong. You're supposed to wear it over your skin," said Michael. "Not on it."

Tristan looked over. "Hey, Michael."

Michael came further into the kitchen cautiously, as if he were trying to decide what to do with an unfamiliar dog. "Hey, Tristan."

"I went boarding at Snow Summit." Tristan wrapped both hands around his glass.

"When did you start drinking?"

"I haven't, really; I've just been cold for four days."

"I see. Did it snow while you were there? It rained here."

"Yeah, it was great, fresh powder. Crowded, though."

"I'll bet. You stayed up there?"

"Yeah."

A silence descended on the room, and Michael shook himself out of it. "Hey, where are my manners? Come into the living room."

"Michael --" began Tristan.

"No." Michael cut him off. He stepped forward. "No. Don't say anything yet, okay?" He was such a coward. "Let me get a drink, and you can get comfortable. You can get comfortable here still, right?"

"Sure. What do you want to drink?"

"I'll get it," said Michael. "Just go have a seat before you fall down."

"Yeah. I am tired, I guess." Tristan left his bag where it was and went to the living room, kicking off his boots and stretching his hands toward the fire.

Michael watched as Tristan sank into the couch tiredly, and he hoped in his heart that his boy felt glad to be home. "Should you call your family and let them know you're back in town?" asked Michael, carrying his own drink and a bag of chips with a bowl of salsa into the room.

"Nah, I called Mom earlier and told her…I said I would come straight here."

"Oh." Michael was surprised. He no longer had any idea what to expect. He pulled a small table up and set down the drink and chips, then found a comfortable spot on the opposite end of the sofa from Tristan and just waited. He hated that he grabbed a throw pillow and covered his abdomen with it like armor.

"I tried to find it," murmured Tristan, so softly Michael could barely hear.

"What?"

"What you saw. You said you looked it in the face, and it changed you. Something…I don't know. Am I crazy?" Tristan raked his hand through his hair, forgetting he'd tied it. He yanked the elastic out and shook his head. He looked so tired.

"Tristan, I don't understand," said Michael, worried a little. Tristan clearly hadn't taken very good care of himself; he had dark, smudgy shadows under his eyes, and he looked ill.

"I rode that mountain like a maniac, Michael. I exhausted myself. I took stupid chances. I kept thinking that if I could face what you faced, then I could find you where you are."

"*Tristan*," breathed Michael, afraid he'd throw up.

"I wanted to know what it was like." He was quiet for a long time. "Anyway, I never found it."

"What could you possibly learn from putting yourself in danger?" Michael tried to hide his anxiety.

Tristan tensed. "Maybe this wasn't such a good idea," he said, putting his drink on the table. Michael noticed he'd sipped it very slowly; half of it was still there.

Michael wiped his tired eyes with the heels of his hands. "Look, no. I'm sorry. Relax. I'm trying to understand."

Tristan sank back into the couch. "The only thing I realized is, it was a hell of a lot easier to give my body to the mountain, with no expectation that the mountain would be gentle, than it is to give my heart to you."

Michael didn't breathe. The only sound was the pop and crackle of the wood in the fire.

Tristan went on. "I wanted to look losing everything in the face so I could stop being so damned afraid of losing *you.*"

Michael moved then, slid and slipped over the soft leather until Tristan was enfolded securely in his arms. He didn't really give a damn if Tristan didn't like it, didn't care if it scared him. His lips found Tristan's in an achingly tender kiss that tasted salt and whiskey and sadness all at the same time.

"Shh."

"No, let me say it."

"Tristan, please, don't."

"I love you so much, Michael."

"What?" Michael held himself perfectly still.

"That's all I know right now." Tristan sagged against him. "That's all I know anymore."

"Oh, *Tristan,*" said Michael. "I can promise you I will never take your love lightly, ever."

"What do you mean?"

"I swear to you that I won't ever put your love last."

"I'm sure you never put my love last, Michael." Tristan waved his declaration away. "I know you never did that."

"I joined the force because I want to help people, to protect people. Right now the thing I want to protect the most is what we have together."

Tristan pushed away from him. "My head is fuzzy, what are you saying?"

"I'm saying I know that the job isn't the only problem we have, but it's a start, yes? I'm saying you're more important to me than the job, and I'll find another job, if you'll stay with me. I'll teach or drive a school bus or something. I'm saying let's start with the job and work from there, together, to build our lives exactly like we want them to be."

"Won't you hate me? Won't you be sorry you're not a cop anymore?"

"Sure, I'll miss it. I like it. But I love you."

"Shit," said Tristan, snatching at the lapels of Michael's robe so he could draw him closer. "I'm so sorry. What a coward I am."

"If you recall, neither one of us is very brave when it comes to losing what we have."

"Yeah."

"Did you even wear a helmet when you went…?"

"Don't ask; you won't like the answer." Tristan snorted with laughter and cried at the same time.

Michael smiled. "I know you weren't looking for this, Tristan, but I'm hoping you want to see where it goes. I don't think something like we have comes along every day."

"No, I imagine not."

"And if you're scared, you ought to know I am too." Michael pulled Tristan closer and held him. "But the thing that scares me most is losing you."

"Me too."

"So everything else?"

"Can be MacGyvered. You know, with a paper clip, a pen cap, the empty foil condom package…"

"I have no idea what you're talking about."

"I mean, if we keep our eyes on the prize we can work on what comes." He rested his head on Michael's shoulder. "Right?"

"You and me, though. That's the prize, right? No matter what?"

"Well, unless you do something stupid, like cheat or die or something. Take up golf and wear those short plaid pants..."

"Me?" Michael said, insulted. "You're young. Are you sure you want to tie it all up with one guy? Are you ready?"

"I don't know," Tristan said honestly. "Right now? Yeah. *Oh, yeah.* But five years from now? Ten years? Scares the hell out of me, man. Five years ago I was banging high school girls in the skate park bathrooms."

Michael felt the color leech from his face. "Oh, Sparky. Too much information. In the bathrooms, really? I've been telling them they ought to install Web cams."

"Sorry. You asked."

"Well. As to that," Michael said almost primly. "It has been established that you aren't the safest place I could put my heart."

"What?"

"Well, I mean, you know, you're young, you spent more time with girls than guys, you hate my job, you play hard and take chances."

"But I love you, you know that. You have got to know that, Michael."

"I do. Because I have faith in you." Michael stroked his finger lightly down Tristan's sunburned cheek.

"Oh."

"And I know that even when it's hard, you'll put us first and be honest if you can't. At least, I'm asking you to promise me that you'll do that. Is that an easier promise than 'forever no matter what'?"

"Yes. It is." Tristan swallowed hard. "I can promise to put us first and be honest if I can't."

"Then I can too. And that's where we start." Michael held out his hands and took Tristan's in them, lacing their fingers together.

Tristan held Michael's hand in his and seemed fascinated by the difference in the texture of their skin. "That's where we start. Yeah…but dude, seriously, could we start in the shower? Because I want to crawl inside you and die, and you smell like something already did that."

Michael barked a laugh and grabbed his sides to help him manage the pain. "Yeah," he said. "Come with me."

Chapter Thirty-Three

Tristan followed Michael into the bathroom, horrified once again by how he looked when he caught sight of himself in the mirror. Not exactly makeup sex fantasy material. Michael turned on the water, and the room began to fill with steam. Tristan started to unbutton his shirt, but couldn't look away from his image. Bruises were visible on his shoulder where he'd taken a bad fall. Tristan knew those weren't the only ones.

"Oh," he said and stopped what he was doing.

"What?" Michael took his hand and turned him away from the mirror over the sink.

"I'm, like, a freak," Tristan muttered. He couldn't look up at Michael.

"You're beautiful," said Michael, kissing his forehead.

"Don't lie." Tristan pulled away.

"Really, Tristan, I think you're…"

"No, you don't, you're just saying that, it's okay. I'm sorry." He began taking his clothes off, hoping he'd last through an entire shower without falling asleep. The alcohol was making it worse; he hadn't had that much, but it was beginning to take effect. "You want to hear something funny? I kind of get off on being, your… I don't know. Arm candy."

"Is that so?" murmured Michael, helping Tristan off with his shirt. He winced as he saw the discolorations, the bruising painfully apparent on his fair skin. "Oh, baby."

Tristan fell into his arms a little when he tried to remove his pants. Large, ugly bruises covered the outsides of his thighs and calves and the big toe of one foot was black and blue; that toenail was sure to fall off.

"Stop looking at me like that, Michael," said Tristan. "They're just bruises. They'll heal." He slid his boxers off and headed for the shower. He was still cold, four-days-in-the-snow, bone cold, and the hot water looked so enticing he almost moaned. It took a special strength of will to lift his leg up and over the lip of the tub. He screwed up his face, but he did it.

Michael came in after him, at his back, and the smooth glide of skin and crisp hair against Tristan made him want more. He leaned into Michael, trying to get every square inch of his body skin to skin. He did let out a moan then; he couldn't help it.

"That's it, baby. Lean on me for a minute." Michael got his hands soapy and ran them gently over Tristan's skin, cleaning him as he cleaned himself, using his hands to sluice the water off and rub warm circles.

"Oh, so good," said Tristan leaning his head on Michael's shoulder.

"You'll have to wash your own hair. I can't really keep my arms up that long yet. It pulls, you know?"

"Sure," said Tristan, turning in Michael's arms. "I'll get yours too." He stopped cold and stepped back. "Oh…*shit*."

It wasn't the first time Tristan had seen Michael's body after the stabbing. He'd seen it, bathed it while it still had stitches. Kissed it and loved it. But nothing prepared him for the end result, the way Michael would look when it was all over. An angry scar marked Michael's perfect abdomen. It pulled at his skin in a strange way, a sad reminder of the pain of the past. Tristan fell to his knees and put his mouth on it, earnestly, as if by kissing it he could heal Michael completely. He was crying, and when Michael tried to pick him up off the tub floor, he wouldn't allow it. He held Michael tightly, arms wrapped around his hips like a python, laving his scars and loving him and crying, until Michael came to his knees too and found his mouth, kissing him back like it was the first time and the last time and all the times they'd ever have between.

"Mine," said Michael, his arms around Tristan's shoulders in a possessive bear hug. "Always…mine. Say it," he demanded.

"Yours, Michael. Always. Yours."

"I need you, Sparky," said Michael, wetting his fingers and positioning them at Tristan's hole. "Let me in; I'm clean, baby. I was tested in the hospital."

"Oh," moaned Tristan. "*Yes*…no!" He froze. "I still have to be tested again, five months. Michael…please?" He didn't know what he was asking for.

"Shit," said Michael, who left the bathroom for a minute and returned, cold and dripping, with a condom and lube. He turned off the water and climbed back into the tub, gathering Tristan into his arms. "Here," he said, pulling Tristan into his lap with Tristan's thighs wrapped around him.

"Yes," sighed Tristan. "Please, Michael. Please."

As soon as Michael had the condom on his cock, Tristan slapped his hands away and straddled him, impaling himself on Michael. It burned and stretched him until he thought he'd rip in two, shocking him and taking his breath away for a moment. He must have groaned, because Michael held him carefully, looking into his eyes.

"Oh, *Tristan*."

"So full of you." Tristan winced and tried a grin, the effects of his rash plunge onto Michael's cock clearly evident in his own limp one. He frowned a little. "Burns."

Michael's brows lowered. "It hurts?" he whispered. "Should I…"

"*No*!" hissed Tristan, wrapping himself around Michael. "Need it. Wanted to feel it…" His vision was blurry, and he licked his chapped lips. "Got you, baby," he said, moving tentatively. "All safe. Got you."

Michael took the invitation to move and slid gently out and in again, testing the connection, hoping that Tristan would find at least a little pleasure. "You've got me," he whispered back, his lips against Tristan's hair. "You've got me."

"Make me feel, Michael. Make me yours." He tightened his muscles tentatively and knew Michael felt it all the way to his toes when he gasped.

"Sexy little shit."

"Uhn," Tristan moaned as Michael shifted him slightly and hit his sweet spot. "Michael…love."

Tristan's cock began to fill again, making itself known against Michael's belly, delivering wet kisses along the ridge of his scar. Tristan was beyond speech, beyond hearing. He was a part of Michael's body, as much a part as Michael's own cock, so deep inside Tristan he wondered if it would get lost there forever. Michael stroked Tristan's arms and back lovingly as he took him soaring higher.

"Oh, *Michael*," breathed Tristan when Michael took hold of his cock and began stroking it with the rhythm of his thrusts, sending sparks crackling through him. "Make me fly, Michael."

"Together, 'kay? Close…"

"Uhn…yeah." Tristan licked his lips. "So full." He let it take him then, over the edge, just let himself go with Michael, loving it, loving him. So much.

"You make me…just," hissed Michael, throwing his head back as Tristan's climax hit, milking his cock. "Oh, Tristan…"

Michael's climax hit him then, filling the latex, filling Tristan; he froze as far inside Tristan as he could get and just pressed himself there, riding the waves of his orgasm until the last pulsing throb of his cock. He relaxed, slumping against his boy on the cold bathtub floor. He lifted to his knees and stroked Tristan's long legs, helping them to straighten so he could lie along the hollow of Tristan's body, and then he plugged the tub and turned on the water.

"What are you doing?" Tristan asked sleepily.

"Wallowing."

Tristan grinned against his temple, lying on his back, both arms wrapped around Michael.

"Eventually we'll have to sit up, and you'll need to turn around or you'll drown."

Michael turned over and shifted Tristan so he could rest against the high back of the slippery tub. Tristan pulled him up against his chest gently. Michael was still protecting his abdominal muscles; Tristan could see the pain etched on his face.

Tristan gently stroked his scar. "Love you, Officer Helmet," he said, lacing the fingers of his right hand with Michael's and squeezing hard. "Always."

"Caught you, Sparky," Michael replied.

Epilogue

Four Years Later

Tristan parked his cream-colored BMW in front of Apple House just in time to see his favorite sight. He'd gone for a sandwich and coffee after school because he knew he wouldn't get dinner until almost nine that night. He got out of the car and walked to a large chicken-wire cage where the residents kept their bicycles. A rough-looking teenager was in front of it, his shoulders tense and angry as he walked his bike back into the cage.

"I'm not the enemy, peanut; it's the law." Michael turned and grinned at Tristan. "You can either wear a helmet, or you can walk. Two options. Pick one." Michael could really smile an evil smile when he wanted to.

"Who cares if I ride without a helmet? What's the big deal?"

Tristan spoke up. "The big deal, little man, is that it's an over seven-hundred-dollar ticket, and you will care very much if you get one of those," he said. "Take it from me."

"Hi, Mr. Phillips." The boy nodded to him.

"Hi, Nathan," Tristan said, waving at Michael.

"I'll walk, Mr. Truax," the boy decided finally, disgruntled.

"Good choice, Nathan," said Michael, holding the bike so Nathan could lock it. The boy turned and started hoofing it out onto the suburban streets to where he worked not far away.

"Officer Helmet is in the house. You know they call you Mr. Ex-Lax behind your back when they're pissed, don't you?" said Tristan, watching the boy go.

Michael laughed and nodded. "The fun never ends, Sparky. I just don't have the badge anymore."

Tristan drank in the sight of his lover, now the administrator of Apple House, a GLBT-teen homeless shelter he'd helped to establish by buying and refurbishing one of the larger, older houses in Fullerton and tapping into the local investment community and government agency grants for resources. "Ah, but you kept the handcuffs," said Tristan, buffeting Michael's shoulder in greeting.

"Yeah, well…" Michael actually blushed, which Tristan found impossibly adorable.

"So, you texted that things got a little wet today," said Michael, who looked like he had enjoyed that story.

"Yeah, well. One of the kids was demonstrating my Van de Graaff generator, and the static charge turned on the automatic sinks, which of course were covered by those sink covers, so yeah, on the whole, it was kind of wet. Nobody got electrocuted, though, so no harm, no foul."

"You are so damn cute," said Michael under his breath. "Aren't you supposed to be home studying?"

"Nope." Tristan grinned. "I've got to go back to the school. I get to help coach soccer from now on."

Michael shook his head. "You realize that you'll be spending hours and hours and getting paid almost nothing for it, don't you?"

"You make that sound like a bad thing."

Michael snorted. "Will you still have time to work on your thesis?"

"I'll find the time. It's soccer, Michael. I'm going to have a blast. It's not like I can't use the exercise, former Officer Sexy. Gotta keep the arm candy sweet, right?"

"I know, Sparky. The porn fairy and the predictable Mr. Truax. I wonder if your students realize that their science teacher is such a wild card."

"I can assure you, they don't. Hey," Tristan said, his eyes going serious all of a sudden. "Regrets?"

"Never," said Michael. He met Tristan's blue eyes squarely with his own. "*Never*, Tristan."

Tristan breathed out, clearly relieved. "Have time for a quickie before I go back to work?"

"Oh, hell, no, Tristan." Michael laughed. "The things you say."

Michael watched as Tristan got into his BMW. "All right, then." Tristan waved. "I'll be home at about nine-thirty."

"Okay." Michael waved. "I'll be waiting."

THE END

Z. A. Maxfield

Z. A. Maxfield is a fifth generation native of Los Angeles, although she now lives in the O.C. She started writing in 2006 on a dare from her children and never looked back. Pathologically disorganized, and perennially optimistic, she writes as much as she can, reads as much as she dares, and enjoys her time with family and friends. If anyone asks her how a wife and mother of four manages to find time for a writing career, she'll answer, "It's amazing what you can do if you completely give up housework."

Check out her website at http://www.zamaxfield.com.

TITLES AVAILABLE In Print from Loose Id®

DANGEROUS CRAVINGS
Evangeline Anderson

DAUGHTERS OF TERRA:
THE TA'E'SHA CHRONICLES, BOOK ONE
Theolyn Boese

DINAH'S DARK DESIRE
Mechele Armstrong

FORGOTTEN SONG
Ally Blue

HEAVEN SENT: HELL & PURGATORY
Jet Mykles

THE TIN STAR
J. L. Langley

THEIR ONE AND ONLY
Trista Ann Michaels

VETERANS 1: THROUGH THE FIRE
Rachel Bo and Liz Andrews

VETERANS 2: NOTHING TO LOSE
Mechele Armstrong and Bobby Michaels

Publisher's Note: The print titles listed above were previously released in e-book format by Loose Id®.